ALL THE WORDS WE CANNOT SAY

Tamar Jehuda Cohen

D1525347

Production by eBookPro Publishing
www.ebook-pro.com

ALL THE WORDS WE CANNOT SAY
Tamar Jehuda Cohen
Copyright © 2024 Tamar Jehuda Cohen

Translation: Tamar Jehuda Cohen

Contact: Tamar@massalaor.co.il

ISBN 9798337742762

All the Words We Cannot Say

A Novel

Tamar Jehuda Cohen

This book is dedicated to:

Shlomo, my wonderful partner, without whom life's wondrous journey would not have been possible.

To my family, a source of endless love and support.

To the believers in miracles, and to those who help make them happen.

And to those who shared their unspeakable with me.

To all those who believe that a crisis opens a window to new opportunities to grow, and the cracks in our life are where the light comes through.

Contents

PART ONE

Against All Odds

ON THE BRINK OF THE ABYSS AND BACK

I opened my eyes slowly as if I was being born again, or maybe as someone who had died already. I did not know the world to which I had arrived: to this one? To the next one? Or to some passage between them? Slowly my head cooperated and responded. The rest of my body refused to move, signaling that maybe I had arrived at the final destination, *Olam Haba* (the world to come), and I was being invited to get off here. My head was screaming, shrieking, letting me know it was alive and kicking. Pain rolled from within, back and forth, like heavy rain clouds weighing on me, until the One who makes the winds his messengers blew them slowly from me, and towards me. Groaning, I moved my head, and a face leaned towards me. A new, yet familiar face. An unexpected face. A face that brought me back to a new and unknown existence. An existence that I had not met.

Prof. Hezkeyah sat next to my bed, tight and alert, at full attention on a high stool with no back.

"What are you doing here?" I asked with a heavy tongue.

"Waiting for you to wake up," he answered.

A clock emerged into my field of vision, 3:24 am "What are you doing here at this hour?" I mumbled in a weak voice.

"The first few hours after the surgery on this long night are the critical hours. I knew that if something unexpected would happen, it will need to be dealt with immediately. If I would not be sitting here, monitoring and watching over you, I would not have been able to arrive fast enough to try to save your life."

I was brought into the surgery room towards two in the afternoon on *Tisha B'av*, the fast day when Jews mourn the destruction of the Temple in Jerusalem. I knew that Prof. Hezkeyah had not slept the night before the surgery, the eve of Tisha B'av. After the complex and dangerous operation, I was not transferred to the intensive care unit in the Neurosurgery department.

"Why?" I asked.

"If we need to intervene, it will need to be done as fast as possible. Every minute of delay could cost you your life," Prof. Hezkeyah stayed on guard, sitting on the narrow, backless stool which kept him awake. When we finished our short dialogue, I receded back into my shell of "nothingness." I sunk into myself. His worrying face was held in my shell of oblivion, a believing, trusting face of gratefulness, and his soft voice escorted me into the dream.

Why and how did I get here? Everything came back to me, as if someone had set the clock back.

• • •

It was the morning of a new week, Sunday of the week of Tisha B'av. In the dark bedroom, Abe was finishing getting dressed, in order to leave early for work in Tel Aviv, before the heavy traffic.

"How are you feeling? How is your head?" he asked. "Still hurting," I answered, "but not unbearable."

"I want you to go to Dr. Levanon on your way to work. He starts early. Go to his clinic before his official reception hours and try to get in before his patients."

Abe left for work while I was still in bed – this was not a common scene. My head was heavy, and begged not to be moved, and my body conceded.

Uncharacteristic of me, I moved very slowly, as my head hurt less that way. I drove to the doctor's office in the near by city. When I got there, the office was open. Surprised to see me, Dr. Levanon invited me in.

"What brings you to me so early this morning?" he asked. It had been some years since he had seen me with anything more than a sore throat.

"Abe asked that I see you on my way to work because my head is hurting. I would appreciate it if you could prescribe something stronger for me than Tylenol," I said.

"How long has it hurt?" he asked. I tried to remember. It was not an easy task, as I have never let pain run my life. It never took center stage, nor did it receive any real attention.

The Friday before had been magical. A day for fulfilling my heart's desire, which had been knocking at the gates of my being for many weeks. I finished all the cooking and baking for *Shabbat* (the Jewish Sabbath day) by the time Abe got back from his Friday morning prayers and *Judaic* studies. We had a wholesome breakfast on our balcony, facing our farm, and breathed deeply. The air was clear, and the view of the olive grove from the balcony warmed our hearts. After the meal we drove up to Jerusalem. I wanted to get to the *Kotel* (the Western Wall, a two thousand years' remanent of the wall around the Temple Mount) before *Tisha B'av*, (the day of fasting and morning the distraction of the Temple in Jerusalem). I wanted, through the large, wailing stones, to touch the sorrow of the people for the loss of their mutual dwelling and feel the *Shechina* (the divine presence of G-d), that has never left us. Approaching Jerusalem, we started to excitedly sing words from Psalms about the holy city, the volume increasing as we got closer. Excitement filled us every time we went up to Jerusalem. For, if we can travel to Jerusalem on a good wide road, then it is obvious that we are living in the time of the actual redemption of Israel. Every time we traveled up the road to Jerusalem, we were consumed anew by excitement, and every time we sang, we fulfilled our aspiration that 'every ascent to Jerusalem will be as a new experience in our eyes.'

On the way to the Kotel we stopped for a short visit at our son and daughter-in- law's home. They were fortunate to have bought an apartment in Jerusalem, and we loved to visit them. They were in the height of preparations for Shabbat, but they put everything down and sat with us in their living room. Rivka the baby cooed happily, enjoying the attention of her grandparents. After some time, despite the great joy and pleasure in the visit, I started to feel shamefully impatient. The urge to get to the Kotel overcame me, and I asked Abe if we could say goodbye and leave. Abe was surprised, but listened to my yearning, and we left their home in unusual haste for the Kotel. We parked our car outside the Old City and walked to the Kotel with prayers and thanksgiving in our hearts: A prayer that the holy city will be magnificently built and the nations will be welcome guests, and a prayer of thanksgiving for the gift of togetherness which G-d had given us on this magical Friday.

The path to the Kotel seemed to leap forward, joining with our joyous hopping and skipping hearts, and we arrived in no time. After each one of us went to "his own" Kotel for his heart's prayer, we went to the Jewish Quarter to eat something light for lunch. When we got up to walk home, I felt heavier and slower. The hopping had turned to walking, and the walking to feet dragging. G-d had shortened our way to the Kotel, but the way back seamed so very long. Abe did not recognize the woman who was dragging herself to the car. It was very rare to see me like this, even on long and hard journeys. But he was not too worried. He thought my fatigue was the common Jewish tiredness, at the end of a long week, before a restful Shabbat. All I wanted was to get into bed and sleep. The excitement of Jerusalem, the yearning for prayer at the Kotel, our happiness as a couple, and our special private "togetherness" – all these wondrous thoughts and experiences seemed to have disappeared. The heaviness and slowness crushed all that I had experienced into crumbs of time, which seemed not to be my own, borrowed and foreign, crumbling under my heavy feet.

On our way home my soul gave in to my heavy body. I fell asleep until it was time to light Shabbat candles. I entered Shabbat calm and quiet, and the Tylenol pushed the pain to the rear of the stage, a gray background to the colorful existence of Shabbat. It was a very different Shabbat. A Shabbat with none of our children at home. After *Mincha* (afternoon prayers), and the women's class on the weekly Torah portion – which I had been giving every other week for the past eighteen years – friends invited us to their home for *Seuda Shlishit* (the third Shabbat meal). The two men were walking in front, and the distance between them and us women kept on growing.

"Why are you walking so slowly?" Abe asked in bewilderment, being used to my fast pace, reflective of my demands on myself.

"Because my head hurts less when I walk slowly," I answered. None of us gave much importance to what I said. Surely not me.

We continued to walk at a slow, friendly pace. When we got to their house, the men had already set the table and arranged the food for the meal. During the whole Shabbat I took painkillers and did not allow the pain to invade our happiness of Shabbat. On Sunday morning, when I had a hard time waking up, my husband brought up the issue by saying, "You have never let pain 'run' your life."

At that time, as in all other times, this was the last thing I needed in my life. A sick body?! Is not the body, as it is, a limiting enough cage for the soul, for the spirit, for the *Neshama* (the devine spark within us)? The headache, I thought, was sent to me as a troublesome noise that steered me away from the essence of my meaningful being, and doing that which I was dedicated to do.

•••

"I want you to go to the emergency room in order to exclude anything major," Dr. Levanon said while writing a referral. He knew me, and he knew that I had no time or place for pain and illness in my life. There were many important issues to deal with – things at the cutting edge of science, things that could save lives, many lives. "To which emergency room would you like to go?"

"I will go to the emergency room in City Center hospital," I answered. Abe, a construction project manager, had been heavily involved in building their new emergency room and this made me feel welcome and at home.

"I am giving you a referral to the City Center emergency room, but I am asking you to go there now, and not after work," he said. I was surprised that he knew what I was planning on doing.

"How did you get here?" he asked.

"In my car," I answered.

"I do not want you to drive there. Leave your car here in the parking lot and take the train to Tel Aviv."

I was surprised; I did not expect this. Just a headache, I had thought to myself. How serious can a headache be? So what if it's a little stronger than a regular headache!?

"Please let me know what the doctors at the emergency room say," he requested.

"Happily," I answered, already with my back to him and on my way out. I parked the car in a parking space by the building where I worked. My office was only minutes away from the train station. This way I would be able to get back to the office afterwards and work, as I had a full day ahead of me.

I boarded the train to Tel Aviv and called Abe, who told me, "When you get off the train please call me and take a taxi. Do not walk. I will wait for you at the entrance to the emergency room."

I did not look sick, certainly not deathly sick, but the team, who knew Abe very well, pushed up our CT request. When we got back to the ER, the images were already up on the screens. The doctors were focused on the images, and much talking could be heard – they had not noticed us yet. We were happy to be finished with the whole process so quickly. A full day of work and meetings awaited both of us.

A senior doctor approached us. We rose to greet him. His face was tight. Before I could internalize what was going on, he said: "You have a 'process' in your brain which is taking up space. It is very large, and it needs to be taken care of."

I have never had patience for beating around the bush. "A 'process which is taking up space' are fancy words to describe a cancerous growth," I said pointedly. "Why don't you call it by its name?" The doctor remained distant and resolute. "I am sending you to the best neurosurgeon for this type of tumor, Dr. Nelson. Go up to him so that he will be able to explain what he needs to do." In silence we took the elevator to the eighth floor.

Dr. Nelson was already waiting for us in his room. The CT images were staring at us on a big computer screen. "You can see that there is a large area which does not look like the healthy brain tissue seen in the other parts of the brain. This is the tumor. It is located on important areas of the frontal lobe of the brain, and it has to be taken out immediately. The images show that there is edema in the whole right frontal lobe, and in much of the left frontal lobe. The edema was caused as part of the inflammatory reaction to the pressure the tumor exerts on the normal brain tissue around it. I cannot perform the surgery while there is inflammation and edema. I am giving you pills to treat the inflammation. Start taking them today. The inflammation will go down within a few days and then I will be able to perform the surgery," he explained.

Before we could absorb the words or respond, he took a model skull from the shelf next to him and said, "Here, let me show you what I am going to do. The tumor is located in the center of the frontal part of the brain. In order to reach it we have to open the skull, raise the frontal brain, go underneath that and then reach for the tumor and try to take it out, along with as little as possible healthy tissue. Only when we are inside the brain will we be able to tell if it is already metastasized, and the pathology analysis, which will be done during the operation, will be able to tell us if the tumor is malignant. According to that information we will clean up the area around the tumor, put the brain and the bone back in their places and sew it up. I see that you wear a head-covering, so it will not be terrible. You will be able to hide the cut and the stitches with the head-covering."

I was shocked. Did he really think that in this moment this was what concerned me? Stitches all around my forehead?

While he was speaking, he picked up the front part of the plastic brain and pointed at the site where the surgeons had to get to. Then he put the plastic brain parts gently back in their places, as if they were a 3-D puzzle, and put the re-constructed head back on the shelf next to him.

I was listening as though I was in a horrible dream. I knew clearly that this could not be real, that it was for sure not happening to me. Abe's hand was cold in mine. My hands were always colder than his.

"What is the effect of a tumor in such a location? What functions does it affect?" I asked. Abe squeezed my hand with his, and his eyes begged me to not ask any more questions, hinting that we already knew more than we would like to know.

The doctor answered me briskly: "In the frontal brain most of the functions and systems which make us human are located.

There is no way to tell today what functions will be damaged during the surgery, but we are well-trained in such surgeries, and we do our best to minimize the damage following the removal of a tumor."

When he finished his explanation regarding brain functions and possible damage to them, he moved onto a topic he felt much more comfortable with: "I am prescribing high doses of steroids for you. Start taking them now. We will set the surgery for a few days from now, to make sure that the inflammation recedes by then. I need for you to have an urgent MRI, today. Only after I see it will I be able to build the final strategy for the operation. The secretary will let you know the day and time for the surgery."

We were in shock. So much had changed in just a few hours. The brain pronounced words to the heart. The words filled the heart until it almost burst. The soul could not contain the words which were said, and which turned the world around us upside down. We were not capable of absorbing anything, of taking in anything. The moment evaded our eyes. Thick screens were trying to dull the "burning bush" of pain. But my soul did not ask for fake quiet. My soul wanted to know where I was standing today, where was I going, and how.

We went back to the emergency room with the answers and decisions of the neurosurgeon, Dr. Nelson. We would need to come back to the hospital for an MRI at 2:00 am that night.

We left the hospital tightly holding on to our strands of sanity, unwilling to let it disappear in an abyss of fear and darkness from the graphic images – how they will cut, take out and destroy part of my brain tissue. Part of who and what I am. Part of what I will soon say "I used to be." What would be, and what would I be, in the future? The fog of a frightening and paralyzing future, thick and heavy, moved around me in circles, and beyond it I could not see a thing. We held hands in silence. We knew that together, we would be able to handle whatever G-d had assigned to us and remain stable and standing tall.

• • •

1:30 am. The hospital corridors are dimly lit and almost empty of people. In the MRI unit the light is bright. Reception at the counter is quick and efficient. "Have you ever had an MRI before?" I am asked.

"No" I answer. People with tired eyes and worried faces are sitting and waiting. I am taken to the MRI room and asked to lay on my back. I lower my head slowly on the hard flat "bed." The pain is strong, in spite of the Tylenol. The knocking sound of the machine hits my brain, echoing inside, intensifying the pain waves, which are already strong.

"Please wait outside until the doctor sees the images and writes her report. In the meantime, we will prepare a disk with the results for you," I am told.

How can I "sit and wait" when I have a big tumor in my brain?

We hear a rumor that there is a doctor on duty tonight who is reading MRI results "on the spot." Instinctively I look for her. The secretary at the counter points to the right door. "But you may not go there" he says in a low, authoritative voice.

"So please have the doctor come out to us," I ask. "It is very urgent."

Something in my tone of voice must have convinced him. The doctor comes out with a worried face and says, "A process which is taking up space is clearly visible, and around it there is a bad edema. I mentioned in my report that there might be something in the blood vessels which could be involved in the process or be the cause. I wrote this so that the insurance company will understand why I thought there was a need to add to the test an injection of contrasting material, so that the blood vessels can be analyzed, and will pay for it." With her face tight, she gives us a copy of her report and wishes us good health. We are stunned, exhausted, yet fully enlisted in the mission of survival. We cannot afford to give space to the doctors' worried faces.

5:00 am. Home at long last. The fact that there was a doctor on site during the night MRI is a little encouraging. This way, the surgeon will be able to get the results early this morning and then already set a time for the surgery. My sense of urgency is stronger now than any worry. With G-d's help the tumor has been discovered, and I can undergo surgery and have it removed. Still, we wise for a second opinion.

Monday morning arrives, the time where distinction is made between light and darkness, between the different gray shades of my brain. In the little time we had left of the night we could not sleep.

Abe takes me to my work so that I can make arrangements for my expected absence. I focus on practical matters: briefing management, canceling appointments and meetings, and discussing the implications of my medical situation on the processes currently taking place in the company and those planned for the near future. Usually, I function well under pressure, but this time my head is somewhere else. I am in survival mode.

Abe calls. With a sigh of relief, he tells me that the neurosurgeon said that it is not a tumor, but rather an aneurysm in the wall of a blood vessel. The MRI will be transferred to Dr. Nir, who is an expert on blood vessels in the brain. Abe thinks that this is good news. I know that a situation with an aneurysm is very volatile and unpredictable.

The phone rings again. Again, it is Abe on the line, and this time he sounds very worried and pressured. "Dr. Nir from the hospital saw the MRI and called me right away to ask where you are. When he heard that you are in your office, he shouted that you must be in a bed in the hospital and that it is dangerous for you to be running around."

The doctor was stressed and Abe, affected by him, got scared. I calm him down. "Let us focus on trying to get a second opinion," I suggest, in order to calm the heavy, pressured feeling which was moving between us.

I call the private medical service at Hadassah hospital and ask for an urgent appointment with the head of neurosurgery, and an urgent appointment with the head of the imaging department. The appointments are set for eleven in the morning and three thirty in the afternoon. Our daughter Devorah, a young doctor who studied at Hadassah medical school, suggests meeting another neurosurgeon, Prof. Hezkeyah, an expert on blood vessels in the brain. She was very impressed by him as a lecturer and as a human being. An appointment with him is set for two in the afternoon. Abe picks me up, we drive to the hospital and Devorah joins us there.

Prof. Govrin, the chief radiologist, shows us the blood vessel, from which a huge balloon full of blood, the huge aneurysm, erupts. He shows us the heavy edema around it, and suggests that it was caused by blood which leaked from the aneurysm through its extremely stretched and thin wall. He explains that we have to see a neurosurgeon "now" and as soon as possible set a date for surgery, and to please keep him informed. We leave his office, heading to our next appointment.

Prof. Hezkeyah receives us warmly, his face full of worry and wonder, reflecting a little of what we are feeling inside us. He points to the aneurysm on the computer screen and explains that it is huge. "This is a giant aneurysm. We do not see such aneurysms in functioning people," he emphasizes.

"There is a need to do an exploratory neuro-endovascular procedure in order to understand the situation better." He urgently schedules us for Wednesday at noon. Everyone, the doctors and ourselves, are hoping that by then the steroids will reduce the edema-caused swelling.

Throughout the day and into the night, "well connected" family members are trying to get a meeting with Rabbi Firer, a genius medical consultant with remarkable expertise in matching medical professionals to specific medical situations. Finally, one of them succeeds. Abe travels to the Rabbi before dawn. When he arrives and opens the door to the Rabbi's office, Abe sees that my medical records are already spread out in front of him.

Rabbi Firer's words are short and definitive: "There are two people in the country who can do this endovascular procedure: Dr. Nir from City Center and Dr. Hezkeyah from Hadassah. Because the situation is complex, it is best to do it in Jerusalem, because there they have a whole expert team needed for this case: Prof Govrin, the imaging expert; Prof Simon, the neurosurgeon; and Prof. Hezkeyah, the neurosurgeon who operates using neuro-endovascular methods.

A decision is made: We will act according to the outline laid out by Prof. Hezkeyah. I deal with the situation on the practical level. I carry out one action after the other and do not look beyond the "doing." My head, brain, and mind act without internalizing the gravity of the situation, and the effect on the rest of my life.

• • •

I am hospitalized in the neurosurgery department, waiting for a diagnostic endovascular procedure. It is very cold in the operating room. I am shaking and trembling. Prof. Hezkeyah is standing over my body, which is laid out on the surgery table awaiting whatever will come. He gives instructions to the team. His calm, authoritative voice imbues the room with a professional and focused atmosphere. A shot of local anesthetic, and after it a deep cut into my thigh, through which they insert a long tube from the artery in the leg to the artery in the brain.

I am left alert and clear headed so that I can cooperate with the doctors. A sheet, hanging on a lead plate protecting from harmful radiation, is laid as a screen in front of my eyes. My sight is blocked but I can hear everything. The voices unfold in front of me, telling me what is happening. I hear the doctors moving around with low voices while injecting, inserting, draining, and transferring equipment from one to the other. My body is in their hands and my soul is roaming free.

"Let's stop here," I hear Prof. Hezkeyah say. This is after many injections of contrast material to the aneurysm area. They are taking a break. Another doctor joins the team. His unfamiliar voice pours into the mixture of dulled speech which is densely packed with concern. The voices re-enter the space where I am laying down, as if they have been called from a nearby mountain top, and then the conversation stops. "We will make a few more tests and then we will finish."

I feel a confident presence next to my head and a gentle voice notifies me: "I am going to hurt you a little, but it will only be for a short time, I am sorry." The doctor next to me presses his fingers deep into my neck, a strong pressure and then release. And again. And again. "We are done," he says. "We will close the cut in the thigh and see you in the adjacent waiting room."

Still on the bed, I am rolled out of the neuro-endovascular surgery room and they call Abe to come in. Abe stands by the side of the bed and looks at me with soft eyes, which are trying not to betray worry. His hand is holding mine. Three serious looking doctors are standing at the foot of the bed.

Prof. Hezkeyah explains the situation. His factual, technical tone keeps us all focused. "The aneurysm is huge and life threatening, and surgery is needed in order to take it out and seal the artery wall." As he speaks, he turns his head to Prof. Simon and adds, "This can be done only with open cranial surgery."

In the corner of my eye, as he is standing at the far side of the bed, I can see Prof. Simon moving his head from side to side, disagreeing. "I cannot go in there surgically. As soon as I raise the brain to reach the site, the aneurysm will burst and kill her. I am not touching her."

He hands the ball back to Prof. Hezkeyah, who raises his hand a bit and draws the shape of the aneurysm on a piece of paper he holds. On this drawing, he shows why the aneurysm cannot be closed/sealed/stuffed/filled with coils, as is routinely done to aneurysms. He points to its opening and explains: "It is too big and completely open, with no neck."

My eyes travel between the three doctors. I try to detect who has some ray of hope. Even a small fragment, a flicker, a tiny spark will do. But they are avoiding my gaze. When eyes rest on them, they each, in his turn, look down. They have nothing to offer me. They have neither an offer nor a solution. I raise my eyes away from them, higher. I know that something has to be done, and despair – theirs or mine – will lead to nothing good.

Abe's voice drops a practical anchor unto the ground of realty. "So, what do you suggest doing? We cannot just leave things as they are and wait..."

Following a tiny nod from Prof. Hezkeyah, Prof. Govrin draws a few lines on another piece of paper, and explains the situation to us. "There are two arteries, which feed the two frontal lobes of the brain: one on the right side of the neck for the right frontal lobe, and the other on the left side of the neck for the left lobe. If we close or block the artery which feeds the aneurysm, the aneurysm will shrink and will not be life-threatening anymore. However, the price is clear. With no blood supply, the right frontal lobe of your brain will die. It is unfathomable to do such a thing."

For a few minutes, the room is filled with silent helplessness. Prof. Hezkeyah bravely breaks the heavy silence of the two other doctors. "Some people have a tiny, thin connection between the two main arteries, the right and the left. You have such a connection. After we saw how seriously bad the situation is, we checked what would happen to the blood flow if the right artery is blocked and sealed. This was the reason we pushed deep into the artery until it was fully blocked. It seems that during the time the artery was fully blocked there was blood flowing through the tiny bridge. Therefore, after the blocking of your right artery there will be some flow of blood from the left artery, via the tiny thin bridge."

"If closing the artery does not lead to the disappearance of the aneurysm, will it then be possible to try the surgical option? Would it be possible to resume blood flow in the artery you blocked?" I ask.

"No," is the answer. "It's a road of no return. Blocking the artery is irreversible."

I look at Abe, and he looks at me. His eyes are full of worry and questions. Questions which needed words. Questions which cannot be uttered. Questions which should not be asked. He presses my hand, which has been in his own all this time. "When can you do the endovascular surgery?" I ask.

After some verbal debate about the needed preparations and the medical team required for this operation, Prof. Hezkeyah turns to me and asks, "When would you like us to do the surgery?"

"As soon as possible," I respond. "I have a ticking bomb inside my brain, and the red figures on its digital clock are running. The problem is that I cannot read the numbers on the display panel, and therefore I do not know how much time I have before the aneurysm explodes and kills me. Please do whatever you need to do, and now."

Prof. Hezkeyah sighs. "It is already late. I can make a special effort and get the whole surgery team for tomorrow afternoon. This is the earliest possible time, and will require great effort and calling in favors from many people."

"OK, so tomorrow you will do the surgery and block the artery which feeds the monster aneurysm," I utter, as much of a command as a prayer.

Prof. Hezkeyah turns towards Prof. Govrin and says to him, "But tomorrow is Tisha B'av. On this day we avoid getting into any risky situations, it is a day prone to tragedies and disasters. Maybe we should delay by a day?"

Prof. Govrin answers, "The patient is in a major life-threatening situation. Not to do the surgery right away is a much higher risk. There is no reason to postpone the surgery because of Tisha B'av."

Prof. Hezkeyah ends the discussion. He promises to do everything in his power to get everything ready by tomorrow afternoon. Again, I am wheeled in the bed, this time to a room in the neurosurgery department, and a "Fasting" sign is hung on the bed. A few hours later, everyone starts to fast over the destruction of our temples. Tisha B'av has come.

The hours pass slowly. Unhurriedly, the ward sinks into nighttime quiet. The only thing entering my conscious being is my heartbeat. I hear it beating as if saying: I are beating, and you are alive. You are alive! This is the message with every beat. Somewhere along the infinite axis of the night I understand that my heartbeat is keeping me alive, but at the same time it is shortening it. Every beat sends blood rushing into the aneurysm, stretching its walls just a little bit more. Every beat, every blood flow into the aneurysm brings my end closer. Life and death held in the hand of a beat.

It is unbearable to hold on to this thought. I divert my mind, trying to focus on prayer. A prayer that the surgery will go well.

A prayer that the blood will flow from the left artery to the right lobe. A prayer that I will live. A prayer that I will remain myself after the surgery. Is one allowed to pray for the impossible? Maybe we may pray only for what is possible? What should I pray for? My head is swaying from the thoughts filling it, from the unfathomable possibilities, from the contradictions within my very own existence. Thoughts are pressed into the bottle neck of reality, into the risks within any possible outcome from the surgery I have agreed to let Prof. Hezkeyah preform.

Soundlessly I pray, "G-d, I really do not know what to ask of you, what to pray for. The only thing I can do is to leave my soul in your hands. Do with it whatever is right and appropriate by you." I close my eyes. "Unto your hands I deposit my soul when I go to sleep, and when I awaken."

In the morning, the family gathers at the hospital. Everyone's faces are stunned, trying to get a hold of reality, an anchor, a cantilever, a rope. They cannot escape from reality, even though they try to scare it away. It flows with blood which is filling an important artery. Soon it will not be free to flow there again, forever.

Towards two pm I am taken down to the waiting room outside the neuro-endovascular surgery room, which I am already familiar with. This is the room where the decision to try and save my life was taken. Abe is waiting for me inside. Prof. Hezkeyah enters. He asks Abe to leave and wait outside. He pulls a high and narrow backless stool towards him, as if trying to create an alert position for himself which will fit the words he needs to say. He pulls it closer to me and sits by my side.

"Sara, I did not sleep all night. I tried to find another solution for the situation in your brain. I read through so much medical literature, and I could not find anything. Sara," he said my name again, and I knew that both his professional heart and his personal heart were finely tuned towards me,]. "Please listen to me very carefully. Even though I have done a huge effort to get the surgery room and the team ready for your operation today, even though I have asked for every possible favor, in spite of it all, you may rescind your consent for this surgery. I will not be angry. On the contrary, I will understand you. This is your brain. This is your life. It is surgery with gigantic risks. Think it over, please. You are alone now. I asked Abe to leave so that there would be no pressure on you, not even the slightest, to consent to this operation."

"I give my consent to the surgery. Give me the required form and let me sign it," I decide, with no doubt or hesitation in my voice. He puts the document, which has been prepared in advance, in front of me. I sign and hand it back to him. He sits next to me again, takes my hand between his own and says to me: "I have ended my fast so that I will have the strength to do the surgery in the best way possible. I am sorry that I could not find another solution. It is important to me that you know that I relentlessly searched for one."

His voice cracks, he does his best to get a hold of himself. "It was important to me to try and take care of the situation in a less drastic, less extreme, less destructive way," he almost whispers, and I think I hear his voice break down.

"I know," I bolster him. "I pray you will be a good messenger. Do not worry, all will be well. Let's go ahead and start."

"Are you sure?" he asks. "I do not want you to feel any pressure, not from me and not from your family. It is your life and your decision."

"Prof. Hezkeyah, with G-d's help all will be well," I promise him.

"OK, the whole team is ready," he answers.

One of the staff comes to wheel me in, but Prof. Hezkeyah stops him. "Where is her husband, Abe? She is not leaving without a farewell kiss from her husband." His stressed voice is decisive yet holds a thin thread of hope. Abe comes into the room, leans towards me with tearful eyes and kisses me. One tear is singed upon my cheek and is my escort to the surgery room.

"G-d, I do not know what to ask for. I want to live! I want to live..." I feel light and clear headed. This is all I can do. I am not afraid. After the surgery I will be told that it is no big deal to not be afraid when you have no real idea of the risks and outcomes. But I do not want to know what will be missing from my being if I will survive the surgery – all I want is to live life as I knew it, as I lived it. As I have lived it to its fullest. I am in a state of complete humility. I have no clear wish beyond the wish to live, the wish that G-d's gift, the soul within me, will stay inside me.

"G-d, I hand my whole being to you. We here on earth will do all that we can, and you will do whatever you wish with me. In your hands I entrust my soul. In your hands I entrust my soul when I go to sleep, and I awake. Please, make it so that I will wake up and live. In your hands I entrust my soul. In your hands."

I wake up for a moment and find Prof. Hezkeyah next to me. I wake up again, this time in the neurosurgery recovery room.

The equipment in the neurosurgery recovery room is beeping at even tones. Abe comes in, kisses my forehead, and comforts, calms me by saying that all is well. "All will be well when I will be given something for these terrible pains," I say and dive down again. Abe receives special permission to remain next to me, and I become submerged again into the twilight of semi-consciousness.

• • •

I am alive! I am speaking. I feel my body. My hurting head held wonderful tidings within. I feel, therefore I am alive! I see Abe and I know he loves me. Earlier I saw Prof. Hezkeyah's face and recognized him. I am alive, and I am Sara! The same Sara that I was before. My whole being is thankful for what remained in my brain, for whatever is functioning. There is no room in my being for those things which are missing, for fears, for questions... only for what there is, and that "is" is huge.

"All of the children are waiting outside this room," Abe says. "I want you to know that Prof. Hezkeyah walked out of the surgery smiling from ear to ear and rushed me into the imaging room to show me the miracle. He also invited Devorah. He showed us the video chronicling the whole surgery, up to the moment he put the coils in. He showed us how the blood flow got totally blocked, and then a miracle happened. From the tiny thin artery which connects the two main arteries, blood started flowing into the continuation of the right artery, right after the point it had been blocked by the coils. He was really beaming and dancing with joy when he showed us this miracle, over and over again. We all celebrated. We broke our fast with food which family members and friends brought, the whole time with huge smiles on our faces. We knew that your life had been saved. We prayed together with Prof. Hezkeyah that the damage to the right lobe will not be too great, but the important thing is that you are alive. After all, this is what we have all been praying for, this is what we asked from G-d."

Everyone is trying to touch the miracle. A miracle for which I am the vehicle. Our sons and daughters, sons-in-law and daughters-in-law, sisters and friends... everyone is touching the bed, and me. It is a determined touch, yet with light fingers, as if they are afraid that if they do not touch me, the holder of the miracle, the miracle will vanish, and me with it.

I am brought back to the ward. I feel that this is my personal time with *Hashem* (the name of G-d pertaining to its merciful personal care). I wish to speak with Him so much. I wish to listen to Him. This is a time for a conversation between He and I, between my creator and myself with no intermediaries, with no written words on worn out, used pages. Why? Because the candle has come back as a halo above my head, and I have seen the universe from end to end. Why? Because I saw everything and nothing, and again reality hit me on the head and left me blind, once again.

On the hospital bed I say to Abe, "It is important to make a Kiddush (a blessing of the Shabbat, over wine, followed by a light meal) for the whole community on the first Shabbat after I am released from the hospital. A thanksgiving Kiddush."

Abe does not understand the rush. "I think it is too soon for thanksgiving. Let's wait a little longer and see how things settle and the situation becomes more clear."

But the need to say thank you to G-d is greater than me. It is clear to me that I am not only myself, but rather that my being extends beyond the limitations of the body, brain and intelligence. I feel that my life is greater than my physical being and that this is beyond any logic, and for that I wish to say thanks. For that I must say thanks.

I am afraid that the miracle will disappear before I will have time to say and show my thanks. It does not feel right to wait "a little bit longer so that we can see how things stabilize and the situation becomes clear." I want to say thanks for this clarity of the now. Now I am here. Alive, and one should be thankful for being alive. I will always be able to say thanks again. I am too small to deserve this generosity and truth. I know with a clear, internal wisdom that miracles come in order to teach us, all of us, about the wonders of personal providence and about "your miracles which are with us every day."

The recovery time ends and I return home. I am surprised and moved to find out that the Rabbi's wife, my neighbor and good friend, heard about the surgery and got the women together to say *Tehilim* (Psalms) during the whole day of fasting and mourning over the destruction of the Temple, a day when reading Tehilim is not usually allowed. A warm feeling spreads within me. I was not alone there. Not just doctors and family, but also the community, they were all in the concealing and protecting hand of Hashem.

Some people have a grievance. "Why did you not tell us that she was in a life-threatening situation? Why did you not tell us that the surgery was so dangerous and high risk? If we would have known, we would have said goodbye in a more meaningful way. If we would have known we would have asked the *Yeshiva* (a Jewish study hall for men), the school, the community, the *Midrasha* (a Jewish study hall for women) – to pray. To say Tehilim."

"Why did you not tell us?" We had no answer. "To say goodbye?" I was not ready to say goodbye yet.

From yours

From yours,
To you it returns
And will return.
I hold on to yours,
It is mine.
What you have given me with compassion
Do not take away
Until it will mean compassion
Until I will admit.

Because
I thankfully thank you,
For you have returned,
And will continue to return,
As long I am within myself
And I can thank
As long as the soul is within me
And my brain is with me
And the language which you have given me, is my speaking soul
As long as my human spark remains whole.

Shabbat. I go to the synagogue. My spirit is strong within my still fragile body. I carry myself with a clear mind, within inner turmoil. During the service, my soul is at peace, settling into the known, relaxed and comforting place of a conversation with G-d. At the end of the service the *Gabbay* announces, "Abe and Sara Davidson have invited the whole community to a *Kiddush Raba* in thanksgiving to Hashem." His words pull me out of myself. All the women around me wish to know what we are thankful for.

What am I going to tell them, I wonder in a flash, that a

miracle happened to me? That I have no idea how, how I am still alive? That I was at the precipice of certain death, but G-d sent an angel to protect me so that I did not fall from the land of the living?

The lady who catered the Kiddush, wonderful and efficient, has set a beautiful spread, with tables full of good food. *Kugel* (a traditional noodle casserole) and *Cholent* (a traditional, slow cooking, meat and beans dish), trays are passed among the people. Those who prayed in other synagogues join us. What are we going to say? Abe asked the Rabbi how to thank G-d in front of the community. The *"Nishmat Kol Chai"* (a psalm which starts with the words: "the souls of all those alive, bless the name of G-d") prayer was his answer.

Abe is standing on steps which go down from the synagogue to the table area, a prayer book is open in his hand and he is reading aloud. Reading and crying, reading and crying. Silence. Even the children stop loading up cups with snacks. He finishes, but the silence continues.

My thoughts are racing. What am I going to tell everyone in the community? My head seals up, my brain freezes and my body becomes petrified from awe in the moment of this occasion and its meaning. I have never had any problem speaking in front an audience, but now, I am flabbergasted (where do I go?).

My soul opens up and speaks. "A time of danger. A time of sickness. A time made for prayer. For almost a whole day and night I had time to think about prayer. To pray, and again to ask and pray, with no limit. I found out that I do not know what to ask for. I found out that I cannot ask for anything. I found myself living the many hours before the surgery in a constant state of '*in your hands I deposit my soul,*' in a deep awareness of '*the soul thou has given me.*' I did not know why, but I knew in an incomprehensible way that G-d is by my side, next to me, with me. I knew that I do not understand what is happening, but everything has a reason. I knew that there are no coincidences in G-d's world, and no coincidences in the world of the Jewish people."

I am not hearing in my ears that which my heart speaks, that which my lips say. I am encompassed by many faces of love, and I see not the faces but only the love. Hundreds of listening ears surround me. The content of my speech echoes back to me from the faces of those listening. I conclude by saying, "I stood in front of G-d and told him, just like the illiterate farmer who stood in front of G-d and did not know the words of the Holy-days' prayer, here are the letters I know, create from them my prayer, as I am humbled by the trials you have put in front of me. Do with me as you please."

A year passes, and another one. Some people from the community have had to deal with terrible diseases and life-threatening situations. They did not show their troubles by their countenance, but they would come to Abe, each in their own time, and tell him that strength was born in them to not give in to the disease, not to despair or give up, even in light of low chances. They found that strength thanks to my words during the Kiddush. Those that have seen in their very own eyes that *"even if a sharp sword is laid upon a person's neck, he should not give in to the calamity."* These people will never forget our courage to embrace G-d's will.

I have become a vessel for advertising G-d's miracles. Me, so small. Can a person live as a miracle and still walk this human path? I thought the miracle will make me light. I found the miracle flying high up on a pole, but its heavy weight threatens to knock me over.

The formal recovery time is over, and I go back to my life, which is loaded with much good, and resume the pace I had been used to.

I must fly to the United States to present a file to the FDA on our system for early diagnosis of viral diseases. Armed with strict medical instructions, to take pills for preventing epilepsy and other conditions, I travel to the FDA meetings regarding the "SMART test-tube" we have developed. I hide the miracle from my work environment. No one needs to know what I have gone through.

• • •

I come back to Israel, and my head starts hurting. As a matter of fact, my whole body is hurting. My condition deteriorates. It deteriorates to the point where Abe takes me on a Shabbat to the Hadassah Hospital emergency room. I am hospitalized in a state of poisoning, due to an allergic reaction to an unknown substance. In the ward they diagnose pneumonia also, which requires strong antibiotics. I develop an allergic reaction to the antibiotics as well. I have become a fertile soil for problems in the immune system, which has been overloaded in the past few weeks. My condition deteriorates even further. It takes time until the doctors realize that I am in severe anaphylactic shock form the anti-epilepsy medicine. My whole body is badly swollen, and I can hardly breathe. I cannot move my fingers; they are swollen and their skin is painfully stretched. My head is exploding from pain, and every movement causes further agony. My body barely listens to me. The situation is terribly dangerous.

In spite of it all I am not sorry, and I am not diverted from my happiness in receiving the gift of my life. I know now, as I knew then, that I will keep on praying and I will survive. I believe that it is not for nothing that I have survived until now. The pain, the helplessness and the endless weakness do not enable the questions "by what right will I survive?" and "why is G-d closing my soul in its prison, even when it is becoming narrower than a strait?"

Recuperation is long, but with G-d's mercies I return to full health. Prof. Hezkeyah's recommendations are clear and decisive: "Go back to doing everything you have done before the surgery, go back to fully functioning in all of your activities and facets of your life. Do not stop using this brain of yours. Keep it active."

I am a scientist and I deal with research and development of new biotechnological innovations. I have collaborations in over 20 countries, from the United States to China. I also lecture at the university and enjoy every minute of it. "My work involves a lot of flying overseas, is this also OK?" I ask.

"It was the unbelievably dense system of nerves and all the brain cells which saved you. It was this high density that did not allow the aneurysm to fully explode and kill you. Continue doing all the wonderful things you have been doing before the discovery of the aneurysm."

I invest every bit of my earthly efforts into "returning to normal life." For over a year I fully function both at home and at work, just I had done before the aneurysm. Without noticing, I invest mental and emotional effort to lower the miracle from its great height to what I thought was its proper earthly place. The attempts to bring it "down to eye level" lead to forgetting the miracle. Slowly but surely, I take for granted that I am alive, fully functioning at home and at work, and continue to advance the system which I developed for the early diagnosis of infections such as HIV and Hepatitis C.

And then the pain appears again in my head. As is my habit, for many long days and nights, I ignore it. Time is short and the workload is heavy, and I have much that I need to get done. I am busy non-stop, from morning till night. But the pain does not let go. It bites into my being, does not let me ignore its existence and climbs to higher intensities. A new chapter begins, much more complex than the previous one. Now, as then, the pain saves my life.

The whooshing of the flowing blood
The whooshing of the flowing blood
The swishing of the thrusting sword
My heart beats echo
Between the walls of my life's prison
Ending my days.

Out of the depths
Out of the depths
I have cried unto thee,
O Lord Because you are with me
In the valley of the shadow of death
Leading me unto my return

To the soul which thou has given me
Which knows the light
From one end of the world to its end
And the time beats in its being
Which praises G-d
Halleluiah

Steps

With confident steps
I climbed to my life's destiny.
My G-d sent me the sun
To light my way.
The shadow stretched
From my past to me,
Wrapping itself on my neck
And getting back to it
Slightly softer,
  Sometimes forgotten.
With a hesitant step
I returned home.
The light of the moon
Echoed within its walls,
Unfolding the story of my life
Unto a closed fist,
Which jumps between the dreams
Unto the reality
Which spills like sand
From my life's clock.

How does one count miracles?

The headaches make it hard for me to function and think. Unlike my usual self, I take more and more pain killers. Dr. Levanon sends us to do an MRI. Again, the results are analyzed that very night, and we are told that there is a huge aneurysm just above the blockage of the right main artery. We are surprised, shocked and worried, as the blood flow to the aneurysm was blocked. We have no choice but to make an urgent appointment with Prof. Govrin at Hadassah.

We walk into his room and find him despondent and worried, with no smile on his face. He invites us to sit down and gets right to the point. On one screen is the image of the blocked artery, the blood flowing through the bypass and the aneurysm, which had shrunk to just a few millimeters within half a year of the operation. The other screen was dark.

Prof. Govrin points to the MRI image and explains: "As we expected, following the artery blockage the aneurysm shrunk, since there was no blood flow through it to the right front part of the brain. However, unfortunately, the aneurysm has grown again."

He turns on the other screen and points to a large aneurysm, located exactly where the previous one was. "This is the large aneurysm which is threatening your life, again. It has to be taken care of, and soon. The problem is that I have no idea how, as the natural access to this aneurysm, which is through the main artery, is blocked. Prof. Hezkeyah went overseas to his family, and he is due back only in a month or so, so we cannot consult him. I think this will need to be done through open cranial surgery. It is important that you see a neurosurgeon to discuss the situation and hear from him the surgery options to get the aneurysm out."

"How can it be, that the aneurysm grew due to deep blood flow inside it, when the artery which fed it is blocked?" I ask, astonished. I ask and know the answer right away. It is in front of me on the second screen. Blood is flowing to it from the bridge between the two parts of the brain. My right frontal lobe is fed from the blood which gets through the narrow bridge, from left to right, in my brain. The blood it receives flows to it via the aneurysm basin. What saved my life, as a thinking, creative and communicative person, is now risking my life.

"As you can see," Prof. Govrin answers, "the blood flows behind the aneurysm clot. This is why the blood is stretching the walls of the aneurysm again and enlarging it, and this is why the wall might tear and cause major brain damage, if not death. At the same time, the blood flow behind the clot threatens to release the clot from the aneurysm, and it could get carried onto the right main artery and block it, above the previous block. Such a situation will cause a serious stroke, with extensive damage."

"Is it possible to deal with it surgically?" we ask.

He refers us to Prof. Simon. Prof. Simon is the neurosurgeon who recognized my aneurysm when it first appeared. This time is no different: he is not willing to go into my brain. "This is a rare and complex situation," he tells us. "This is entering the Holy of Holies of the brain. A surgery like this is always complex, and in this case, it might be impossible to do without major, and broad, brain damage, with a high risk of death during or following the operation. In my opinion, there is no one in this country who will be willing to go into your brain in this situation."

We do not know what to think. Emotions flood us, without control. Yes, he had said already the first time that there was nothing to be done, but this time there is no other option, there is no way to reach the aneurysm via the arteries, as the artery leading to it is blocked. The only way to survive this terrible verdict is to not give up. I knew of only one way to keep despair away: to seek a solution even when we were told there is none.

We fix a meeting with Prof. Hed, a neurosurgeon "with hands of gold." On his screen, in his office, is the aneurysm, which has grown further. His face promises nothing good. He explains in detail how serious and complex the situation is. "Since this is a very rare occurrence, there is no experience in this country with a surgery like this. Maybe there are surgeons in the United States who have done a few such cases. You should look into it, and fast. I will write my opinion down, and you should hand it to your health insurance as soon as possible so that they finance the overseas surgery. I hope you will find someone who will be willing to do this procedure. This is a grave and rare situation, usually people do not live to get to such a state."

He writes the letter, then he takes another piece of paper and writes a prescription, while explaining, "I see that you are in a lot of pain. It is not good nor healthy for you to be in a state of stress or pressure. I am writing a prescription for medication with morphine. Take it and try not to be a hero. You must be relaxed if you wish to survive this aneurysm."

The Essence of My Life
Within the pain The hope
To know the essence of my life
Before I will not know a thing.

The pain, the effects of the medication and the consternation on one hand, and the need to act in a focused and efficient way to find a place for the surgery on the other hand, forces me to stay home. From the house I do my best to answer questions from work. Due to my state, I do not know if my answers have any value. I am doing my best. Finding a medical, surgical solution and carrying it out – these are my goals. In the past, I always functioned well under stress and today my life depends on it. How does one do all this without stress?!

We call Prof. Marino, a friend of ours from the days I did my post doc in Atlanta, some twenty years ago. He used to be a top neurosurgeon in a leading hospital in Boston. We explain the situation and we ask for his help to find a surgeon who would be willing and able to perform the needed operation.

"Right away, by overnight courier, send me five copies of the whole medical file, including all the MRI and MRA imaging done to date," he asks. "I will transfer the material to the relevant hospitals." Before he disconnects the call, he says, "I know this sounds impossible, but you have to stay calm. Any tension can kill you." Silence. "Or cause brain damage which might be worse than death," he adds.

Five envelopes with all the information are sent urgently. Within 24 hours he transfers them to the leading neurosurgical departments in this field: in Boston, Atlanta, Texas and the West Coast. Thanks to his personal friendships with the department heads, he succeeds in getting my case an urgent review in the next big meeting at each of these neurosurgical departments. "There are only two centers which are willing to perform the surgery at their hospital," he tells us over the phone. I think to myself that two centers are more than none, and I need only one.

"Both teams which are willing to perform the operation warned that the risks are high. There will clearly be great loss of function, but, due to the severity of the situation and the urgency to treat it, they will be able to know the actual scope of the damage only once inside, in the area of the aneurysm, with the details right in front of their eyes." I get off the phone. Abe continues to talk with him.

Abe is invited to stay with Prof. Marino and his wife for the whole duration of the surgery and recuperation period, until we can go back to Israel. How long will it take? There is no way to know, until the surgeons go inside.

The surgeon from Boston calls us in order to explain all the risks, and set a date for the surgery, as soon as possible, in the next week or two. There is a surgeon. There is a whole team which is ready to save my life. But we have to finance it, immediately. It is a fortune.

"I have no doubt that the health insurance will cover all the costs," Prof. Hed promised, "but you need to start the wheels of bureaucracy turning right away, so that they will approve the great expense of the Boston surgery and pay them."

Am I allowed to fly in my condition? The question is on my lips, but I swallow it. It is a question one should not ask. We have to do whatever it takes to save my life.

In the health insurance offices, I fill in all the forms required for requesting an approval for overseas surgery. Because of the complexity of the surgery and thanks to the letter from Prof. Hed, there is no doubt as to whether it will be approved. The question is, how fast we will get the approval. The office staff is cordial and takes care of the paperwork with efficiency and empathy. The pity on their faces and in their tone of voice are foreign to me. I am not in a state which warrants pity. I am in a state which requires action and doing, and this is what I am doing, to the best of my ability, and in a focused and efficient way: to live, to get to the surgery before the aneurysm explodes, and to pray to come out of the surgery alive and functioning. To remain "Sara" after it.

Unlike the first time, now we are not doing everything alone. I ask my sisters to meet with us. We describe the situation to them. The aneurysm is back, in a huge way. The surgery is complex and dangerous and can be performed only in the United States. The shock on their faces and the fear in their eyes rattle me and pull me from the "doing" bubble, which has surrounded me like a protective wall and blocked the fear. It is hard for me to breathe. It is hard for me to think. I cannot look them straight in the eye. They all look so distraught.

I try to pull them out of the paralysis which has overtaken them. "We are truly fortunate. Thank G-d there is a possibility to operate. Thank G-d there is someone who is willing to perform the operation. With G-d's help the doctors and surgeons will be good messengers, and all will end in the best possible way."

Slowly, their breathing returns to normal and they find words. At first words of sorrow, fear and deep pain for the suffering and challenges which Abe and I are going through. However, after a short while, they shake all this off, and move onto practical issues. "Do not worry about the money. Leave this to us. We will take care of the money for the surgery, until the insurance will come around and pay. This way you will not delay the operation. It sounds that it is extremely dangerous for you to wait. The most important thing is that you two focus on the things only you can do. Fix a date, as soon as possible, and fly there."

I am emotionally flooded, feeling protected and loved. I knew all along that they would always be with me, but here, the "knowing" becomes real. I can touch it; I can see it. It is important for me to hear, with my own ears, that they will do everything, all that will be needed, so that the surgery can be done as soon as possible. It is important for me to know that Abe and the children will not be alone during the complex challenges ahead of us.

We are talking about hundreds of thousands of dollars. We are talking about an operation with a long and hard recuperation. We are talking about going there as the "Sara" I am today, but there is no way to know what kind of "Sara" will come home. We are talking about hard times, in which Abe will be alone with me in the United States. It meant that the children staying in Israel will be 7,000 miles away from us and from whatever happens to us, both to Abe and to myself. All these things do not sit well with us. Our hearts rebel.

The family's warm embrace and the community's support are important components in our life, and of our ability to do, to be, to live, to cope.

After much deliberation we decide not to go overseas for the operation. Here, there is no possibility to operate. The only remaining option is to try to treat the aneurysm by the endovascular route, meaning, to get to it via the only available blood vessel. A small and narrow vessel, but it exists. It is important to me to be in Israel, at home, among family. If we wish to survive the operation beyond physical survival, then there are factors which are much more important than the technical abilities of the surgeons.

We are trying to reach Prof. Hezkeyah. No answer from his office. Where is his secretary? We are helpless.

We go back to Prof. Govrin. He does not have good news. "Prof. Hezkeyah has postponed his return to Israel, due to his father's condition. There is no date yet for his return."

What do we do? We must not fall into despair, but it seems that all it would take is just the slightest push and we will fall into a deep black hole. "Look," he says, "until Prof. Hezkeyah comes back to Israel, all the cases which demand neuro-endovascular surgery are transferred to Dr. Nir in City Center hospital."

I am afraid of the unknown. I have full trust in Prof. Hezkeyah, because he sees himself as a messenger, and is aware that the surgery results do not depend only on him. He is very modest, and he knows how to say, "I do not know," when needed.

In another meeting with Rabbi Firer, Abe is told that Dr. Nir is an expert on endovascular procedures in the brain, and that we need to treat the aneurysm as soon as possible. Armed with Abe's personal acquaintance with most of the department heads at City Center, and with Rabbi Firer's recommendation, we soon have an appointment with Dr. Nir.

In his room the big screen is filled with the terrible aneurysm. "I can perform the surgery in two days," he promises.

"And what is the risk that you will not be able to reach it because of the blocked main artery?" I ask. He waives the concern away with his hand. "Wherever the blood can get to, I can get to," he answers, full of confidence.

He tells us about the risks involved with the procedure, such as full anesthesia and blood vessel damage during the catheterization but estimates the risk of death as a very small percent. Unlike Prof. Hezkeyah, he sees no need for a diagnostic endovascular procedure prior to the surgery.

The operation is set in two days' time, at two in the afternoon. I must come to the ward first thing in the morning for pre-operation tests, and be ready for surgery as soon as Dr. Nir finishes the first surgery of the day.

These two days are way too long, because of the fear. These two days are way too short, as I am failing to focus my wishes and prayers. Something is following me around, not letting go of a hard hold on my sanity, trying to choke it.

The morning of the surgery arrives. We leave early for the hospital. During the morning hours our children arrive, each one at his or her own time. My sisters have also come. What are they all talking about? I do not know. I am here, but not here. I am with them, but really not with them at all. I cannot relax.

Something is pulling at the hem of my consciousness, and undoes whatever little confidence I had gathered, one crumb after the other, since the aneurysm had become a monster again.

"Please change to this hospital gown and wait on your bed," I am told. We all gather inside my room. The conversation continues to float somewhere above and below me. I am here, but not here.

A nurse comes into the room. "Dr. Nir would like to see you. He is waiting for you at the nurses' desk."

"Why does he need you now? You are supposed to go down to the surgery room by now, did they not say it will be at two?" my sister is impatient. I think she is actually mirroring what we are all feeling. "I am coming with you," she says, and does.

"I need you to re-sign the consent form for the operation," the doctor says.

"Why?" I ask.

"The risk assessment has changed," he answers. At the bottom of the page the risk estimate is five times higher than what he had said before.

Regretfully, I sign. "In just a few minutes they will take you down to the operating room," he concludes and goes on his way.

My sister is enraged. "It is outrageous and irresponsible to let you know that it is much more dangerous only at the last minute, when you are all ready to go for the surgery. What, did he not know it beforehand?"

Abe is nerve racked and stressed to the maximum. "What happened? Why are you so upset?"

My sister is on the verge of tears. Then she is actually crying. "He no longer thinks it is a surgery with a regular level of risk. He had her sign on a risk of death five times higher than what he told you and what he had her sign earlier. How can he do such a thing, with no explanation or apology?! As if it is normal practice to change your mind a second before you start cutting."

Abe is silent. He looks at me and his eyes are asking what should not be asked: do you still have the courage to go through with it?

There is no sense in talking about it, not with her and not with Abe. There is no room in my heart for anger or disappointment, certainly not towards the person who is supposed to be G-d's messenger to fix me, to save my life.

I go back to my appointed room. It's clear to me that only now did Dr. Nir really look into the situation in my brain. That only now he has come to realize the full problem of going through and performing surgery through a very tiny blood vessel. A blood vessel with a diameter which does not enable a simultaneous passage for all the ultra-thin tubes and wires which are needed in order to perform the operation. A blood vessel which no one has ever tried to go through, anywhere. I have a bad feeling. I have been put into a situation where I am "a hostage" of the surgeon. I have no other option, and the bomb in my head is ticking...

What am I supposed to do? What?

I sit on the bed. On the bed at least I look "on the way to surgery." Everyone gathers around me. The nervous chatter from the morning moves into a burdensome silence. From the silence rises our daughter Bruryiah's voice, singing slowly and quietly "HaMalach HaGoel Oti" ("The Angel Who Protects Me", usually sung before sleep at night). Others join in the prayer, singing a song of faith and hope. Again and again the Malach HaGoel is invited to bless. I am due to go into a deep, deep induced coma, and I need all of G-d's possible help and support. In the silence, between the verse repetitions, a song emerges which describes what I wish to feel, what I have been trying to feel. How can one "force" the soul to feel the presence of the Shechina (G-d's merciful presence) next to it? We sing "On my right is Michael and on my left is Gavriel, in front of me is Uriel and behind me is Raphael, and above my head is G-d's presence the Shechina." No tears. No crying. Just a prayer coming from a deep and clear conviction that all is in the hands of G-d, "the healer of all flesh and the One who does wonders." We pray that He will do wonders for us too.

The minutes turn into an hour and still no one has come to take me. There is no longer a feeling of helplessness in the room. I have entered a state where it is clear to me that *"Even as I walk in the valley of death, I will not fear, for Thou are with me."*

A nurse and an orderly come through the open door of the room. "They have come to take you down to the surgery room. Are you ready?" the nurse asks.

Behind her stand two more nurses. I am confused. Why does it take such a big team to take me down to surgery? "We came to see you. We have never seen a surgery preparation like that. Since when does a person sing before surgery?" said one of them. "It is actually quiet charming to wait like this," added the other.

We go down in two separate elevators. The orderly, Abe and the bed with me in it in one, and the family in the other. At the entrance to the surgery area, we meet and part again. We will see each other, G-d willing, after the operation.

A Burnt offering

Behold the fire and the wood
But where is the lamb for the burnt offering?
What will live and what will die?
What will intensify and what will become orphaned?
And what will be deprived?
Until it will walk stooped?
A burnt offering you will be, my daughter
And the knife is waiting
And the flame is rising to the heaven
In rhythmed pulses
That do not let go From the thin walls
That maintain the existence
Until...

At the threshold of the end
I kneeled on its threshold
And could not see its end
Will there be a ladder
To bring me back to the world?
And if there is none?
And if not?
And if my hands will slip on the rope?
And if my legs will tremble under me
And shake me until I will not know
To differentiate?
Between the depth of the blackness
And the light at the end of the abyss?

The Valley
Even though I walk in the valley of the shadow of death
I will fear no evil for thou art with me
And if the valley spills to an abyss
Which resided there below
From times immemorial?
And if not all the waters have been gathered
And the earth will not be seen?
And if you will be with my soul
And leave me behind?
Then who will know
And who will admit
And who will confess
That he is tired?

• • •

In the waiting room they let only Abe stay by my side. After a while Devorah also comes in. We wait and wait. The big hand of the clock above my bed completes a full circle and starts another one. Someone comes in and tells us that Dr. Nir has been delayed due to an emergency operation, a head injury in a bad car accident. The clock hands keep going in circles. After many hours have passed, since I was brought to wait, we are told that "Dr. Nir went in for an emergency surgery of the person with the head injury, and will not perform your surgery today. You will need to stay in the ward, and he will do the surgery tomorrow."

The junior doctor goes on and explains: "On Friday, the day after the surgery, the doctor will be leaving for a conference overseas. But he asked to let you know that you have nothing to worry about, the recuperation from a catheterization is fast, and you will be released to go home after just a few days."

Many feelings are whirling and cascading inside me. Stupefaction, disappointment, surprise, shock. I feel detached from reality. I am like someone who has been taken to the scaffold, her head is on the block but the guillotine has not come down. I am like someone who has a gun pointing at her head, and the gun has made the sound of the firing pin hitting the bullet, but the bullet did not fire. In a haze I go out to the family. Everyone seems paralyzed and speechless. "I am not staying here. I am going home," I say, and do.

The tears break out as I am getting dressed. Bitter tears. Angry tears. Tears of disappointment. Tears of pain which have remained inside me, as part of the preparations for the additional and greater pain which will come after the surgery.

We all walk out of the hospital, shocked. It is cold. I feel that I have been saved. The tears of pain turn into tears of thankfulness to G-d, "For you have saved my soul from death, my eye from tears, my legs from collapse; I will walk in front of G-d in the land of the living..."

All along I knew that Dr. Nir did not see himself as a messenger of G-d. Now I knew that he did not have the humility required to change from his original plan for the surgery steps, even at a very high functional cost for me, maybe even an unreasonable one, just in order to remain "right" as to what he said to us in his office just a few days ago. "Wherever the blood can get to, I can get there also," he had said.

An opening
An opening
A moment
An eternity
A world

One buys his world in one moment
And the moment, what is it, compared to eternity?
A man stands at the opening of the world

Peeks for a moment
Affected forever.

One passes to eternity
In one moment
And another stands at the opening
At the end of the word.

The family starts to disperse. Devorah calls Prof. Hezkeyah's secretary at her home, on her private number. The secretary gave it to us as soon as she heard from Prof. Govrin about the new situation. Devorah wishes to know if the doctor has come back already.

"He will return from overseas tonight," she says.

"We need an urgent appointment with him for an endovascular surgery," Devorah tells her.

"But I was told that you are going to Dr. Nir."

Devorah describes what happened. "We decided not to wait for Dr. Nir, but rather wait for Prof. Hezkeyah."

The secretary sounds wide awake despite the late hour. "No problem. The doctor left the first few days after his return to Israel open, in order to enable any urgent surgeries he might need to perform." She asks for a moment to check his schedule. "He will do an exploratory procedure on Sunday morning, and based on that, you will go into surgery the following day."

I am back in a familiar world. A world where the stars move in their tracks and there are no eruptions or screeching. A world where doctors also pray for their successes. A world where even doctors, and especially doctors, understand their difficult job and are aware that it is a job which requires hard decisions, which have to be taken with humility. I am back to myself. I am thirsty. I am hungry. After all, I have been fasting for more than a day. My body and its needs enter my awareness. My soul wraps itself within my body as if it was an armor, and settles in patiently to wait.

Friday and Shabbat pass slowly. I am feeling that I am in an unfathomable existence: hanging between heaven and earth, without a hold on either one. Within my body, and outside of it, my soul shifts from a prayer of hope to a prayer of supplication, from pleading for the mercy of heaven – and not of humans – to a plea that He will not judge me in the measure of justice.

When I say goodbye to the *Neshama Yeterah* (the additional G-dly spark a Jew feels on the Shabbat) which is walking away with the Shabbat Queen, the space remaining fills up with fear. Alone, I will not be able to fight my enemies: fear and anxiety.

We hold onto each other, forming a space which connects

between the heavens and our earth. The silence twists around the cry to Hashem, hitting the walls of the space between us, filling it with a huge sound. *"Not in the sound G-d appears."* Only towards morning the fine, accurate and clear notes of the soul emerge from the silence. The gentle vibrations of its vocal cords rock us. We are submitting the music of our lives to the hands of the Creator, that all is His.

Again, I find myself naked under a thin hospital gown. Again, I am in a waiting room which opens to the endovascular surgery room. Again, I sign a consent form for the surgery, a consent for the anesthetization, a consent to totally disappear, except for my body, which will remain naked and bare of spirit and soul, of mind and character.

Prof. Hezkeyah calls for Abe to go into the surgery imaging room. The aneurysm, the very thin bypass from which blood flows into the aneurysm and to the remaining artery which feeds the right side of the brain – all these are stark, in every possible angle, on all the big screens. The doctor again explains what he has already told us earlier. He points to the blood vessels around the aneurysm and says that he will try to get to the aneurysm through the very thin bypass. It will not be a regular catheterization process, because there is no room to put all the fibers and microscopic tools needed for the mission through the very thin blood vessel, which feeds the aneurysm and the whole frontal lobe of the brain. He will try to get to the aneurysm with a fiber lead, and on it guide the coils for sealing the aneurysm. He will try hard, but it might not be possible to deal with the aneurysm in this way, and he might need to go out after achieving nothing.

Abe leaves the imaging room, kisses me on my forehead and whispers, "I love you. Be strong, and good luck." The door to the corridor opens, the children come in to wish me good luck. This time everyone knows how dangerous the situation is, and how risky the surgery. They are crying, but they are trying to hide the tremors and tears. They are trying to protect me. I love them all very much, but in these moments, I have already curled into myself. The words, the scenes, the faces, the tears – they all fade from my consciousness, disappearing the way they came. They did not find me. They found only a void, a gaping abyss, with the spirit of G-d hovering over it in the dark.

Again, two nurses are handling the bed, one at the head and one at the foot, to take me into the surgery room. Again, Prof. Hezkeyah stops them. "I am not doing the surgery until her husband parts from her with a kiss."

Again, Abe comes in, kisses me and says that all will be well, and that he is right here, outside the door, waiting for me until I come out. Only this time the farewell sounds like a farewell before death. Again, Prof. Hezkeyah asks me, "Are you ready? Are you sure that you are ready? We have not started yet; we can call off the surgery."

Again, I respond to him, "Do not worry. G-d willing, you will be a good messenger, and all will be well."

This time everyone who knows me, or my children – people from the community, synagogues, Yeshivas, school children – everyone is praying during these hours, and everyone will continue praying for success throughout the duration of the surgery, and beyond.

Again, I submit my soul into G-d's hand, and again I ask that He return it to me in
the future – the future which will arrive when I wake up from the anesthesia.

Again, I sink into nothingness, naked from knowledge and without any senses or belonging.

Blocked and Bleeding

The thrust of the sword swung high
The whistle of the air being cut
By the sharp edge of the knife entering my head
And its penetrating look turns my flesh
Filling it up with prickles.
The questions rise with the flows of the scream,
Farther and farther away from me,
And I remain blocked and bleeding
The puddle of blood curled unto itself
Leaving the red question
Open, every day anew.
"In thy blood live!"
Really?
Till when?

I am suffocating. I am fighting to breathe. I am on a respirator. At the fringes of awareness, I remember that they had told me that they would insert a tube into my trachea. I remember the anesthesiologist explaining that he will have to control my breathing and heart rate during the surgery. They will slow my heartbeat so that they might have a chance to fix what needs fixing.

I am confused. If I am already awake, then why don't they release me from the machines? I am squirming under this suffocation, trying to take out the tube from my throat. A hand stops me. "Mother," she whispers, "please do not pull, you will only hurt yourself. You woke up too soon, I will call the anesthesiologist."

The moments until the anesthesiologist arrived seem like hours. A few more seconds of being awake, before sinking back down to the unknown and the unconscious.

From the deep, I have called Hashem and I knew not that I had called.

I wake up in an empty bed. Only a heavy, hard, fossilized head lays on it. And the head is empty, it has no thought inside it. Only a pain which rules all, whirling in the hollow of my brain, hurls itself unto the walls of its prison, and screams towards the nothingness, "help!" As the pain intensifies, the bed fills up. Feet, legs, hands, arms, a body and in it, a beating heart and lungs which burn at every breath. A hand is placed on the forming body. A warm hand on my cold body.

"All is well. I am here," Abe's voice seeks the openings of my ears, but I have no ears, and the voice invades a painfully pulsing space. I am supposed to also have a mouth.

With great effort I find it, and with it I discover my face. "I am cold... where am I?" I weakly ask.

"You are in the neurosurgical intensive care unit. Thank G-d that you have woken," Abe answers.

The awareness comes to me as a hot wave within a terrible cold – I am alive. I am alive!

"I am cold. I am in pain. I am nauseated," I say. Abe calls the nurse without removing his hand from my body, as it slowly fills up with live organs. There is a blanket on it. The blanket is heavy. It pulls me down to the netherworld, to a place with no air. I am shivering. Another weight is spread on my body, which is begging to escape from my head. Now, it cannot run away. All that it is left is a rattling shake, and I do not know if it is so because it does not have the strength to run away, or that this movement is all it can do as the start of an escape.

"I am cold. I am in pain. I am nauseated," I say again.

Abe whispers, "The nurse is putting into the IV something for the pain. She also injected something for the nausea." Why is he whispering? Does he actually hear the banging sounds on the walls of my empty head?

He whispers me into the nothingness, which distances my body from head again. The head remains fossilized, as before, on the bed, sitting on it like a stone which no one could turn. Will I ever hear its whisper again? Is it important?

From this question rises the lioness which has been sitting, somewhere, on the ladder between heaven and earth. Yes, it *is* important! It is important for me to get back from the silence between the words and the wait for the next word. I leave the stone of my head in its place, and float to the place of the hands, which are waiting to pull me up from the netherworld. My hands search for his. Abe's hand, heavy and relaxed, lays on me as a promise, and I believe.

The monitor's beeping deafens my not-ears, with no response. I cannot contain it in the space, which is filled with terrible pain, diluted with a belief that grows from the cracks of this hesitant existence. All of a sudden it is important for me to know what time it is. Abe tells me, and I absorb the time through my skin. I have time. How wonderful. I have time. I am alive.

Hours pass and I am wheeled out of the intensive care unit. Worried faces. Smiling faces. "Trying to smile" faces. Crying faces. They all roll into my eyes, which have fully opened, to greet their fellow eyes. Hands are reaching out.

Hands are touching, and not. Heavy hands, warm hands. Hands that invite me to be a mother. To be. And I know, through all the thousands of screens, that I am a mother. I am alive. A smile connects my mouth to my face, as it tries to enclose my head in the folds of the skin of my face, which are born together with my lips, forming skin around my head and creating an existence, a being. I have elastic skin which can move on my hurting head. I have a face. My head is alive, and it has feelings. Tears role down my face.

"Mother do not cry. All is well. You are here. We are here."

The tears whisper, "We are tears of joy. Tears of thanks. Tears of life." But their voice is not heard. Their ears are full with their own words, and there is no place in them for the tears' voice

of thanks to G-d, who has not yet demanded my soul from
my body.

An Existential Discussion
Come, return to the rock from which you have been hewn,
To your place.

I will not come, not yet
The work has not been completed.

Shed off your coat of skin,
Get free from your shackles.

The shackles –
your shackles
The vessel –
your vessel.

I am calling you to me
Sending my angel to you.

You have sent him to uproot me from the Garden of Eden,
To plant me in the soil of this earth,
To put down roots,
To grow branches,
To carry fruits and seeds,
To remember the Torah which has been made forgotten,
And to discover the wonders of your creation.
No angel does two missions,
Hands off.

An elevator. Its door opens. I am rolled in. "There is no room for everyone," says someone behind me. He does not understand that there *is* room for everyone. That I can squeeze the pain and make room for everyone inside me, in my heart, in my soul. There is room for everyone. My tears repeatedly whisper, "there is room for everyone."

"Please wait outside while we receive and process her." On my right is the orderly and on my left is the ward bed, in front of me is the nurse and behind me is the man that said, "There is no room for everyone."

"Ready?" My body is laid on a cold bed, devoid of tears, devoid of words. My main guard has gone, and with him the orderly.

"My head is hurting."

"I will check to see when you last received a painkiller."

"I need something for the pain now, no matter what."

The nurse has already left. Who will hear me?

"I am here. All is well." Abe kisses me on my forehead, as if checking that my face is real. Kisses again, a welcome kiss. Kisses again and says, "I love you." Kisses my hand and says, "You are here, and this is all that matters." I am alive. I am loved.

Abe is next to me, I – I am.

"You can come in, but she really needs sleep, and more sleep." Faces. My daughters' faces. My sons' faces. Loving faces. Disbelieving faces. Faces which tell the wonders of the wonder.

The pain rules my hours with an iron hand. "Can I please get some morphine?" I ask.

"No morphine in the neurosurgery ward. We keep the brain active. It's forbidden to subdue whatever survived the surgery," the nurse answers.

If I am not allowed to subdue my brain, that means that I have something to feel blessed about. The pain sends my words directly to the foot of G-d's seat. The words twist around themselves, get entangled and climb towards Him, all mixed up. But the minister of prayer undoes the knots, gently frees the words from each other so that their fine threads will not tear, and with infinite patience arranges the words, each spoken in its exact order.

"My G-d, I have beseeched you and you have healed me, you have pulled my soul out of the netherworld, you have brought life unto me, keeping me from going into a pit." My speaking soul comes back to me, light and sure of its place within me. I hug it and whisper to it: "I love you. Thank you for staying with me. We have so much more to do here in this world."

Abe also stays with me the following night. After this the children will take turns to be with me and help me. I think I can be alone. They know that I cannot, and they are right. But only for a while. Right?

Prof. Hezkeyah arrives at my bed, hesitant and concerned. "Prof. Hezkeyah," I try to say, "please do not worry." It seems to me as if he straightens up a bit. Or is it my imagination?

"How do you feel? The procedure was extremely complicated, it was very hard to get to the aneurysm. I almost gave up. But then I remembered that you never give up and I knew that I may not give up. Not with your brain."

He continues to talk while looking into my thin smile. "When I finally succeeded in reaching it and was able to fill it up with coils, I found out that the coils filled the whole aneurysm, as necessary, but they also blocked the blood flow to your artery. This left the right frontal lobe without oxygen. I had to clear some of the aneurysm's neck from the coils, so that you will get blood to your right front brain. This took time. Parts of the brain remained without oxygen for beyond the allowed time. Parts of your brain have been damaged, but we have no way to know which parts were damaged, and what functions they are responsible for."

"Thank you for not giving up," I search for his eyes. "I know that you did everything possible, and beyond." His eyes meet mine. "All will be well," I say. Tears well up in his eyes. "Thank you for being a faithful messenger of G-d."

"I only did what I was supposed to do," he says. "To save your life is already not in my hands."

Inside me my soul forms words: "To guard your life is *my* job. To live them is yours."

"I am begging you not to be quick to leave the hospital," he continues. "Give yourself as much time as you need. Be patient with yourself. Your brain has undergone an extremely severe trauma. I believe you when you say that you will be okay, but please listen to me, and believe me that it will take time, a lot of time."

He turns to leave but comes back. "You have a wonderful husband, Abe. He is a good man and he loves you very much."

In the evening, when Abe comes, I tell him about Prof. Hezkeyah's visit. The lines on his face spread and become deeper. Fear fills his eyes, and my soul reaches out to him, wishing to hug him and exchange his fear with hope.

"Now I understand why he came out of the surgery room the way he did," he says and sits down heavily next to me. "After the previous surgery he literally danced his way from the surgery room as we sat and waited for good news. At that time his face was one big smile. He pulled us into the adjacent imaging room and showed us the miracle of the blood flowing from the left as soon as the main right artery was blocked. The miracle appeared on the screen again and again, while he shared with us the unbelievable." Tears come and well up in his eyes.

"This time, when he came out, he looked tired, shattered, almost broken even. He said that the surgery is over, and that you will soon be transferred to the neurosurgery intensive care unit for recovery and monitoring. He did not want to say anything more and turned away from us leaving no option for conversation. When he turned to walk away, I saw that his whole back was wet, I understood that he had sweated a lot, yet then I still did not know why."

He sighed. "It's fortunate that I did not know why. I needed to be totally immersed in the awareness of your being alive. At that point in time, I could not deal with any challenge beyond keeping you alive. It is better it happened so. This way my thanks to G-d were complete and whole."

"Our thanks need to stay whole. I am alive," I say. "I am not less alive just because there were terrible complications during the surgery. G-d willing I will be fully functional and will be able to do all the things that I plan and wish to do."

I want to be a loving mother, a hugging grandmother and a supporting wife. I want to leave a mark of goodness and of life-saving on this world. I want to fulfill my life's mission, and I am sure that I know what it is. I cannot imagine a situation where I cannot continue to be the chief scientist of my company. And I know that I will continue to teach in the Technion and give *Shiurim* (classes) on the weekly Torah portion on Shabbat.

I know, I just know, but where does this knowing come from?

To be born anew
To be born anew?
To be born elderly? Tiny?
To be born new – old.

To emerge from the womb,
From the mercy, from the 'almost death,'
From the darkness and the fear,
May be even from being frozen.

To a world that sees, hears, thinks
To speaking and doing
To life flowing from an upside-down vessel
To the knowledge of death in every single breath.

To be born into a new light.
To count days and not years.

I am seven hundred and thirty days old,
Have I become wiser?
Have I grown from the test?
Into a different growing being?
Into an existence within a richer good?

And maybe I was never born again?
Maybe I was never saved?

Shards

I saw my life
Dissolving into thousands of shards
And my hands sent
To hold onto them
To gather them
Into my tightly closed fist
And they stream from it
Quenching the thirst of the earth
Which will grow a soft green fine hair
Over the stubble of the past
Which is stretched unto nothingness
To wrap my soul
Which is escaping from between my fingers.

•

I am released from the hospital with written instructions to take a sick leave of many weeks, recuperating at home. If I would have told them that I do not need the official sick leave documents, because for over two years I have not gotten a salary for my work at the company, they would not have believed me. If I would have told them that I did not plan to slow down, to cut back my challenges or reduce my workload, they would not have understood me. I stay silent, but in my heart, I am determined to get back to work and to the full scope of my activities, and soon.

For a very long time after the surgery, pain is a domineering partner in my life, stealing from my strength and my abilities. But I do not intend to let it rule me forever. Over time it subsides, until it almost goes away. Once in a while, I discover something which in the past I could do, and now it is hard or impossible. When the pain subsides, the excuse of blaming all my inabilities on the excruciating pain fades away. Again and again, I find myself dealing with a damaged, deficient existence, and now it

67

is very clear that it is not "only a matter of time until you fully recuperate."

Now I realize that I have incurred both neurological and structural damage. Minuscule damages to the brain have major implications for different functions. I am determined to regain the abilities I have lost, and strengthen the functions which have become weak, but in spite of my determination, some wrongs cannot be fixed, some losses cannot be recovered. I learn to compensate for the deficiencies and cover up the damage. To the whole world I am the same Sara that I have always been. Inside myself, I know that much has changed, not only in my mental and intellectual abilities, but also in my social and emotional ones.

Touch me
Touch me
I am alive.
Touch me
I am in pain.
Touch me
I am afraid.
Touch me
I am in love.
Touch me,
Do not fear.
I do not break
I do not crack
I do not fall So easily
Except from loneliness.

Over time the "new" Sara becomes *the* Sara, and the changes that occurred in the recent past continuously shape a presence which creates a different reality of "Sara." I try to be the best Sara possible, until all the damaged parts of my brain are forgotten, as they become part of me, and that is that. I feel no sorrow, but rather have a feeling of achievement. No one but me knows the battles, the hardships, the coping, and the wrongness that can never be fixed.

Sometime after the second surgery, one of our daughters asks me, "Mother, why did you not tell us last time, when they discovered the giant aneurysm, that your life was in danger? If we would have known, we would have come more, prayed more, worried more, understood more."

Why not? "We ourselves did not comprehend that from a moment of good health, we moved into a moment which revealed a clear and immediate danger of death," I answer her. "We also, in the several days between the diagnosis and surgery, did not really have the presence of mind to think of both the near and far future ramifications of the unfolding situation. When it was clear that the surgery had to be immediately done, when the ticking bomb in my head was already on a very short fuse, there was no time for fear or worry. In the twenty-four hours between the diagnostic catheterization and the surgery itself, there was no room, in our state of mind, to think of the moment after."

First I answered, only afterwards did I think about it. The more I think, the real and innermost answer recedes further from me. I think that maybe this was part of the gift that G-d granted me, that He did not leave us time for indecisiveness, doubts and worries. I think that maybe this was a safety mechanism to avoid a choking of the engine due to fear. A mechanism which focused on "what needs to be done." A survival mechanism in which I am fully practiced – doing, doing and doing without a break. I think that maybe I really did not have a true and realistic understanding of the situation in my brain, and how high the risk was. The thoughts pile up in a dark corner, like items no one wants. In each thought there is a part of the truth, but the essence of it was missing in all of them.

The day arrives when I am not thinking about my daughter's question anymore, and the truth sprouts, rises, and grows inside me with all is grandness, with all its simplicity. It was clear to me that I will continue living, and therefore, as far as my inner being was concerned, I was not really in mortal danger. I had a clear and true conversation with G-d, and I had no doubt that all would go well and this nightmare will be gone, as if it never was. The possibility that something in me would be damaged was not at all real, not even in a passing thought or for a fleeting moment.

What was true for the first surgery has absolutely nothing to do with the second one. My total confidence that all was solved and fixed from the root, with no possibility of damage, was an apparition. I did gain another year and a half of a complete life, but at the doorstep of the second surgery I was more aware of the frailty of life in general and of my own in particular. The long wait for the surgery, and the repeated insistence of each and every expert as to how complex and dangerous the surgery was going to be, left no room for doubt as to the long-term effects it would have. It was not clear if I would even remain alive as a human being at all, and not a vegetable, G-d forbid.

The clear feeling of great salvation, which I had when I walked out of the waiting room for surgery in the City Center hospital, had left me with no doubt. It was clear to me that I will only let Prof. Hezkeyah operate on my brain. It was clear to me that only a person who would dare go into my brain, with a clear understanding that he is a messenger of G-d, a messenger of the One who gives life and takes it away, only that person would be able to save my life. It was clear to me that the only way to try to fix the complex and dangerous situation was from a place of great humility and awe for the wonders of creation, of life and of the creator.

My brain is quiet for almost two years. But from the silence, a giant call for help starts rising, with my body waving a giant black flag of pain. A giant flag which could not be ignored.

We are in the emergency room again. We already know the drill. We do not agree to do a CT, as there will be a need for an MRI and MRA anyway, so why expose the head to so much damaging radiation with no actual benefit? Again, we are released with a referral for an urgent MRI and MRA. We receive an appointment for that very night.

The following day we are in Prof. Govrin's office again, for a private consultation in order for him to professionally and accurately study the imaging results with no undue delay. As is his way, he has already studied the images before he calls us in. As we walk in, we can see that he does not have good news. The truth is that I did not expect good news. A strong pain in my head has already saved my life twice. I knew that this time, too, the pain is a warning bell. I just did not know that this time the problem was in another artery.

How does one count miracles?
How does one count miracles?
From the beginning?

From the end?
As a whole? Every detail?
They tell me
And I hear

That they hear me and understand
But I do not always understand.
They are impressed that I am moving
(due to the pain it is really a miracle),
They complement me that I look really good.

I touch the vessel carefully.
It is much more transparent than it used to be.
I tilt it on its side,
To figure it out.

I stare at what is visible,
Wonder about what is hidden.
The 'myself' of the past,
Has it passed? Gone? Remained? What endured,
Is it long?
Or short?
Is it 'myself',
Or just its shadow,
Unfamiliar,
A stranger?

Measured Beats
To go fast
Because only little remains?
To slow down
To experience what there is?
To change
And have time to be different?
To maintain
My existence, my being?
To forget
That we are dust and to dust we will return?
To record
The impressions of the days which go by
Which are more precious than gold
Getting lost like sand grains
From between my fingers which are slowly opening
To erase
The anger, the disappointment, and the pain.
To dip my quill pen
In a sea of love, acceptance and giving
Full heartedly,
For as long as it beats.

To Caress The Dream

I wanted to touch everything
To caress the dream
To see it blooming
To pick its fruit
And to role on my tongue
The sweetness of its wishes
The bitterness of its seal
On the tablet of my heart
Which is crumbling into ink stains
Which I know not their meaning.

Limited Time

I knew that the time was limited.
Only a vessel of pure oil remained
One Small
Sealed with the seal of the High Priest,
With the seal of the angel of death.
Will I leave it sealed?
Will I undo its string?
Will I expose its oil?
A flame flickers
Holding onto the wick
Hugging it with a halo of light.
Will I know to see?
To come to the flying away letters
To hold unto the moments
To engrave them into my heart,
Which is beating
Its last beats,
Until it will be extinguished
With the last
Candle.

How Will You Support Me?
"When I said my foot slips
Thy steadfast love, O Lord, held me up."
Do words create a reality?
'My foot slips' I said – and so it was.
And if I will not say?
My foot will not slip?
G-d will not hold me up?
Let me feel your hand
Your held up-hand to cover up
With my hand
Which is supporting the feet of the bed
And holding on to G-d's care
Which is envisioned as a cloud
And ungraspable like it.
Which is felt like a column of fire
Which is untouchable.
And I will know
That I am in G-d's camp
Every man by his own standard,
Every man by his camp.
And I, in my narrow camp,
How will you care for me
When the whole world is full of your glory?

GREAT EXPECTATIONS

Prof. Govrin looks at us with a serious face and very worried eyes. He goes through the MRI image slices, from the back of the head to the front, and explains the situation as he points to the changing screens.

"The tumor in the back is growing, and it is important to do the surgery soon and get it out," he says. "It was a mistake, in my opinion, to ignore it until now, because as the tumor grows the risk from surgery grows, too. A larger tumor increases the risk and magnitude of the damage to the areas adjacent to it. In your case we are talking about the motor abilities on the left side of your body. I think the tumor is already too large to treat with a radioactive implant, which could kill the tumor from within without the need for major surgery. In any case, you will need to consult with neurosurgeons and hear different options on how to treat the tumor."

A great feeling of relief fills my heart. A tumor is not a ticking bomb. There is time to study different options, to get ready for the implications from surgery, to choose an appropriate time, to deal with the problem and remove it from my life. I am so relieved that I almost miss what he says next.

"Unfortunately, today the tumor is not your immediate concern. No one will perform the surgery on you today, because your life expectancy, according to your brain history, is at the most five years. In your current condition it is doubtful that you will be alive even a year from today."

"Why is my life expectancy so low?" I ask, while my ears are not willing to hear what my mouth speaks.

"It is because of two aneurysms on the ophthalmic artery," he answers, and moves to transfer the pictures in front of us onto two huge screens in front of him. "As you can see, these aneurysms have grown since your first MRI in 2009. Then, they required no handling since they were small and their risk, compared to the risk of the giant aneurysm, was marginal." My eyes wander to the other screen, which shows the current MRI. There is no need to measure in order to discern that they are much larger today than they were two and half years ago.

I remember a conversation with Prof. Hezkeyah when the ophthalmic aneurysms were growing more and more. He told us that there are different schools of thought regarding the closure of aneurysms of this size. In Europe they will not touch them. In the United States they will recommend and put pressure to go in and close them.

"Personally, I recommend not to have an operation, but rather just continue to follow the progress," he told us back then. "The risk involved in surgery is greater that the risk of the aneurysm exploding. This is my opinion." During that conversation I immediately adopted his opinion, and he repeated it in every follow up visit we had with him.

Therefore, I almost miss the rest of Prof. Govrin's words.

"What worries me is not their size but rather their shape. It seems to me that there are blobs coming out of their walls," he continued. "This means that there are areas in the walls of the aneurysm which are weaker, and they are becoming weaker and thinner at a higher rate than the rest of the walls. It is like a balloon. If there is an area which is thinner than the rest of the balloon, then when we blow it up, this area will stretch more than the rest, will become thinner faster, and the balloon will explode from this place. If this is the situation here, then we have to deal with these aneurysms right away."

To deal with aneurysms, again, immediately? This cannot be real. I cannot handle another emergency. I cannot see again the numbers of a ticking bomb inside my head, without being able to read them. I cannot handle this. No! No! No!

"In order to see the situation in detail and to understand what the treatment options are, we need to do an exploratory catheterization. Prof Hezkeyah is not in Israel, but I can perform it."

"When will Prof. Hezkeyah be back?" I ask.

"At the end of the month," was the answer.

"And will you be able to do the exploratory catheterization?" I am moving into operational survival mode and practical-technical thinking.

Prof. Govrin eyes soften, as someone who can help, wants to help and will help. "I am giving you a referral for the procedure. Go to Prof. Hezkeyah's secretary and she will schedule the earliest possible time for the catheterization."

The secretary in the neuro-endovascular unit already knows us. "Prof. Hezkeyah is not in Israel. He will be back only at the end of the month. Should I schedule an appointment with him?"

We explain the situation to her. She sets a time for the catheterization in a few days. "I am reminding you that the hospitalization is for an additional day after the catheterization, in order to monitor and make sure that the artery through which they entered closed and sealed properly, with no external or internal bleeding."

"Thank you. But I have another request. Can you please set up a meeting with Prof. Hezkeyah already, as close to his return to Israel as possible?" I know that she cannot, but I hope to at least embed an understanding of the possible need for urgent surgery. To my surprise she says that she is putting me on the list of urgent cases to be dealt with in the first week of his return. A more accurate date will be given closer to his arrival.

Prof. Hezkeyah has saved my life twice, and he did not wish to leave any cracks through which more risk loaded situations could penetrate. His secretary knows it. Prof. Govrin knows it. Who else knows it?

The exploratory catheterization shows that there are blobs, and more than one, on the larger of the two aneurysms on the ophthalmic artery. These aneurysms are threatening my life because they are on a main artery in a very central location in the front of the brain.

I hear the diagnosis with ears which cannot hear, again hanging between heaven and earth. The facts enter the heart which is already experienced in complex situations. The heart is experienced but not immune. It will not know how to keep on beating as if "all is well" when every heartbeat brings me closer to my end, G-d forbid.

What will happen to my prayers? Recognizing the good, where did it disappear to? Don't I already know that human life hangs by a thread? Did I not know how to live and do, while my life is hanging in balance in front of me?

In the days of the waiting, I learn something important. I have the ability to adapt to this situation – and yet, may G-d never test with me with impossible situations!

Time after time, I have succeeded in continuing my life "normally," thanks to miracles that have been done to me, and I have tried very hard not to let them confuse me. I know how to adapt and not complain.

Notwithstanding all the above, I do not know where I will find the strength for another surgery. I do not know, yet I know in the most clear and complete way: I have a grand desire to live, and this desire will soon find the resources needed for it. Somewhere, in the being which has no words and no logic, except for the contemplation of the soul, I have found confidence that the surgery – which I know has to be done with no delay – will go well and be successful. Where does this assurance come from? I do not know. But yet, I do know. In the conversation between my soul and G-d, there was beseeching from my side and a great compassion from the other.

Again, Prof. Hezkeyah meets with us as soon as he returns. Again, I am in mortal danger. What does he think, inside his head? He explains the need for surgery and for putting a diverter, which still will enable blood flow in the artery but will be dense enough so that it will not allow blood to flow into the aneurysm. "Up until today, we did not have such a diverter which could fit these aneurysms. However, just recently the FDA approved a new diverter which was developed exactly for major surgery on aneurysms like you have. I think I could get permission to use it in your case, without waiting for the approval in Israel. This is the only device which could save your life."

The sigh of relief has a short time span. He continues: "I have to tell you that the diverter was designed to be an excellent, even perfect answer to all of our dreams and requirements. But I have to warn you that this is not the first diverter which I thought to be perfect, only to find out I was wrong. Every diverter has unforeseen problems. We have no way to know the risks and the benefits before we collect information and experience from many such endovascular surgeries, with a perspective of years. All we can do is to follow this artery frequently and closely after we put the diverter in place."

Oh my G-d, so many miracles! I do not deserve any of them. I do not have enough virtues to be granted one miracle. I am already in deficit from the second miracle.

Oh my G-d, with your great benevolence, please answer me and save me. I do not have any merits, but you have mercy, benevolence, love and truth which are beyond our human understanding. G-d, You have already "managed" so that there will be a diverter which can save me. You have already insured that the FDA process would end just in time for me. G-d, You prepared the cure for the disease, so surely you are not going to leave the miracle orphaned from success and lifesaving.

Tranquility comes down upon me.

The surgery date was set for right after Prof. Hezkeyah received, especially for me, approval to use the new diverter.

"Are you ready?" Prof. Hezkeyah sits down to the left of my bed.

"Are you ready?" I ask.

"Only if Abe is also ready," he answers. Abe is standing next to me on the right of the bed and remains silent. The silence was simultaneously infinite and as sharp as a blade.

"Yes Prof. Hezkeyah, I am ready, and I pray that again you will be a good messenger."

Abe kisses my forehead and turns to leave the room. But he returns, turns his face to Prof. Hezkeyah and says to him, "Please take care of my wife. Take care of her because she is more precious to me than anything I can put into words."

"I will do all I can in the surgery room. You pray and ask all the family and friends to pray. Pray as much as you can, and then some. I hope that with G-d's help all will be well." The sliding door opens, Abe exits, the door closes.

I thank Prof. Hezkeyah for all the effort he has put into getting the new diverter, and so quickly. He does not raise his eyes to mine. I try to lighten up the heavy atmosphere in the room. "All will be well," I say.

He nods his head and says: "Pray!"

Again, I am alone. Just G-d and I. Everyone else in the operating room is busy with last-minute preparations. The room is cold. I am shivering, asking for another blanket, and then another one. I know that soon they will strip all the blankets from me, but they will do it only when I can no longer feel anything. The blankets are heavy on my body. The sheet touches my skin, clinging to my body. The skin absorbs the promise of warmth and stops it's demand to shiver. I sink into a conversation with G-d. 'Please let Your mercy rule all Your other attributes. Not in vain have you brought me all this way, right? I have so much more to do, please, let me do your will here, on this earth'. In the nothingness which engulfs me, G-d nods his head towards me.

I am in the recovery room. "Thank G-d, all has gone well," Abe says as he sits beside me. I can see... The pain is excruciating. I am nauseated. "I have asked the nurse to come," Abe says as he tries to calm me.

An attempt to bear the pain. An attempt to sink into oblivion. In spite of the drug I was given, the nausea is terrible. It overcomes me as if there was no other suffering inside or around me.

"I will call the nurse."

"Yes, the medicine I gave her causes nausea, I will give something through the IV, it will help her quickly."

Dozing off. Sleeping. Dozing off. "I am in pain."

"Soon we will move you to the ward and they will give you something for the pain." But I am hurting now. Where is Abe? I am without glasses. I cannot see one meter away. Everything is a blur. Anyone here?

There is someone here. The One who encompasses the whole world and fills it with His glory. His hand conceals and protects me from the strong light, and from the pain which is even stronger.

I am being rolled. Abe is at the side of the bed. The children are holding on to the sides of the bed, helping to roll it and me on it. I am in pain. I am hanging unto the movement of the bed, and the pain which accompanies it, in order not to fall asleep. Not to close my eyes. I want to see everyone around me. Each one special. Each one loved. Each one nestled deep inside me. My sisters are not here. For how many miracles can one wait outside one surgery room?

Recuperating from the surgery. Coping with the pain. Going back to work in the company and to lectures at the Technion. Sometimes I cannot concentrate on the conversation enough to hear the questions. Sometimes I do not remember to answer. Once in a while there are "disconnections," and then the world around me retreats, all is black and devoid of movement and sound.

The disconnections become longer. Many of our telephone conversations at work are with the United States. We are in a process vis à vis the FDA, while doing large scale clinical trials. In one conversation it happens that I come back into full awareness when they are calling me on the other side of the line, "Sara, are you there? Sara, are you there?" and I hear them say, "Maybe the line went dead, maybe we should dial again?"

I pull myself from Nowhere and ask them to repeat what they have been saying "just before we had problems with the communication," as I put it.

I write scientific articles, protocols for clinical trials, the FDA filing dossier, and statistical analysis of data from clinical trials around the world. I have been writing for years. Hundreds and thousands of pages of scientific documents. I am writing now, too, but the writing takes me much more time. The thoughts do not race forward as they used to. The thread of my thought gets cut off once in a while, and it takes me back to the beginning of the sentence, the paragraph, or the document. What used to take an hour now takes a day. What required a full day of work takes a week or two.

But no one – almost no one – feels it. In the past I functioned at a speed level way above average. Now I am less capable, much less, and slow, very slow. But as far as the world and those around me – except for the immediate family – I am, in their words, "really OK and functioning very well." I am still a brilliant woman, but they have no idea how much internal energy I need in order to radiate "brilliance." The brilliance has faded, but it still carries the burden of leading people forward. I do not give up. I have things to give to the world and to humanity. Early detection of diseases can save lives, as simple as that. It cannot be that the abilities to invent and develop such important tools have been given to me in vain. The feeling of destiny does not allow me to give up. I continue to do it all, but I start to show signs of the constant effort, which is beyond my strength.

I continue to lecture. Long lectures of four hours at a time. As always, I go through all the material and prepare new lectures for every academic year. Even though these are the same courses, the students are different, each one arriving from a different background and learning experience. But in spite of my preparations, it is hard for me to remember the material in a continuum. I prepare more detailed presentations in order to help me along. When my thought process is completely paralyzed, I turn my back to the class and draw a graph or turn to the slide on the screen as if getting ready to talk about it. The long seconds of silence are hidden behind my back. I do not give up. Why? Because I love teaching. Because it is meaningful to me to broaden the students' horizons and see the wonder in their eyes in understanding the wondrous creation. Because my life, the way I define it to myself, must go on. Teaching is part of my definition of self.

My being is bent over, under the burden of a life that was right for me once, but today this life demands huge, almost illogical effort. I am literally bent over under the burden, the tension and the demands of those around me and my expectations of myself.

I Will Lift My Eyes To The Hills
I will lift my eyes to the hills,
I thought.

From there my help will come.
I will bow my head to the valleys,
I thought.

From there my being has come
And in the landscape of my birthplace I saw
The end of my being
And the beginning of my existence
Like any human being
Who repents
A day before his death.

Restraints /Shackles

I long for the quiet
And am afraid of death.
I search for the light

And hide in the shadows.
I aspire high
And cling to the soil.

I want the freedom
And curl up in the fishing net.

I seek the notes,
The music,
The singing.
I desire to move,
To dance,
To be.

But the rattle of the locks on my shackles
Gets entangled with my chains,
Gets fogged up in the space of my prison
And strangles the prayer
In the bud.

I have healed from the third brain surgery; this is what the doctors said. This is what the medical records said. This is what the decreasing doses of pain medication said. It is good for me this way. It is good for me not to be "sick" or "handicapped," G-d forbid. It is good for me to be "okay."

Every day is a new ordeal. The vessel looks whole from the outside, but it is cracked and dripping. At the end of every day, in spite of many long hours of intensive work, I come home knowing that I have hardly gotten anything done. Every morning I pull my prayers over my head like a prayer shawl, and wrapped in them, I can be both inside and outside at the same time. Every morning I don the robe of my belief in my ability to get back to myself, and under that title I function in the world of articles and documents, of protocols and calculations. Every night I gather myself and pray that I will be able to go on. I know that I am no longer the "knowing self," sharp minded and quick to respond. I try to accept this new state, but I am really not able to comprehend the simple fact, that three brain surgeries do not leave you "whole."

I function and perform, but no one knows it is a Sisyphean, daily battle. I survived the surgeries, but no one knows at what price. I nurture my life to be a life which is beyond mere survival. I am "myself," however my "self" winds between my fingers, between my toes, blocking my way, slowing my moves, evading and coming back to pull me by my hand and to say, "This is you. You are weak, but you are still you." I hear but do not comprehend.

And the others? They are all blind and deaf. Everyone sees a functioning whole/complete body. No one touches the hidden stitches holding together the broken pieces. No one smells the sweat of a soul which is functioning from within corridors which are becoming narrower and narrower.

Unknowingly, some healing emerges from this state,. I finally recover from the third brain surgery. We almost sighed a sigh of relief. Now, after what was in the eyes of the doctors a full recovery from the surgery, the time has come to deal with the tumor I have in the back of my brain. A tumor which has continued to grow all this time with no restraints, affecting me in unclear ways.

During the neurosurgical-oncological consultation, we are presented with three options. One: to radiate the tumor from the outside, by using a series of beamed radiation treatments. The second: to insert a small grain of radiation, by using a simple surgical procedure of creating a small hole in the skull. The grain will radiate, continuously, for a very long time. In both of these treatments the radiation damage will increase over time. Its ramifications will be uncovered over many years. The third option is to do open cranial surgery and take the tumor out.

Prof. Hezkeyah suggests doing the craniotomy, even though he is principally against opening up the skull because "the person that comes out of such a surgery is not the same person who went into the surgery. The mere exposure of the brain to air, even before we go into the brain tissue itself, causes a change."

"So why do you recommend the open brain surgery in this case?" I ask.

"Because as far as damage to neighboring tissues goes, the risk of this surgery is much smaller."

We consult with another expert neurosurgeon. The location of the tumor enables it to be reached relatively easy in open brain surgery. However, the tumor is already pressing on the main vein, and might have already invaded it. It will be necessary for a brain surgeon specializing in blood vessels to be present on the surgery team, in order to deal with damage to the wall of the vein.

My sister knows an expert neurosurgeon, a department head in a prestigious medical center in the United States, who is due to arrive in Israel for a short visit. She helps us arrange a meeting with him. The expert examines the MRI images, which were downloaded onto my computer. Every time he pulls up a tumor image, my heart skips a beat. In the end, he confirms all that we have heard from the experts in Israel. The tumor itself is located close to the back of the skull, but tumor is also entangled within the main vein in the brain, and that makes the surgery much more complex.

"What about the timing for the surgery?" we ask.

"Look, I think that before surgery, it is imperative to check if the diverter that you have in your ophthalmic artery is functioning well. Based on these considerations, we will be able to weigh if, in your condition, it is at all possible to perform the surgery."

Another lifesaving tool which has become an obstacle.

"I have a friend, Dr. King, who heads most of the FDA clinical trials for stents, diverters and anything else which might be inserted into the brain. I suggest that you send him the disks from the MRI and ask for his opinion," the expert summarized.

We send the disks and await his answer. At the same time, we are getting ready to spend a month's vacation at Sandy's summer house in north Montana. Sandy is a distant relative. We now feel that meeting her in a family Shabbat, over half a year ago, was a gift from heaven. Sandy told Abe about a summer house, a vacation home which she and her husband bought in a forest in north Montana, close to a tiny village named Whitefish. The house is close to the Glacier National Park on the U.S. side, and close to the Canadian Rockies just over the Canadian border. She told Abe that ever since her husband passed away, she does not go there, but she lets friends vacation there if they want. "It is a wonderful ski area in the winter, and with stunning scenery in the summer," she said.

Abe asked if the house will be available for us for a few weeks, and when she said it was, he asked her to keep the month of July for us.

All this happened before the ophthalmic aneurysms swelled and changed their shape, and before we knew that the tumor has been growing and growing. When talking to Sandy, Abe thought that it was a wonderful opportunity for a vacation, in a beautiful place with no rental cost. Quite far, but for a long vacation it was a reasonable distance to travel. We ordered tickets as soon as we got back from that family Shabbat, and it was good we did so. Soon after, the storms and strong waves which took hold of our lives and shook us relentlessly would have cut this opportunity right from underneath us.

When the tests showed that my life was in immediate and clear danger from the ophthalmic aneurysms, we felt extremely fortunate that we would have a place to recuperate after the additional surgery in my brain. When I went back to full activity, after the insertion of the long silk diverter that covered the two aneurysms which threatened to explode, it was clear to us that this vacation would be a total must for us. We had a lot to talk and think about together. So many of our life's plans called for re-evaluation, and we again found ourselves at a place where major decisions needed to be taken.

Now, after the meeting with the expert, we needed to make more decisions. Open brain surgery is not a simple matter. Surgery to remove a tumor which is on the main artery or already inside it – it is much, much more complex. Our visit to the U.S. would enable us to meet with Dr. King. We fixed a meeting, in a hospital in Baltimore, towards the end of the vacation.

When the time for the flight to the U.S. arrives, we are already restless to leave to the vacation house, deep in the Montana forests. The flight to the U.S. is long, and this time it is especially long. A few hours after take-off, I lose control due to a strong seizure, and everything turns black in front of my eyes, taking me into a deep, infinite dark space. There was no place for me to lay down. There was nothing Abe could do, except hug me and drag me to my seat, all the time talking to me to keep me next to him, grounded and not sinking.

We land, Thank G-d, in one piece. The first thing we take care of is to get a local mobile phone, and give this number to Dr. King's secretary, so that she can contact us.

We rent a car and head out to a three and half-hours' ride from the airport to the village Whitefish, and then another quarter of an hour to the house. We pass through gigantic open spaces. A few lonely farmhouses dot the open land. Silence.

Everything is green. The forests are thick and dark. Far away in the horizon we can see the high Rocky Mountains, with their tips still covered with snow. Sandy sent us detailed and accurate instructions on how to get to the house and suggested that we stop in the city on the way, so that we can stock up on food and other supplies. We are tired, but we stop and fill a cart with initial needs. We want to get to the house and see what it looks like already. We hope that it will be in a condition which will enable us to relax and rest. We pass through Whitefish, a picturesque, pleasant, and tiny village. We go on dirt roads between farm fences. No names. No signs. No marks of distance. How are we going to find the place?

We have directions from Sandy. When we read them at home, they were cute, detailed, and different from anything we had seen before. Now, the long sentences start to make sense. "If you go to the farm with the big sign 'The Smith Family' over the gate, then you have gone too far. Go back, and when you see the sign 'Jack's Horse Farm,' turn onto the narrow road into a forest."

After many twists and turns, we saw on the left the roof of a house, and a shed full of wood for the hearth. From there the road continues with no signs or posts. We are looking for a sign that reads "A House in the Forest." The first time, we missed it, at our second go around we drove slower and discovered the almost hidden entrance to the wooded land where Sandy's house is located. Another two hundred meters, and the house can be seen in a clearing in the forest.

The house awaits us, unlocked. It is well equipped, clean and filled with greenish sunlight filtered by the trees of the forest. Large windows into the silence. The closest house is a kilometer or so away, and the lane to it is a narrow, one-person path which leads down the slope onto another forest clearing and a small house.

This vacation house has everything. A dream house. Abe is exhausted from the flight and the long drive on unfamiliar roads. He checks out the mattress in the master bedroom and falls asleep, as is, shoes and all. I am too excited, unable to close my eyes. I walk around the house to get to know the place we will be staying in for a month. I arrange the clothes in the closet and the food in the kitchen and make a pasta and vegetable meal.

Abe wakes up when his hunger encounters the aromas from the kitchen. We sit within the silence. We see the forest from every window. In front of us are wide green horizons guaranteeing a month of meditation, preparation, thoughts, understandings and hopefully, conclusions.

Silence. And within the silence we seek the inner peace, existence and being within, which have formed from all the tribulations we have gone through. There is no mobile phone reception in the forest. The landline in the house is, as far as we are concerned, only for outgoing emergency calls, and for the children, if they will need to get in touch with us. Living without mobile phone reception scares us, but also contributes to the peace and quiet of just being. In the house, next to the land-line, there is a page with emergency phone numbers. The number of the local ambulance, and the name and address of the main hospital in the area, in case there would be, G-d forbid, an emergency. Emails? Surfing? There is no internet. Silence. A new-old silence. A blessed silence.

The following day, a Thursday, we drive to the village and walk along its main street. All the stores are well-kept, and the signs announce a building supply store, a souvenir store, a restaurant, a coffee house, a pizzeria, and an ice-cream parlor. There are stores for shoes, children's clothing, and vacation equipment. There is also a pharmacy, a veterinarian, a post office and a small courthouse.

Cute. For food, one has to travel to the nearby town. There

is a bookstore on the street corner, so now our vacation can be perfect. We walk into the bookstore and get acquainted with the owner. We leaf trough some books and buy four. *Shabbat* (the Shabbath, the seventh day of the week, the day G-d rested from his creation, and said that 'what is, is enough'. The day we also rest and abstain from creative work) is approaching and it is good to have something to read, and enough books for one Shabbat or more.

There is a coffee house with free internet next to the bookstore. The place is plainly furnished and the atmosphere is pleasant and inviting. A wedding planner is leafing through shiny magazines, and pointing at this page or that page while speaking incessantly about the importance of the right design for a wedding "as we get married only once." A handyman is finalizing work details for the home of an elderly man, while his daughter sits next to him and makes sure that everything is okay, "as she is the one who writes the check at the end." At a nearby table, two girls are studying statistics together. Young people have cold drinks, and adults drink cups of hot coffee. Other patrons are sitting at tables, reading, writing, or working on their computers. This corner of the village enables us to communicate with the outside world – with home, family, and with friends in the U.S., whenever we want, and only whenever we want. This will be a good place to visit once every few days during our stay in Montana, to write and answer emails.

Friday, we go to the town, to a big grocery store, and buy things to cook for Shabbat, as cooking is not allowed on the holy day. We rush to leave the house early, so that we will have time to talk to all the children before Shabbat comes in in Israel, as we do not use the phone on the Shabbat. There are eight hours between us, and more than a ten-hour difference between the times when Shabbat begins and when it will end. We will be able to call them only after we get out of the forest. Standing in an area where there is mobile phone reception, we call each one of the children and wish them Shabbat Shalom. It fills our hearts with joy to hear everyone's voices. Now it is time to prepare our Shabbat in the forest in Montana. Fresh salmon for Shabbat, fresh fruits and vegetables and different treats.

We are in the car on the way back to the house in the forest, and I remember that we did not buy rolls or pitas for Shabbat *Lechem Mishne* (2 loafs or Challahs, just as the Manne from heaven was double the portion on Friday, and none on Shabbat). We drive back to the city to buy what we are missing.

Burning words

We are on the way back to the house again. At the edge of the forest the phone rings, and Dr. King's number appears on the screen. My heart stops and then flutters. Abe stops the car immediately so we do not lose reception.

We sit in the car, alone, on the edge of a giant forest in Montana, while the secretary transfers the call to the doctor. I am afraid of forgetting the things he will say, so while listening carefully I write on every piece of paper Abe can find in the car. The words burn the pages, and their burning hot ashes carve them into the tablet of my being.

"I have reviewed the material you sent me, after your conversation with my friend and colleague. You do have a tumor, and under regular circumstances it would be necessary to perform the surgery to take it out, but you have a much more severe problem: the diverter which was put into the ophthalmic artery. It is reasonable to assume that weak blood flow will enable blood to clot in the aneurysms, and they will become inactive aneurysms. However, there is a very high risk of a blood clot forming inside the diverter itself. This will cause great damage to large areas in the right frontal lobe of the brain. In order to prevent this, or at least to reduce the risk to a minimum, you have to continue taking the anti-coagulants."

Dr. King stops his flow of words and asks me if I understand all he has said so far. I understand. There is silence on the other end of the line, and then he continues to speak.

"The clinical trial results from this diverter are very good, but the follow up, based on which the FDA approved its use for cases like yours, was only for six months. We are continuing to follow up, with those whom we have inserted the diverter, and unfortunately within the following six months there are blockage problems with the diverter. There are risks in taking strong anticoagulants for a long time, however in your case, the risk in not taking them is several times greater. Way too high for you to take the risk."

Due to the anticoagulants, which I have been taking at very high levels in order to prevent a potential stroke due to an obstruction of a main artery, I am covered with blue, black, purple and yellow bruises. Every small bump or injury turns into internal bleeding, which stops only after a relatively long time. I think of my life with the pain of these internal injuries and marks, which stay on my body for many weeks. Prof. Hezkeyah has told me to stop taking the strong anticoagulant six months after the surgery to insert the diverter. I share this fact with Dr. King. He is silent and time stops. There is no movement, no sound, no life. It is a heavy, thick palpable moment, as if G-d has folded all of Time and has put it as one big heavy stone under my head.

His silence lengthens, as if he is making sure that it reaches me. It does reach me, and encircles me. It encircles me so as to protect me from the rest of his words. The silence becomes an entity of its own, asking to remain there, as it is.

"I am deeply sorry, but the diverter and the aneurysms it is supposed to protect are not your main problem. The giant aneurism that you had in the ACOM – the arterial bridge which provides blood to the holy of holies in the brain – is not closed, and it is growing again. The medications which slow clotting and dilute the blood might loosen the clot that has formed in it or break it into smaller clots. One can see, already, blood flow behind the clot. If you continue taking these medications, there is a very high risk that the clot will detach and travel to the artery. This will cause broad, major damage, to the extent that it is doubtful you will survive. My expertise is endovascular brain surgery, but there is no way to treat the aneurysm in the ACOM again, which receives blood from the very narrow bridge between the open, left main artery and the blocked, right main artery. There is no way to prevent the clot detaching and then block the blood flow to the whole right frontal lobe of your brain. The truth is that open surgery in this area of the brain is also very complex and dangerous. In any case, there is nothing which can be done, because of the coils which have already been inserted into the aneurysm."

He is silent. For a minute I am afraid that there are problems with the reception, but while driving in reverse – Abe is trying to improve the reception – the doctor's voice comes back, and we can hear him. "Do you understand the implications of what I am telling you?"

I nod my head, not aware that he cannot hear the nodding. There is silence on his end. "I cannot help you. There is nothing out there that can be used to reduce the danger. Maybe there will be one day, but right now there isn't anything, not even in clinical trials. I am really sorry. There is no need for you to travel especially to see me. I have nothing to add beyond all I have said to you in this conversation."

"You told me that the ACOM aneurysm is growing again," I ask. "You said there isn't anything to do about this. If I continue to take the anticoagulants, I am at risk of death, or at least death of all my higher functions. From you, I understand that due to the risks from the ACOM aneurysm, I should stop taking the anticoagulants. But, as you have explained, without the anticoagulants a blood clot will form inside the diverter in the ophthalmic artery, and blood flow to parts of the brain will be blocked, causing major brain damage. Did I get it all right?"

In the silence on the other end of the line I see with my mind's eyes Dr. King nodding his head. "Do you have any more questions?"

Questions run around inside me, and knock on my walls of consciousness, asking to break through protective barriers. Many questions, but none of them are related to communication with Dr. King, or any other doctor.

"Please do not hesitate to contact me if you have any more questions," he continues, "but I have to admit that I have nothing to add. In your current condition you have five percent chance to survive the coming year." I write it down, but I do not comprehend. I thank him for his time and his professional analysis of the overall situation.

"There are all the time new developments in the field of brain blood vessels. Many of them fall under my purview, as a leading researcher in the clinical trials required for their approval. If I hear of anything that might be of help in your situation, I will be happy to let your neurosurgeon know. Maybe sometime in the future there might be something like that. Right now, I do not see any possibility or way to solve this complex situation."

Due to the reception issues, the conversation was held without the loudspeaker, and thus Abe could not hear the other side. He sat next to me, trying to read my facial expressions and learn what is happening from the words I spoke. When he heard my summary of Dr. King's message, he went into shock.

I inhale deeply, exhale, and breath again. I need to feel that I am alive. I need oxygen so that I will have strength to exist. Abe's head is laying in his hands on the wheel. He has no strength to start the car. He has no strength to bring the car to the clearing in the woods. He has no strength to prepare for Shabbat, to receive Shabbat, to sanctify Shabbat.

• • •

The power of small things. The power of banal obligations. The power of a decree from above. The power of the tradition of Torah and *Mitzvot* (the commandments that guide the life of a jew). We drive to the house because we must put the groceries in the refrigerator. We drive to the house, because we have to get ready for Shabbat, to cook and bake, to set the table and prepare the candles. Thoughts and talking are pushed aside in favor of Shabbat's honor, in favor of an existence which is beyond any deed, in favor of "And the heavens and the earth were completed," in favor of the One who "Spoke and the world was created," the One who commanded "Six days thou shall labor and do all your work; and the seventh day, Shabbat to the Lord your G-d."

Fish into the oven. Rice on the stove. Vegetables for baking. Grains for cooking. A tablecloth on the table. Candles on the marble top. A bottle of wine to open.

Plates, cups and cutlery to set, wildflowers in a drinking glass, a kettle full of boiling water to wrap well in towels. The sun is going down below the treetops, it is already late. Nightfall comes late in Montana, Shabbat comes in after nine pm and goes out after ten the following evening. We thought that we will bring Shabbat in early, but this was in our thoughts "before the conversation with Dr. King." Now we are in a different place, in the place of "after the conversation with Dr. King."

Everything swirls around us in wide circles and with incomprehensible slowness. The circles become more crowded, denser, all of them gathering into a core of time and space, wrapping themselves around me, united and ensnaring. I cannot receive

Shabbat this way, with a heavy millstone of fear, helplessness and death. Death is standing at my doorstep and the tip of his foot is already preventing the door from closing. It is already impossible to leave him outside, behind lock and key. He is already here.

But it cannot be. It cannot be that death is here. He is not invited. He is just an intruder with paralyzing strength. I do not have to admit death into my life. I do not want his breath on the back of my neck. A lifesaving rope squeezes its way from the fading light of the sun into the open window. A known and familiar lifesaving rope squeezes its way from the fading light of the sun unto the open window. A familiar and well-known rope, the rope of the Shabbat Queen. I reach out to Her and she wraps her soft shawl around my shoulders and says: "I am here, I am here." Wrapped in Her glory, I light the Shabbat candles, and their light pushes away the darkness and with it, Death and its choking and petrifying cloak.

Shabbat. "And G-d completed, on the seventh day, all his creation which he has done." During Shabbat, our whole being is as if everything is complete, whole, full of good. G-d has given us a beloved gift, a time which comes down from heaven and invites us to rise up with it. To rise above the secular and the routine, above needs and tasks. To be elevated to a state of being where we can be happy with the way we are, with no inner need (which is somewhat distorted) to be perfect. The act of creation has been completed, and now we have to build the world which has been given to us, and to act within it. The world which has been laid at our doorstep on that Friday afternoon at twilight, threatening to destroy all of existence and be rebuilt from its ruin. The Shabbat commanded it to stay at the doorstep and did not allow it to move from one domain to another.

Shabbat in an isolated house in the forest in Montana, with no other Jews. The two angels (a legend tells of two angles who come to every Shabbat Table and bless it, if it is set well, and curse it if it is not befitting),which escort us to the Shabbat table are relaxed this time, and are not quick to reach a verdict regarding the table, next to which we are standing and singing, asking for their blessing. Their presence is relaxed, and peace and tranquility exists in their company. Shabbat's robes are spread over us and over them, like a *Huppah* (a square cloth, held up, in the corners, by four poles, under which stand the bride and the groom, with their parents, for the wedding ceremony.), which invites the bride to her beloved. The candles are flickering, and the dark night remains far away. We are enveloped in light, relaxed and receptive, absorbing Shabbat into our being, accepting our world as complete, for a whole day.

During Shabbat day, we walk in the forest. The scattered houses make for a long and pleasant walk. The tall trees, the deep and endlessly green grass, the small crystal-clear lakes, the quiet, the butterflies and the birds, all together create an essence which can contain even the world of "after the conversation with Dr. King."

We start to see how great and exceptional G-d's personal providence over us is. Half a year ago, we booked a month in a forest vacation home in Montana with no special reason, simply because it was an opportunity. We had never taken such a long vacation, but we felt, at the time, that it was right for us. We even bought our tickets all those months ahead of time, in order to guarantee good prices. There were no aneurysms, additional endovascular surgery, diverters in a blood vessel in the brain, additional risks or additional brain damage on our minds then. And here we are, when the time came to fly to Montana, this vacation was desperately needed – far away, detached, and quiet!

Also, the appointment we arranged to see the doctor who might be able to help us, was only for the end of our planned stay in the USA.

During that Shabbat we realize that the fact the hard news arrived now, at the beginning of the vacation, is a great gift. We have almost a month to absorb the challenges which were put in front of us and to deal with them. A month to cry, to accept, to make decisions and to prepare ourselves for the life which will follow, in light of the decisions we will make. A month of powerful togetherness and great love. A month to build our joint inner world from within the predicted destruction. A month to reinforce our home with all the supports and columns we will be able to find, to gather, connect and place them, so that we will be able to stand under a stable and protective roof.

• • •

We are so fortunate. It is almost impossible to believe the magnitude of our good fortune. We feel blessed with a personal and wondrous divine providence. In the days and weeks following the conversation with Dr. King, I re-discover the beauty of life. Without being aware of it, I start to take pictures with my phone camera. I take pictures of flowers and weeds, rocks and trees, light on the water, and the trail that a boat, with two children rowing, leaves behind it. The world looks different, special, more beautiful, more mysterious, more loved. In this beautiful world I have a place. A place of happiness and a good eye, a place for a different prayer, greater than me, so far and so close, simultaneously.

I am taking pictures incessantly. I do not notice that I start taking pictures with more and more detail. I become aware of it only when it is hard for Abe to stop every minute and wait until I take a picture of a fracture in a rock or of the lichen on it. After a relaxed conversation at the end of the day, Abe understands that I really wish to take many pictures in the coming days. He is a very special person, and he respects it. Photography becomes, for me, an important part of our vacation in Montana. It becomes a part of my life, granting me another dimension of living, thanks to the good eye which is growing and growing, until it swallows my eyes of blood and flesh, covering them with a transparent lens. A transparent lens which filters the light and feeds the brain, the emotions, and my soul with an overflowing and growing goodness.

In Montana I learn to see. In Montana I learn to be blind. In the isolated house in the forest I shed a layer of coarse skin, which protects from too much close contact with the world. In the house in the green forest patch I learn to live with my new skin – maybe it is the original one, the old one? – I feel it between my fingers, taste it with my tongue and hug it very tightly, so that it will never disappear again.

Now, once we have passed the days of shock, mourning and accepting, it is time to make some heavy decisions, with life and death ramifications, and all that is between them.

The facts are startling. To stop taking the strong anticoagulants will mean there be a good chance that the big aneurysm will stay relatively stable, preventing an embolus from the clot inside it, and we will hope that the clot will re-attach itself to the aneurysm wall. If I continue to take them, the aneurysm will be exposed to the blood flowing through it. Without the protection of the blood clot, the aneurysm will tear and cause major hemorrhaging in the brain, massive brain damage so terrible and irreversible that it will end most probably with death. If I stop taking the anticoagulants, within a short time the new diverter will get clogged, and the whole area which receives blood from this artery will be terribly damaged. This will cause disabilities of an unimaginable scope.

Before we left for Montana, we received instructions from Prof. Hezkeyah to stop the anticoagulants after six months. I send him a summary of Dr. King's words and ask for his response. In a return email he says that there is nothing new in what Dr King said. Yes, there are articles about the diverter's shortcomings and problems, but this was the best which medicine could offer me. He wrote that it was important that I stop taking the anticoagulants, because taking them puts me at risk of internal bleeding, with all that comes with that. Moreover, he repeated

again, the anticoagulant risks affecting the situation in the ACOM aneurysm, and this is the highest risk to my life at this time point. The six months will be over a week after we get back to Israel. We need to make an appointment to see Prof. Hezkeyah as soon as we are back, and as close as possible to this mark.

When we return home, we will be living with constant fear and under the shadow of the unknown. In spite of this, it is clear to us that we will overcome. Life is too precious, beautiful and wonderful to give up, even for only one day. Slowly, our conversations move also to mid- and long-term plans. We stop planning only for the next day.

I continue taking pictures. Every leaf is a greater miracle than the one before it. Every pebble tells its tale, blue skies, green slopes, black cliffs decorated with white beards, and above it all the sun with its healing wings. I am taking pictures. We walk in beautiful paths in the Rocky Mountains of Montana, and I take pictures. We travel up north for a few days, to the Canadian Rockies. I take pictures of the road, the cliffs which block the entrance to the high mountains, the clouds that hug them and suck from them strength and existence. We circle magical lakes in colors of deep turquoise on foot. Around us is rich, colorful and fascinating vegetation, and I continue to take pictures. I photograph it all in my mind's eye. The camera can capture only flashes of what my eyes see, of what fills my soul. The grand beauty of G-d's world fills me with joy and thanksgiving. In all this good there is no room for fear. In all this wonder there is no room for sadness. In all this beauty there is no room for sorrow. And the pain? It found its place a while ago, and we treat each other with mutual respect, stemming from the realization that we are entwined together, my life and the pain.

The mornings in the north are cold, even in the summer. Every morning, I exercise on the wooden floor of the living room. I open the shutters and swallow with my eyes the luscious green of an earth which has never known thirst. The sun climbs up between tree trunks, sending hesitating, cold fingers to the sealed window. The walls of the room hug the vapor of my breath and passionately absorb it, and they slowly become transparent and hospitable.

I roll up the mattress and put on a coat. It is time to combine the inside with the outside. I go out to the balcony with my *siddur* (prayer book). From Montana, Israel is to the south-east, just like the direction to Jerusalem from our home in Israel. The familiar prayers have a new flavor, the words roll on my tongue, familiar yet different. How many more times will I be able to say *"Shema Yisrael"* ("Hear O'Israel") and hear them reverberate inside? How many more days will I be able to stand and choose to accept the yoke of Heaven? How many more opportunities will I have to ask for the complete healing of my people? To ask for revenge against our enemies? To ask for our people to return to their land and its judges to their places as in the past? To ask for mercy on the people and the land? How many more days will I still be me?

I want to be me. I have learned to love myself. I have learned to cherish my life. I have learned to honor my abilities. I have learned to be thankful for my world. I have learned to see that my world today is greater and more whole than my world yesterday, the day before, and further back. I have learned to taste the color, to drink the scenery and to nourish my being with the beauty of the world that The Master of all beings has created. The G-d who creates worlds and destroys them in order to rebuild them again. A thin, transparent yet strong shell has cracked. Through those cracks my being flows into my consciousness, until I know that I have a part in this world, a part of a whole, which for the time being will be incomplete without me.

Going back home, we are more loving, connected and closer. We know what there is to know and believe there is a reason and cause for everything. We are thankful for the part which we have in the present – between us, in our family, in our community and in this world.

• • •

I stop taking the strong anticoagulants. A headache starts after a week and gets stronger and more difficult to bare. Prof. Hezkeyah says that in his opinion, there is no need to follow up using diagnostic catheterization, but Prof. Govrin is worried because of the headache, which has already saved my life three times. A diagnostic catheterization is scheduled in a few days.

I am fasting. Someone is preparing the area where the catheter will be inserted. I am wearing a hospital gown. A rolling bed barely avoids the walls, corners and the elevator doors, and I am on it. My head is screaming in pain from the movement, my body is asking for relief from the pressure, I am trying to relax the muscles a little, which are trying to protect me from becoming scattered. My soul is murmuring in its cage, its wings are hitting the bars of tomorrow, which are locked on both sides, in the lower and the upper worlds, as if deliberating onto which direction to turn its face.

You have given me all that one can ask for and a thousand times more. You have given to me with no restraints. You will give me more, I know, but in what form? In what identity? And until when?

I know that His mercy is abundant. I know that His expectations are immense. I know that I am unworthy, but I also know that it does not matter, that I will do whatever I can. "The foundation of *Hasidut* (expecting excellence from yourself) and the root of *Avoda Temima* (wholesome worship) is that a person will clarify for himself what his true obligation is in his world."

How will I know what my obligation is in this world? How will I find within myself the true wish to know my duties in my world, and from my world to beyond it? I am trying so hard to know, and I know nothing. What more can one ask of You?

The waiting room. The process I am so familiar with returns. Signing the consent for catheterization. Being rolled into the room, which is so cold, so familiar and yet foreign, to the point of horror. Disinfection, local anesthesia in the thigh. A cut. The catheter goes in, aiming for the main artery in the frontal brain. Contrast material, a feeling of heat in my neck, flashes of light between my eyes and my eyelids. I listen to my heart, which is beating and drumming on the membranes of time, which are stretched from one horizon to another by the ropes of my vacillating consciousness.

Prof. Hezekiah's voice, sharp and tight, tears into my inner thoughts and brings me back to the cold room. "When did you stop taking the anticoagulants?" he asks.

"Two and half weeks ago. Why are you asking?"

His voice gives away great tension, anger, disappointment and maybe even fear. Fear from what? Disappointment from what? His words cut through the air like a whip: "This is not the time for talking, you must start taking it again, immediately, for at least another half a year. Start taking it right away, and with no breaks. Is this clear?"

I have never heard him speak like that. "Yes, it is clear," I answer as my thoughts swirl in my head and fear settles into my heart.

I did not receive an explanation as to what was seen and what was said. Taking out the catheter. Pushing on the artery for 15 minutes. The technician, whose finger is pressing to let the artery seal itself without internal bleeding, is trying to pass the time with idle talk, but I have no time to pass or waste. I know what has happened. How wonderful, yet how terrible.

In the two and half weeks since I stopped taking the anticoagulant, the diverter started getting clogged up with coagulated blood. The diagnostic catheterization saved me from a major stroke. I was immediately put back on the anticoagulants, which prevented a complete blockage of the ophthalmic artery. They have saved the image of G-d within me. They have saved the "me" that I know.

They have put me back on anticoagulants, which risk my life because of the volatility of the giant aneurysm. Small injuries with large marks. A constant prayer that the blood clot which saved my life will not be the one which will eventually kill me.

After six more months, the moment of truth has arrived. Continuing with the anticoagulants risks my life, stopping them puts me at risk for major disability in many important functions. We are debating, the decision is hard. At the end we decide to not take the risk of death, but rather the risk of a major disability.

How can I explain our decision? The truth is that we really did not need to choose, seeing that we are commanded "And thou should choose life." We were guided from above: "And thou should choose life;" "And you who adhere to you G-d your Lord are all alive today." It is impossible to cleave to G-d without being alive, without living life. We chose life, the life of cleaving to G-d.

But this is not a simple thing. There are hidden situations in this choice which could come about and affect the whole family, mainly the children. We chose life "at all costs." But the cost could be charged to our dear ones also. It is important for us to let our children and their spouses know. It is important for us to enable a discussion about it, to make room for their questions and listen to their thoughts and feelings.

My birthday is on the eve of *Sukkot* (the feast of Tabernacles). Even though the family has grown, thank G-d, we all continue to gather for the first day of *Chag* (holy-day) in our *Sukkah* (a temporary dwelling under the sky, outside our roofed home) and celebrate happily. Some of the children's families would sometimes stay another night, so as to take a trip together *Hol Hamoed* (the middle days of the holiday), and others would go back to their homes.

This year I ask everyone to plan to stay another night, so that I could talk with them on *Motzaey HaChag* (at night, after the holiday ends). From the moment I asked for a time to talk about my condition, many thoughts begin running through my head. I wish to share with them the experiences I have gone through in the past few years. It is important to me that they will understand me, but I know it will not be simple.

Writing poetry has been my companion through the challenges, the miracles and all the experiences which were between them. The writing exposed the turbulent world inside me, which sought serenity. The photographs expressed this through color and shape. I sat down and created a book with some poems and photographs and ordered copies for everyone.

Preparing this book was an intense experience which I had never undergone before. Typing in the poems, which had all been written by hand, transfers them from a private, inner space to an open and exposed place. At the time, the poems were written at the pace of my existence, in those moments of seclusion and coping. They were part of my inner self, which is usually hidden even from my own consciousness. The heart wrote, the hands drew on the paper and the eyes followed the movements of the pen. The conscious brain seemed to be out of the picture.

Only now, when I read them, months and years after they were written, do I hear my inner being speak.

Putting the poems into a computer file brought me, sometimes for the first time, together with what I wrote. I hardly touch the poems, I do not wish to edit them and change the flow of being, which has entwined the words together and arranged them into lines, like beads in the chain of "me."

The photos from the summer in Montana tell the story of eyes which have learned to see and of a heart which has learned to love. The poems invite them to join the pages. Words, shapes, colors, and textures form a delicate embroidery, thin yet concealing, soft and clear. All these pages gather and come towards me, bringing in front of me a reflection of the rate of my turbulent heat.

Preparing the book is a wonderful way for me to meet me. To meet the miracle of my being. To meet the world which I am granted to see and live for another day, and another. I am overjoyed.

I get excited, as the evening, in which I will let my children know me as a poet, approaches. Until this day I have not shared my poetry with anyone. I am worried about seeing my medical situation through their eyes. I want so much for them to share their feelings with us, their thoughts, but am I capable of containing them? Understanding them?

As the night approaches, the tension inside me grows. I have never been good in social gatherings, and definitely not in leading them. How will the evening go? Will I be able to maximize the use of the moments of quiet granted to us by absent grandchildren, the pre-arranged time we will have?

The end of the Chag has arrived. All the grandchildren change into pajamas, and they are all happy on our bed, watching a Walt Disney movie together. For them it is a real party, and the parents are free for the conversation. We have an hour and a half. Everyone is sitting silent, tense and ready to listen. I do not know what to say or how. I have spent so much time preparing for this opportunity. I have spent so much effort trying to arrange my thoughts in a manner so that I would be able to speak of them in an organized flow. I am speechless, pressured. What if all the plans and preparations go down the drain? Silence. Silence of questions.

Silence of restlessness. The silence before the storm.

I tell them about the situation in my brain, as it has been unfolding for the last year. I share with them Dr. King's words about the dangerous situation with the giant aneurysm, which has already almost killed me twice. I explain the risks from each one of the choices: Continuing the anticoagulants means a risk of death from the giant aneurysm, and stopping the anticoagulants means a possible stroke due to the blockage of the ophthalmic artery, causing major damage of an unknown scope. I share with them our decision to choose the risk of a stroke and disability, probably a major one, and not to risk death due to destabilizing the giant aneurysm. I explain that it is important that they know both the debates we have had and the decisions we took.

"Do you have any questions?" Silence. "Is there anything that you wish to know in more detail?" Silence. I do not know if they are frozen in shock or are paralyzed from horror? I invite them, I ask them, to enter the circle of my being, but they cannot. The words flowed from me, draining me from willing, from wishing, from begging. These words formed a barrier which they cannot overcome. All of a sudden, words are not my friends, and it is terrible, because without them there is no chance that they will understand me. I must not get sucked into the feeling of failure. I must not give up, even if all of my family is feeling hopeless/ lost. Something wakes up inside me. The lust for life rises inside me and fills me up with a simple yet complete joy, the joy of life. I smile.

"*Ima* (mother) why are you not crying?! Why are you smiling all the time?! Why are you behaving as if it is not so terrible?!" The words are said with so much frustration that for a moment I recoil. Where does this anger come from? What does her pain stem from? But I start to understand that a bridge, a very narrow bridge, has been laid between us.

"I am smiling because I am alive. I am happy with the daily gift of life that I get. I am smiling because I am here, and you are all here. You are a wonderful gift, and I am proud of you, of each and every one of you, because these are not simple times for you."

"Ima, you are in pain, it is hard for you, why don't you speak about it? Why are you presenting the situation as if all is well?"

Only now I understand. My bravery is understood by them as arrogance, haughtiness, patronizing. My acceptance of the verdict seems to them impossible, and therefore they cannot accept it to be completely true. My choosing life puts them in a very complex spot. My choosing life puts in front of them that there is a high probability there could be situations where they will need to rise very high in their inner being, in order to turn an obligation to a prerogative.

I have failed to connect between us, and I have no way to find out why. A very narrow bridge was created, and it remains narrow. As the distance grows, the bridge stretches more and more, almost threatening to tear. I am desperate by my inability to connect to them, to connect them to me. I try to fill the empty space with words. "Are you afraid that it will be hard for you with me disabled? With an entity which will not be me anymore?"

"Ima, it is absolutely not so. We do not want to even think of a situation where you are disabled, handicapped, but if there will be a need, G-d forbid, then we will take care of you with full acceptance and no anger at all."

Silence again. The promises fall onto an earth saturated with tears, with fear and with prayer, melting the crust of the earth in which G-d breathed the breath of life. I feel helpless, empty, and so disappointed with myself that it hurts.

I bring out the copies of the poetry book and hand one to each of my children. Maybe this will help to connect us. Maybe this will form a bridge between us. Maybe this will enable my words to be heard in a way which is less direct, less threatening, less sharp and less painful. They hold the books as if they are red hot coals that are already burning the tips of their fingers. I read a few poems to them and thank them for listening, for being here and now for me.

A wave of little children rolls down the stairs and glides into the Sukkah. Tired children. Happy children. Children who want a kiss and a hug before they go to sleep. Children who see only what their eyes see –the tears, the bridge which is being built in the space where parents, children and grandchildren meet.

During the Sukkot Chag, as in every Chag, we have a sisters' meeting. With time, the children grew up and most of us have married children and grandchildren. The meetings do not include everyone now, but we do not give up our "togetherness." I speak with each and every one of my sisters. I did not spend much thought prior to the conversations with them. I share with them the medical situation and the decisions we have made.

The responses are varied, and some are surprising and un-expected. Some listened with empathy and love. They tried to contain the new challenge that is at my doorstep. They tried to understand, accept and to be there for me in the good and in the less good. If there was wonder in them, they tried to contain it and closed it inside them.

And there were others: "Tell me, did you fall on your head? Is it not better to simply die and that's it?! Why do you need a life with major disabilities, which cannot even be fathomed today? Why do you not live the best life you can in the time you have, while you are healthy and functioning and that's it? Why continue beyond that? Is it not better to just go at once? Is it not better that you will be remembered like this, normal and not handicapped? What, you really want to be a burden on your children? Is it not better that they remain with good memories of you? Why are you fighting death? There are situations when it is better than life, don't you think?"

In total shock the words are thrown into the air without thinking. The words come from the gut. But their guts are different than mine. "Is it not clear to you that I want to live?' I scream in a whispering voice, which is seeking its way from my gut to their heart. I look into their eyes, and I say, "I want to live. I lust for life. Why is it so weird in your eyes to prefer life, even with a major disability, over death?"

"I want to live!"

Eyes are looking at me as if I am crazy. I am no longer their strong hero sister who stands through life's challenges and does not become broken. I am no longer the big sister you can always rely on to be there for you. I have become someone to whom a terrible and frightening thing might happen, which will be terrible and frightening to them too. I have become a burden, before anything has even happened to me. I wish to say: look at me, it is me, your oldest sister. It is me and I have not changed. I love you and love the moments we share together. Let us put the fears aside and live. Let us live with happiness and gratefulness for the daily good which G-d has bestowed on us in His great mercy. But the words echo in the hollow space where there was once a bridge between us, until it was desecrated. The words knock on the limits of my being, as if looking for a way out from nothingness to the reality of light and heat and touch and breath of air and sounds and words and containing and accepting silences. The words search, they do not give up, even though I am exhausted.

I did not ask for anything
I did not ask for anything.
Not a miracle,
Not a challenge.
but I was summoned,
and I came to the unfamiliar.
From the unfathomable
I grasped the miracle
And I hugged it into my bosom.
It sucked with no end

Actually,
With no beginning.
Sucking my marrow
Making me his own Without words.

Absorbing my being Making it his being
Beyond anyone's comprehension.

And I,
I only wished to live.

I try to get into the "after the holiday" routine. I try to get back to work full-time. I am present in the office, I participate in conversations, I write scientific and regulatory documents – but at a different pace. It is a pace which does not fit that which is expected of me, of what they were used to receiving from me. The hardship becomes more and more real. From a distant relative, the hardship becomes my brother, who sits in my lap and is asking to suck the marrow of my life. No one wants to see it, so it does not exist. I insist on continuing to do "everything," but this demands a high price from me, which grows higher every week.

I have always given a series of lectures, in the accademia, where every meeting was for four hours. Now, in the winter semester, it is hard for me to maintain a line of thought throughout the four hours of lecture. Short-circuits occur in my thoughts and in my contact with my surroundings. As short as they might be, they damage the quality of my teaching. I exchange presentations which held only some bullet points and graphs for presentations in which almost everything is written down. I hope that this way I will not lose my train of thought. The semester goes by okay, but I share with my family how hard it is for me to teach. This hardship frustrates me so much, because I love teaching these courses. I love teaching, period!

Spring semester has arrived. I walk into the first lecture of a graduate course in biotechnology. I have given this course for the last two years and enjoyed it. But it is hard for me to concentrate, I have disconnections in my thoughts and speech. I try to hide my hardship by turning my back to the students and drawing graphs on the board. I hope that they will not notice how hard it is all for me. I hope that the lecture is going okay, but it is very hard.

It ends up that this hardship is only the beginning.

MUTE

I am in the playground with two of our grandchildren, who live next to us. Recklessly, I rise from squatting and bang my head hard against the parallel bars. I fall and lose consciousness. I wake dazed and in pain. It is clear to me that I have to get back home with the grandchildren, but I have no idea how. Thank G-d that they know the way, and it is mostly on a sidewalk. I deposit them at home, while I am still confused and not really "here."

My speech deteriorates and within a few days I lose it completely. I enter the circle of the silent ones. My world, a world of lectures and presentations, teaching and group learning, conference calls with researchers from around the world, conversations with the children and grandchildren – everything has stopped. The stroke leaves me unstable. It is not clear to me on which ground am I standing, where can I go and where I might fall.

The doctors forbid me to enter into any state of tension or pressure and warn me that this is a matter of life and death. I cannot go back to work, but the demands from the company do not stop. Abe needs to protect me from the unyielding demands of the company. He makes it clear to them that I cannot deal with anything until I recover.

The situation is unfathomable. My world has changed so much that it is barely recognizable. Deep in my heart, I know that at least some of the brain damage will be fixable or compensated for, because the brain is elastic. I cannot know what we will be able to rehabilitate, but in some unexplained way, it is clear, deep inside me, that I will be able to speak again. I am willing to put in any effort required in order to rehabilitate my speech. Abe and I head into a long, complex, and unexpected road of rehabilitation.

Telephone communication is exchanged with messages (SMS) and email. In face-to-face communications, hard-back notebooks and a pen are my mouth. But not only my speech was damaged. I am all battered inside and out, I am so tired of living as though I am all well.

I discover the world of visible handicaps, which is so hugely different from the transparent, invisible handicaps. Everywhere I go, I hold a hardback notebook and a pen in my hand. At the head of each page it is written, "I cannot speak but I can hear." It is unbelievable, but no one believes what they read. In a commercial center I write, "Is there a bookstore in this area?" and I show someone who is passing by. He answers me in slow, simple words and repeats the explanation several times. My inability to speak has been translated in his mind to being retarded.

Never before in my life have I found myself in a position where people thought I was retarded. Living like this is a great lesson in humility. I learned, and I continue to learn this lesson every day. After hitting my head and losing my speech, I have moved, in the eyes of the world, from one end of the spectrum of mental capacities to the other.

Shabbat arrives. I can communicate only by pantomime, as writing is not allowed on the Shabbat. Shabbat, and another one. At the Passover Seder they skip over me when taking turns to read the *Hagadda* (the story of coming out of Egypt as a nation) . Without my notebook and pen I am caged within myself. I accept my fate. Between death and being dumb the choice is clear, and in this case, no one even asked me.

Friday, the phone rings. I am already used to the fact that it is useless for me to answer it. Devorah is on the phone, and Abe puts her on a speaker so that I can also hear. "We asked a rabbi regarding your situation on Shabbat, with no way to communicate clearly. The rabbi said that you should use your smart phone and write on it everything that you wish to say." Abe thanks her in my name.

It is clear to me that I will not write on the Shabbat, not only in my current state but even in a situation of great need. During the whole Shabbat I have no need that is great enough to warrant me writing on the screen of my mobile phone. As far as I was concerned, the Shabbat remained whole and pure. (religious Jews do not write on the Shabbat, nor do they use the phone or other screens).

On Saturday night, after Shabbat, they call and ask, "How was the Shabbat with writing on your mobile?"

I write and Abe reads it out. "I had no need, so I did not write."

"Ima, we asked the most stringent rabbi, and he unequivocally said that you should write everything you wish to say. Two-way communication is important, and in the way that he told you to write, it is allowed. Not to cut down on writing. This is a tool that you should use on Shabbat. It is important that you have a 'normal' Shabbat, just as it should be."

Apparently, there is great importance in direct communication between people on Shabbat, too.

The next Shabbat I try. It is so strange to write on Shabbat, after knowing for over fifty years that it is forbidden, and that this prohibition is an important part of the Shabbat atmosphere. At home with the family, it is somehow okay. But to put my mobile phone in the Shabbat bag I take to Synagogue? With the Siddur and the Wrap? This is so strange. Still, I take it. After the services, I try not to get into "purposeless conversations" and thus not need to use the writing for unimportant words.

Some friends wonder how I can continue my life, happy and well. "How come it does not pull you down? How come it does not break you?" the children ask. "Ima, how come you are not sad? We know how hard it is for you to be dumb."

That night I sit and write, to myself, an answer to their question. I read what I wrote, and I start to understand that I received a great gift from G-d. That not being able to speak could be an important lever in *Tikun Hamidot* (improving one's deads, making oneself a better person), especially in the realm of all the issues connected to speech. In the morning I send what I wrote to all our children. When the Rabbi's wife asks me how I am coping, I send her too what I wrote, the understandings I have reached via inner observation into the space devoid of speech. The Rabbi's wife asks for my permission to show it to her daughters. Others also ask to receive what I sent her. My personal, inner contemplation becomes the property of many. For the first time in my life, I do not feel that the exposure is foreign to me, and it does not diminish me in any way.

Everything I wish to say I have to write down, and this leads to the fact that now I weigh my words carefully before I write them. Is saying these words worth the trouble of writing them? Very quickly, I find out that most of the things that I think of saying are neither important nor necessary. Sometimes, the words are not even worth saying at all, and sometimes it is better not to say them. Having to write them prevents them from being said. Every day I have a practical course of *Shemirat Halashon* (Guarding the Tongue – a book against slander and gossip), through guarding my hand and appreciating the great value of time. It is unbelievable. In the past I have spoken so many words with no purpose or benefit.

Up until the blow to my head, I studied the Jerusalem Talmud with a wonderful friend. How shall we continue to study? Times set aside for Torah study are sacred. They are the air and oxygen for my soul. Fixed study times are part of my living soul. Would I ever consider stopping to breathe? To stop maintaining the soul? I walk to the *Chavruta* (study partner) with my laptop in a backpack on my shoulders. She reads out the words of the *Yerushalmi* and we discuss them, trying to understand and discover their deeper meanings. She speaks, and I type on the computer my thoughts, explanations and the myriad questions that arise.

My words appear on the screen, she reads them and responds. Entire chapters in *Masechet Pe'a* (one of the tractates of the Talmud) are studied together in this fashion. We continue to study, uninterrupted, except for days when my medical condition does not allow me to go to her house. Thank you, G-d, for enabling the "dumb" to converse.

For some eighteen years I have been giving an hour-long class on the weekly Torah portion to the women in the *moshav* (an agricultural village) where we live. Ever since the stroke and my loss of speech, for the several weeks, my friend Shlomit has been giving the class (we were giving the class on alternating weeks). One Shabbat after synagogue, one of the women from the class turns to me and says, "We miss hearing you. Why don't you write the *Shiur* (lesson), and someone will read it out? I am willing to read it aloud to everyone."

I am happy to study in order to teach. Reading the *Parsha* (the portion of the week), and studying the commentators on the subject I choose, are done on a different level in the weeks I study for the sake of teaching, as opposed to the weeks I study only for the sake of study. All those years previously I used to read the Parsha on Friday morning, before I went into the kitchen to cook for Shabbat. Afterwards the Parsha would circle inside me until I would find a topic for the Shiur. While cooking, I would develop the idea for the entire lesson. During Shabbat I would focus on the topic I chose and mark with stick-on notes the sources I would bring with me to the Shiur. All in all, the preparation took two to three hours.

What will I do now? First, I must prepare the Shiur early in the week so that the woman who will be giving/reading it will have time to go over it and ask questions should they arise. I must put all the commentators and *Midrashim* in a written document. But this is not enough. I have to write the Shiur word by word; in the way I think would be best to deliver the ideas. This is the request of the women who volunteer to read the Shiur aloud on Shabbat.

I try, but it is extremely hard for me to get to a level which will meet my expectations. Short circuits in my thinking and communication hinder and burden the preparation of the written Shiur. What I could do in just a few hours on Friday and Shabbat, now demands from me many hours during the days of the week. But still – with much effort I go back to giving Shiurim in Torah. Blessed is the One who frees the imprisoned.

As part of my work, I established collaborations with government bodies and academic institutions in the USA with the company, but now I cannot continue to manage and lead these efforts. I try not to cut them off completely, but there is nothing I can do, I am dumb. When there is a need for scientific meetings, people from the company come to my home and conduct conversations by having me write answers to questions which come up. Someone from the company reads them out loud to the party who has been waiting on the other side of the line. The effort is tremendous, as it demands concentration and focus for long periods of time, skills which are becoming harder and harder to hold on to.

After a few weeks I am exhausted, and I cannot do even that. These conversations, and others involving the company, are loaded with tension, which costs me my health. Conversations regarding company management issues are not conducted from my home anymore. As a matter of fact, such conversations have ceased to be conducted with me at all.

• • •

Dear loved ones,

You have asked me how I manage with the loss of my speech. I told you that losing my speech was very hard, as it came as a shock and turned my whole life upside down. However, I found out that the silence forced upon me also has a positive side to it. I tried to understand how, and I found out that from this loss there is growth within me, and that daily I learn an important and wonderful lesson. I try to remember the fundamental truths which have been clarified to me, and I am sharing them here with you, with great love.

1. I believe that I will be able to speak again, with G-d's help, in the not so far future. It demands intensive and diligent work with professionals, and much patience. I am used to the first demand, and I am acquiring the second one – patience – in large portions. Patience is a gift I am learning to give to myself.

2. Surprisingly, the world is not a lesser place without spoken words and without my voice. It makes me wonder how much of regular conversation and words are really needed in the cosmic/worldly order of things.

3. Today I have to think about what I want to say before I write it down and ask others to read it. I realize that so much of the talking I would have done in my normal state is actually not needed at all.

4. The need to write down my thoughts and my responses creates a pause for rethinking and created a good sieve for sorting out what is really worth saying. The saying "the boundary of wisdom is silence" brings with it an additional meaning and dimension.

5. To be quiet, really quiet inside, is a good way to learn to listen better. Listening is a key to good communications, and thus I find myself unexpectedly in a situation in which I improve my communication skills.

6. To say less is a good way to reduce the need and effort to control things and people around me. It is a good exercise in letting go, in stopping to hold on to things where there is no good reason for me to.

7. This does not invade my life and does not stop me from doing whatever I chose to do at a given time. Messages remain on the screen until I choose to read them later. I hope to maintain this situation even after I learn to speak again. That is, to maintain that whatever I am doing at a given time is not less important than whatever someone else wants me to do at that same time.

8. Without speech I have more time to myself. While I do not seek to become an introvert or isolated, I do need to show more respect to the passing of time. This is true as time is short, both as a rule and in relationship to me in particular.

With all which is written above, I pray that speech will come back to me as soon as possible.

I also pray that I will not forget the lessons which I have learned during this period and therefore, will not feel that I have had to go through this challenging time for nothing.

NOT DISAPPEARING

Shabbat. My daughters and their families, and my sister and her family, have come to us for Shabbat. Full and relaxed, we are sitting at the Shabbat table and discussing the Torah portion. In a little while I will serve desert. I get up to check something in the kitchen. I am confused, what did I get up for? What am I looking for? My body betrays me, and I fall on my face on the floor. The floor is cold, and then it disappears.

My sister tells me later that they saw me convulsing on the floor, and then falling unconscious. I wake up to faces who ask me what happened. My body is hurting, my head is in pain, I am confused and weak.

Someone yells, "Call an ambulance!" I wave my finger to say no.

"She does not want an ambulance."

"Are you crazy? Do not listen to her." Again, my finger waves in refusal.

"She had an epileptic attack. I know how it looks. A doctor needs to see her. I am calling."

"No need, I already called."

Without talking, I beseech them: "Please call it off. I will be fine." Someone picks me up and puts me on the sofa. The men from the ambulance arrive. I am already recuperating.

"There is no need to take me to the hospital. I fell. I got up. That is all," I explain in pantomime.

Someone brings me a writing pad in order to communicate with the medical staff. I am taken to the ambulance. Abe and my sister come with me. In the emergency ward the effect of the attack wanes, but my head hurts unbearably. I am given something for the pain and left under observation for the night. Abe and my sister try to doze off in the emergency room, with their heads and hands on the side of my bed. It is impossible to sleep, but impossible not to. The night passes with all three of us in a twilight zone.

In the morning they are willing to release us, but how will we get back home? Will we have to stay on the hospital premises the whole Shabbat? Asking around, it turns out that there are Arab cab drivers who can take us back home and will wait for payment on Sunday (we do no commerce or use of money on the Shabbat). I am rolled in a wheelchair to the cab's door. At the gate to the moshav, next to the sign which reads "Entry on Shabbat and on Jewish holy days is forbidden," the cab stops. Abe and my sister support me on both sides, and I can barely drag myself between them. My legs do not carry me. I pray that the walk will be over soon and that I will be able to lay down.

9:00 a.m. on Shabbat morning. Everyone is at prayer in the synagogue, including a few women who go to the synagogue for the Torah reading.

We schedule an urgent appointment with a neurologist. He asks, "What exactly happened?" and Abe describes the scene in our kitchen. The doctor explains. "This was an epileptic attack, a very big and strong one, which is called Grand mal. I am giving you anti-epileptic pills. The dose needs to be raised gradually. Let us hope that we will find a reasonable dose which will alleviate the attacks."

This was my first epileptic attack. In the following months I will have several difficult epileptic attacks both in the house and outside. In the shower – it hurts terribly and is embarrassing, and in the kitchen, when my head almost hits hard the corner of the table in the middle of the room.

I fall on the stairs in the house, lose consciousness and slide down on them. Abe does not dare to move, because he is stopping my head with his foot. If he moves, I will continue to roll down the stairs. But he has to move in order to put me in a safer and less painful position. I cannot stand up. Abe brings a "secretary's chair" with wheels, and with it he transfers me to a bed in the guest room on the main floor, the entrance floor.

Shabbat. I pray in the synagogue. After the service, the women gather outside by the main entrance to talk and catch up. This one had a grandson, the other had twins; this one is planning the *wedding* of her daughter, the other one the *bat mitzva* (a party celebrating her coming into the age of Torah obligations) of her granddaughter. A collection of ages and countries of origin, fields of interest and occupations. Some are discussing the Shiur that we heard at the end of the service, and what we can take from it for our daily lives. I am standing next to the wall in the plaza outside the synagogue, listening to the Rabbi's wife and two of my friends. Suddenly, I collapse. I disappear.

Voices of fear. Voices of panic. Words float through the air: ambulance, first aid, resuscitation, doctor, oxygen, a stretcher, to move her, not to move her.

Somewhere, in a world parallel to mine, these words are floating like balloons which are connected with transparent strings to whomever said them. Time is bubbling in a boiling pot of scared people who wish to be, or rather not to be, near me. Bubbles bubbling, rising to the surface.

I wake up laying on the cobblestones of the synagogue entrance and my head is hurting, the pain unbearable. My daughter leans towards me and her lips are moving, but her voice is unheard. Slowly, slowly I take in my surroundings. Under my head there is something soft, padded, merciful. Above me are white, gray rays and blue skies, all quiet. All the noise is inside of me. Around me are whispers, segments of words, syllables, and tones of people.

"You are okay Ima; you had an attack. You are by the synagogue and we are with you." My hands move to my skirt, wanting to cover my legs. "Ima, you are covered, all is well, rest a little."

I sink and resurface, hearing and not hearing. Seeing and not seeing. I wish to move, to get up, to sit. A hand on my shoulder, "Ima, please remain laying down a little longer. You had a strong attack, and your body is weak and needs to collect itself anew."

Above me people are having a discussion. An ambulance should be called. No, she has attacks and there is no need for an ambulance for that. She hit her head when she fell. She is okay. She will be okay. Who knows what happened in her injured brain? Such a fall is dangerous to anyone, even more so to her.

Why? Because she has had several brain surgeries. She almost died in the past. She could die now too. But she did not, so let it be. Is there any way to help? To bring a wheelchair? A wheelchair is a good idea. Who has one? I do not know, not sure. We will look for one. We will find one. We will bring her a chair. How will you get home? There is no need for anything, thank you. We are here with her. She will recover, and we will help her get home.

The voices, the colors and the people who bore them move further and further away, until only we were left, the epileptic victim and her family.

On that Shabbat there was a grand *Kiddush* (a blessing of the Shabbat over wine, followed by a buffet of light food and cakes) after services, and all those praying in the various nearby synagogues joined together to celebrate and wish *Mazal Tov*. The plaza was full of friends, people of the community and their siblings, *Hassidim* and traditional Jews, *Bene Akiva* and *Ezra* youth, newcomers and the old timers – one large fabric full of human life, with a big heart and brimming with charitable deeds and charity. I had an attack with convulsions, I fell and lost consciousness in front of tens, or maybe hundreds of people. I recover after two or three days and get back to my routine of study and writing. The community carries the memory of my epileptic attack for a very long time.

Surprised looks greet me in the synagogue the following Shabbat. I do not know what there is to be surprised about. I fell. I got up. After the services, women ask about my well-being and tell me where they were and what they were doing when I fell, when I convulsed, when I remained lying unconscious on the stone floor of the entrance plaza. Mothers of babies, tell me that my daughter asked for soft blankets to protect my head and limbs from getting hurt during the strong convulsions. The small blankets all gathered into one big blanket. I am told that women's shawls protected my arms.

"You are really brave," a friend says.

"Brave? How come?" I am surprised.

"That you are not ashamed to come up to synagogue after what has happened."

The astonishment on my face is still wordless. With one sentence, a mirror has been put in front of me, the mirror through which others see me. Seizures and falls are a scary, shameful matter. Such things you do not expose to the outside world. How dare I allow myself to return to my routine after such major humiliation and helplessness, only a week ago?!

It is not the first time in which I understand, through other people's eyes, that I deal with the situation differently, very differently, from what others expect from me. I seek the opportunity to grow in places where others expect me to wilt and wither. I am not willing to let my body control me, and it does not represent me. The body convulses, not I. The body falls, not I. The body is weak, not I.

A Cobweb of Fears

I am torn from within With invisible tears
And thus, not important.

I am scared at the foundations By unnoticed scars
And thus, nonexistent.

I am fractured through my whole being
With hidden branching fractures
And thus, not affecting.

I am wounded in the depth of my heart
with silently bleeding wounds
And thus invisible.

The tears I connect and survive.
The scars I oil and dance.
The fractures I fill
and erase.
The wounds I bandage and smile.
But,
The fear in your eyes from a visible tremor,
The worry for my sanity due to heavy stammering,
These I cannot erase.
These I cannot silence.
These I have to survive,

Without the ability to shake off the cobweb of fears
The threads of worry
That your pity weave around me to imprison me.

To cast me
Into the form of the nightmare in your eyes.

Budding Out
The hems of Winter's cloak
Touched my face
Raised to the sun.
I did not know
Who diverted from its place
The rain knocking
On spring's door
Or me.
I started budding out
From a pained heart Yearning
For flowers
And long days
Of fruits
Wrapped in prayers.

Longings
Longings for what was
Bring to the present
Their offering
Like a ball
Which could be bound
With iron chains
To my feet
Or sit in the palm of my hand
Ready to be
Thrown
Into the future Pulling me with it
Onwards Climbing
Towards that 'good'
Which I knew I will know
At due time and course
And not a moment earlier.

A SUPPORT CHAIN

Abe is working. Now he is the sole bread winner. He cannot be with me all the time. I also do not want someone to be with me all the time. Most of the time I am well and can take care of myself. Most of the time, but not all the time. We buy an emergency alarm button which is connected to the *Yad Sarah* (a national help center for the injured and handicapped) telephone service center. When I push the button, they will call right away and try to talk with me. But I will not answer because I cannot speak. Whom do I wish them to call? I give them the number of our daughter who lives next to us. And whom should they call after her, should she not answer? The neighbor, who works from home, agrees to be a link in my chain of survival, should the need arise, may it never arise. If the neighbor will not answer? To a family member by ,marriage, she is like a sister to me. She is already retired, and thus she spends a lot of time at home. If she does not answer? To Abe, to his mobile, but most of the time he is in meetings in Tel Aviv or in other cities. Each one of the women in the survival chain is equipped with a key, Abe's phone number and the phone numbers of the other links in the communication arrangement. If there is no answer from any of the numbers, the person at the call center will call an ambulance to my home.

I am marked as a handicapped person, as someone in constant

and immediate danger, who has a flag flying over him announcing that existence. I wear the emergency button on my arm. It is effective at a distance of up to 100 meters from a special phone in the kitchen. A superbly constructed set up, yet with one major problem with no solution: I have no early warning prior to having an epileptic attack, and therefore I will not be able to push the button before I fall and have a seizure.

I try not to think about it, because there is really no solution. It takes two to three days to recover from a grand mal epileptic attack. After that, I try to function in the house. Cooking means the risk of a burn in case of a seizure, especially when cooking over a gas flame. I give it up. I maintain a healthy routine, mentally and physically. The fourth day after a major attack, I can go back to swimming, one hour a day, five days a week. I let the lifeguard know that I have epilepsy. He is not worried. "You have been swimming here for a long time and everything has been fine," he says.

In the pool there is a lifeguard who can see me, at home there is no one. It is not a good situation but there is no other option. The family tries to get organized for the first day or two after a major epileptic attack. Much of it falls on the shoulders of our daughter who lives next to us. They are all brave. It is harder to see a person fall down than it is to fall down yourself.

On the other days they make sure to send me messages throughout the whole day, until Abe gets home in the evening. Some good friends also participate in this setup for maintaining contact with me during the long days. I have to answer every message right away. If I do not answer, and a second and third "are you OK?" SMS are left unanswered, they start trying to find out where I am and whether there is anyone who knows why I am not answering. There are times that one of them comes to my house to see what is going on. Maybe I fell? Maybe I got hurt? Maybe... Maybe...? When I lay down to sleep, I have to let them know first, so that they will not worry if they do not receive an immediate response. When I wake up, I let everyone know that I am up and ready to be "followed up" on and protected again.

Weeks go by. Now, when I leave the house to go to my Chavruta, I SMS her so she will know when I am expected to arrive at her house. If I do not arrive, she will know to go and look for me on the sidewalk or street, between my home and hers. When I leave her house, she becomes worried and tense, until I send her an SMS as soon as I have reached my home. I learn with another relative by marriage in a *Midrasha* for women. Once in a while I have an epileptic attack during a class. Almost always, there is no loss of consciousness, or a loss for just a second or two. She is brave. She continues to drive me in her car, to sit next to me and not to lose her wits when I start trembling or my body becomes rigid. I am blessed, as I am surrounded by brave and loving people.

Abe and I barely go to crowded shopping malls, as they destabilize my brain and this could lead to, or cause – and it does – an epileptic attack. It is embarrassing to find myself helpless on the floor in the middle of a shopping mall or in a store. It is even more embarrassing for the one who accompanies me. Abe is a real hero. At some point Abe puts a veto on my entering crowded places. Weddings and other affairs in closed halls are also not good for me. We come for the *Chuppa* (the actual wedding ceremony, which takes place under a cloth canopy held up by four poles) and stay after the Chuppa only until the bride and groom come out of the *Yichud* room (the room where the bride and groom go to, once united by the wedding covenant, spend the first private time together, before the dancing and socializing with the guests). The notes the orchestra plays prior to their entry to the hall are our notes of goodbye from the celebration.

The neurologist continues to increase the anti-epileptic drug dosage. The drugs dull my thinking, but the attacks are dangerous to the brain, inside of which the aneurysm has started to grow again. The attacks are also dangerous to my body – the falls are hard, and I have almost no control of the way I fall. The injuries can be difficult. Sometimes, in our bedroom at night, Abe discovers dark marks on my body, bruises acquired upon falling. Sometimes I have no clear memory of how it happened. Over time I have a collection of marks, black and blue, purple and yellow, until they disappear, "making room" for more bruises which will eventually come. I try to function through blurring screens of different anti-epilepsy and pain drugs.

One day a week, at two o'clock, I pick up two grandchildren from their nursery and day care. I serve them lunch. After that we play a quiet game or draw. Their mother has said it is okay to have them watch a children's show on the computer on a day when I am too tired to play with them. On one of those days, when they are at the computer, and I am clearing dishes in the kitchen, – I fall. My head is hurting badly. I am laying on the floor. When I return to consciousness, I hear the four-year-old, first-born whisper, "Grandma, are you okay? Grandma, are you okay? Grandma, are you okay?"

I open my eyes and nod my head. I am okay. I sit up on the floor. I wait. Soon their father will come to pick them up, and I will lay back down. My heart aches, I have caused my grandchildren trauma. In the evening, my daughter comes to see how I am doing. "How are you, Ima? The children told me that you were on the floor today. I asked them, and they said that first you strongly shook your arms and legs, and then you just laid on the floor with your eyes closed."

I told her how sorry I was to have caused them trauma. "You had a trauma. They did not," she replies. "They know that you have a problem in your brain and that it hurts you when it is noisy or there is a commotion, and that sometimes you fall because of it, but later you get up. For them it is a simple fact of life. Please do not worry, they are just fine."

The rehabilitation of my speech is moving along. I still communicate most of the time in writing, but I can already sound some syllables and parts of words. With time, I can be understood a little. For a long time, I am "stuck in one place" regarding improving my speech. It seems that all am doing is reducing the effort it takes to sound the words out and to get them out of my mouth clearer.

Abe does not let up. Every doctor that might be able to help is recruited into the rehab effort. I work hard, I do not give up, deep inside I know that my speech will return and that I will speak clearly and fluently. Many months go by. The intervals between big epileptic attacks become longer and longer. Partial attacks, without losing consciousness, happen several times a week, at different intensities. When it happens, I usually have enough time to sit down on the floor or at least lean against something.

The situation in the company deteriorates without me, in spite of everyone's efforts. The stress rises, and this tension is dangerous for me. I try to totally dissociate myself, but it is hard. I really do not wish to disappoint them. So much effort, time, money and years of my life, and some of theirs, have been invested in this, in the company. At the end it becomes impossible.

After a difficult conversation with the CEO, he drops me off at my house and I walk along the entrance path. I feel bad, unstable. I continue on the grass a few more steps and I fall. After some time, half awake, my right hand finds my left hand, above my head, and I push the emergency button. I return to oblivion.

My daughter leans over me, "Ima, you are very hot, you are in the sun, you need to move away from the sun." I hear and but do not hear. I try to move but cannot. She pulls me on the grass towards the shade. It is hard. I am heavy and I am not helping her. I am like a rag, or rather like a heavy bag. My head is now in the shade, but it's not enough. She needs to get me into the house, to lay me on a bed or a sofa. My eyes close.

Later, I am told that my daughter received the call from Yad Sarah while she was at a friend's house with her three boys. She took her friend's car and went to look for me at home. She found me laying down with my face buried in the grass, burning in a hot and fierce noon sun. She estimated that I had been lying in the sun for at least forty minutes before she got to me. She was afraid that I had a heat stroke. When she could not move me by herself, and certainly not get me into the house, she called the neighbor who was the next link in the chain of warnings created to protect me. Together they pulled me up the outside stairs and laid me on the closest sofa in the house. My daughter and the neighbor alternated watching over me until Abe, whom she had called, got home. I remember telling them that I was okay and that there was no need to be with me, that they should not waste their time, and I dozed off again, emerging and sinking, a little here and a little there.

Out of The Frying Pan into The Fear
Out of the frying pan into the fear,
Out of the abyss into the oblivion,
In invisible steps,
In disrupted breaths.
Out of the rescue into the pain,
Out of the success into the despair,
Like tears dripping salt
On my wound which is bleeding
To death.

My Tears

A tear
And another tear
Burning its way
From within my being
Unto my narrow world.

And from the cracks in the walls of my existence
G-d peers at me
Silent and accepting
The shards of earthenware.

Collecting in them
My tears
Creating from them
My world

Which is renewed every day In its goodness
In its pain.

That evening we completely cut off communication with the company and its staff. I am not allowed to take any more risks on my life, beyond total necessity. The company has been a source of high tension and stress. There is a lot of bitterness from their side and much frustration from mine. My life's enterprise is going down the drain, and from this point on it will not be possible to rehabilitate it in the future, but there is no choice.

I recover and go back to speech rehab. Every day, I gather one small achievement. Every week I bring a perceptible improvement with me to Shabbat. The month of *Elul* (the last month in the Jewish year. When it ends, the High Holy-days start)) arrives, the time for evaluating the year which is coming to an end and to take upon oneself commitments for the coming year. My speech is improving and with it the risk, G-d forbid, that I will fall into the pits of *Lashon Hara (speaking liable and gossip)*. I read again and again what I wrote when I was unable to speak, what I believed in and what I took upon myself for the time when I will speak again. I take upon myself an intent to minimize my speech, even now when it is improving more and more. I wish to put holiness into the words that come out of my mouth. The gift of speech which G-d has given us is part of "His Image" as "in His image He created him." G-d created Adam as part of the world, which was created by ten sayings, so that the Ten Commandments could descend onto it. In this regard G-d is recreating me, breathing into my soul the words and into my throat the sounds, the syllables, the pronunciations.

Holiness. I seek Holiness. Holiness. But it is so far from me. I am too small for all the mercy and truth that G-d has given and is giving me. I am too small, and therefore I must accept the merciful gift of speech with an appreciation for the magnitude of the gift. A gift which is beyond any right which I could have ever gathered to bring in front of Him. A gift which no one believed could be replanted in my brain and brought back to full function. Speech is still hard, tiring, and my voice is still weak and strained, but the words are already clear. Even if the sword of dumbness is put onto his throat, man should not despair from this calamity.

My birthday is on the eve of *Sukkot* (the feast of the tabernacles, when we live in temporary dwellings to remember our forefathers living like that in the dessert after going out of Egypt some 3,500 years ago). In the month of Elul I hoped, on *Rosh Hashana* (the first two days of the new Jewish year, when the whole world is judged for its deeds) I decide, and during the Days of Atonement I implement. I prepare a Shiur for the women, which I will, G-d willing, give in my Sukkah. For many years I have given a special, large Shiur, to which dozens of women come. Many of them do not come to the regular lesson on the weekly portion, but make sure to come to the special study on *Shavuot* (the day we celebrate the giving of the Torah, to the nation of Israel, on mount Sini) and Sukkot. On Shavuot, at our house, Shlomit gives a Shiur on aspects of the Shavuot holiday or the scroll of Ruth. On Sukkot, in our Sukkah, I give a Shiur on aspects of the Sukkot holiday and the book of *Kohelet* (Ecclesiastes). Last year I did not do this. On Sukkot last year, I did not have the gift of speech.

I prepare a Shiur about the joyousness (*simcha*) of *Beit Hashoeva* (on Sukkot we pray for the blessing of the water (which is scarce in Israel) and about Hillel's words in regard to the big simcha and in *Pirkey Avot* (The Sayings of Our Forefathers). Hillel says: "If I am not for myself then who is, and when I am for myself what am I, and if not now then when?" Hillel who knows his place and says: "If I am here – all is here, and if I am not here – who is here?" Hillel who says: "To the place that I love, to there my feet take me." Hillel who speaks with G-d: "If you come to my house – I will come to your house, if you do not come to my house – I will not come to your house."

I am trying to examine and fine tune the feeling of joy where the "self" expands and is erased simultaneously. I try, through these words, to hold onto the belief in the creator of the world and its manager, together with the belief in man's ability, as a creature with free choice and a role in the working of the world and its keeping. These understandings emerge and grow from study, and with them an excitement towards giving the Shiur, and sharing with my women friends and students some of my lessons from the long journey back to speach.

I write a message on the moshav website: "With thanks and gratitude to the Creator of the world I will, G-d willing, give the traditional Shiur on Shabbat of Sukkot, in our Sukkah. Sara."

The hope moved on to become a plan, the plan to a study, the study to a shiur, the shiur to a deed. And this deed, the words of the message, creates a being. The written message becomes a living entity standing on its own. A Shiur is going to be given. Waves of anticipation and excitement towards it glide into the shores of consciousness of those who hear and wish to learn. The voice comes and goes and comes again, wave after wave onto the beach, which is waiting there between one wave and the other, sure that there will be another wave, and another one, and between them silence. Come oh *Kallah (bride)*, come oh Kallah, come.

The first day of Sukkot. I say the blessing over the candles and also *Shehecheyanu (a special blessing for surviving to reach that special day)*, that He has maintained us, kept us and brought us to this time. I say the words of the Shehecheyanu slowly and with great, deep intention. This blessing, which has been imbued with a special meaning for me on every holiday since my life was saved, rolls off my tongue with a wonderful sweetness, and creates an awareness of life, with great wonder. Life within a miracle which has been done for me, to one so small. Life which has not yet stopped and therefore demands an importance and meaning which will justify this gift to me.

After the evening service I stand with most of our children and grandchildren next to the holiday table in our beautiful and spacious Sukkah. Abe sanctifies the Chag, blesses over the wine, and says Shehecheyanu, that G-d has sustained us and kept us and brought us to this time, and for sitting in the Sukkah. I wish to bless the creator and thank Him aloud, but my lips are trembling, and I can say nothing. I say the blessing in my heart, and my heart says Amen.

I sit surrounded by beloved and dear children and grandchildren, happy with the holiday and happy with each other, and I can speak with them! Blessed, being blessed and blessing everyone in circles of warmth and love, gratitude and thanksgiving for the great and wonderful being inside us and around us. I know that I am unworthy of the benevolence which has been bestowed upon me. My heart is fearful and joyful, unwilling to believe that I have survived this trial, too.

Oh my G-d. How does one live with miracles? G-d, how does one live without them?

And There Was a Miracle
And there was a miracle
And another miracle.
It is not possible to run away from the miracle.

It ascends upwards
And uproots the roots of the existence,
Raising them higher and higher and more.

The sheets swell up and wail.
The cords stretch till they are gone.

The pegs tremble,
Imbedding their sharp tip into the earth,
Calling her clods not to leave them
To sighs
To loneliness
To miracles.

The Revealed Miracle

No one sees the revealed miracle.
Everyone is busy creating it,
As if it is nothing but a passerby.

In the routine of the regular good life
No one hears G-d's living words.

Everyone is busy fencing them and protecting them,
As if they are nothing but details of laws
In the course of ideals of restrictions upon restrictions.
No one feels the shielding and protecting G-d.

Everyone is busy describing His almightiness,
As if there is nothing in Him but strength and power,
In a world of the wicked who knows no rest.

No one wraps himself in the big soft embrace.

Everyone is busy distancing and acclaiming Him,
As if because "the whole earth is full of His glory"
There is no place for His cloak and His prayer shawl.

But sometimes, for tiny fragments of time,
We see miracles,
We hear the words of the Lord
Feel that "the nearness of G-d is my good"
And wrap ourselves in his arms
And say: "Here I am."

Sukkot is the holiday of visible miracles. The holiday of clouds which protect us from the sun, clouds of honor, which filter and soften the supreme light which glows upon them from the heavens. A holy day remembering our one garment and one pair of shoes, which did not wear out during forty years in the desert. A holiday of "Your walking after me in the dessert in an unsown land." A desert, but with the Well of Miriam. Unsown, with Manna from heaven and all the flavors of the earth and its delicacies within it. A holiday of a temporary dwelling, which rises when the cloud rises and settles back onto the desert ground upon its descent and rest. A holiday where the cloud which covers is the cloud which enables the light to be seen. The cloud which hovers over the Tabernacle is the cloud which marks G-d's descent onto this earth, and the rising of the people to become a priestly nation and a holy people. A holiday which is entirely a memory of an existence of the present, without the knowledge of what tomorrow will bring.

It is not possible to preserve a miracle from one day to the next. A person cannot draw from today's miracle to establish the miracle of tomorrow. The miracle is a measured existence "for each day, its portion." "On the day you should pay his fee," On the day you should give thanks for His miracle. We have shown G-d kindness by being willing to live like this, when we do not know if there will be food to sustain us tomorrow. Kindness which we have shown G-d by willing to live in the shadow – or the light – of visible miracles.

It is hard to constantly live within a miracle. "The kindness of youth" ends upon the people's entry to the Land of Israel, and daily, visible miracles are transformed into hidden miracles. From prenuptial engagement to marital relations. The connection now is via our "doing" in this world. We raise our eyes to heaven to ask for rain, to ask for conditions which will enable us to obtain our bread and our life from the earth.

We do not raise our eyes for Manna which will come down from heaven. It is time for constant work, for life which is itself, by its very existence, a miracle. But these are "small," regular daily miracles. They are around us and with us so much, we are not really aware of them. They are a needed and familiar part of daily existence in this world.

When Moses raises his arms to enable the victory over Amalek, his hands are heavy for him to hold up on his own, and Aaron and Hur need to support him, or else the miracle will be lowered and disappear from the vision of Israel and its fighters. When a person fights for his life, he needs someone who will enable him to lift his head upwards and focus his heart on his Father in Heaven, so that he will be victorious. A miracle upon a miracle has been pilled upon my shoulders.

Tall miracles, which can be seen from afar. Heavy miracles, which crush me and teach me humility. If my soul has been rescued from death and my eyes from tears, it is surely not because of my deeds. And if it is not within my right, but rather an act of mercy, then the mercy of G-d has nothing to lean on. I am too small, but I still have been asked to carry miracle upon miracle. So it must be that I have to raise my hands up high and ask for G-d to support my arms from both sides, so that all will see and know that "Even if a sharp sword is laid upon a person's neck, he should not give in to the calamity."

"If I am not for myself who is, and when I am for myself who am I?" G-d has given me the gift of life, but it is up to me to see this with a good eye. From the state of thanksgiving, I feel obliged to make this gift the property of the many.

Shabbat of Sukkot arrives with candles and Kiddush, sitting in the Sukkah and inviting the *Ushpizin* (special spiritual guests from our past as the nation of Israel). After clearing the big table from the day's meal, we spread elegant white tablecloths on it, and two rings of chairs are arranged around the living room area of the Sukkah. Piles of plastic chairs, stacked one on top of the other, are waiting at the corner of the Sukkah.

I cannot sleep. I cannot rest. I am excited about giving the Shiur. I pray that I will be able to do it and do it well. I prepared a Shiur on the Simcha of Beit Hashoeva, which was the epitome of true simcha/joy. It was the highlight of the Simcha before G-d in the exact and complete connection to the Torah and via that, to G-d. The Shiur includes an attempt to understand the words of Hillel, who makes conditions for G-d: "If you will come to my house I will come to your house, and if you do not come to my house than I will not come to your house." And I, what do I ask for? How can I come to your house empty handed? Please bring me to Your house in this world, let me dwell in it for a long life, a life of blessing.

The women trickle into the Sukkah. Each one is like a drop of water, together they are like a blessed rain. The chairs fill up, including all the extra ones. The women who come late stand at the entrance to the Sukkah.

"Shabbat Shalom and Chag Sameach to all of you." Silence. I cannot raise my voice. Everyone leans forward, trying to hear every word. My words fall on thirsty, yearning ears, like rain drops on green meadows.

I say the blessing *"Baruch Roffe Cholim"* (Blessed is the healer of the sick), *"Hatov V'hameytiv"* (Belassed is the Good and the Benevolent),"and *"Shehecheyanu V'kiyemanu V'higianu L'zman Hazeh"* (Blessing the One Who has granted us life, and sustained us, and brought us to this time).

My voice chokes, trembles, seeks its owner, its creator, the one who breathed the breath of life into it, the one who taught it, already in my mother's womb, the holy language, and gave him the ability to create an existence. A spiritual and holy existence. An existence which clings to her Beloved through some one hundred eyes and ears, which are asking to enter with her the gates to the garden of the king, to the king who sits on a high and mighty seat.

Since it is hard for me to maintain my thread of thought and keep things in order, while focusing on pronounciation of the words, I read the Shiur word by word. I seek the women's eyes between one sentence and the next, including them in my being, wrapping them with words of Torah, with sentences of Simcha. Happy eyes, listening eyes, absorbing eyes, hearing eyes, understanding eyes, tearing eyes, praying eyes, thanking eyes. The letters do not fly away from the page, and it remains light in my hands, as it was before. My voice, which trembled at the beginning, finds its place in the space of my being, and settles wherever it settles, with me, here, in the Sukkah.

The words end. There is not a dry eye. With the end of the words on the page sentences flow towards me, sentences of joy, of thanksgiving to G-d, of belief in the One who heals and does wonders. The relief at seeing me alive, from within the Torah, inside it and thanks to it, which has saved my life from falling into the pit. Rivers, rivers of light wrap me and the women in semi-light of *Olam Habah* (the world to come) of Torah, while sitting in the Sukkah, which G-d put us in on our way out of Egypt. The words carried with them, foaming and tumbling, the stones which blocked the way, enabling to request "G-d, please open my lips and let my mouth say your praise," clearing a space for the One who created the world with his words, for the One who said "no more" to silence and gave my soul and body back the ability to thank, to praise, to adore, to extol and to acclaim.

I sit in the Sukkah, on the road on the way out of Egypt, out of the narrow straits of my brain which has asked for a rest, which I did not grant, and I did not give up. A Sukkah made of growth from ground which has been uprooted, in order to

enable another type of growth. In the Sukkah I told of the glory of G-d and His benevolence, through the story of Simchat Beit

Hashoeva, the joy found in the proximity of G-d, in the fact that He has come to my home, even if it was only for the duration of time in which a drop of blood can stand on the tip of a sword until it splits, part of the drop to one side and the rest to the other.

Remember Me for Generations to Come
Remember me for generations to come
My life's song
In the corridors In the valleys
In the low tide and the high tide
On the precipices of time
From within the rock I have been hewed from
From the hidden place in the cleft of my rock
Raising my voice upon a high mountain
Whispering out of the depths
"I have cried unto thee O Lord."

Out of The Depths
Out of the depths
I have cried unto thee O Lord
As you are with me
In the valley of the shadow of death
Leading me onto my return
To the soul thou has given me
Which knows the light
From one end of the world to the other
And the time beats in its being
Which praises the Lord Halleluiah.

A Morning Prayer
"My G-d, the soul you have placed within me
is pure.
You created it,
You fashioned it,
You breathed it into me,
You safeguard it within me,
and eventually You will take it from me,
and restore it to me ..."

Please watch out that they do not carry it
Outside the Shabbat bounds
Please see to it that they do not render it defective
That the burnt offering will be unblemished
Please listen to its life humming inside me
And say 'it is good'
In the meanwhile ...

Until the Time to Come.'

A Being With a Hole
When a piece of being is missing
Is it still the same being
Just with a hole
Or a new being all in all?

After a year and half of bad epileptic attacks, and after an increase, and another one, in the doses of medications to prevent them, I have reached a balanced state. I have no more grand mal attacks, which come with loss of consciousness, hard uncontrolled falls, strong shaking of different body parts and then a body which stiffens uncontrollably. Those difficult attacks used to leave me bruised and hurting, with a head screaming in a loud voice that it is suffering and barely surviving.

I enter a blessed routine. I study alone and with a *Chavruta*. I hear classes from the *Midrasha* (Torah school) for women and from taped Shiurim from different Rabbis. I study the portion of the week already on Sunday, and spend many hours every day preparing the Shiur so it will be ready by Thursday. When I feel that the pain is worsening – it has never stopped trying, not even for a minute, to take the scepter of control out of my hands – I study the Sayings of our Fathers. I try to keep my sanity.

My constant, internal motto is "He who's head hurts, should immerse himself in Torah." For over two years and more I have taken this saying at face value: a good medicine for a hurting head is the study of Torah. Recently, the clock has come back to ticking inside my head, parading Time in front of my face, sliced to thin, almost invisible, yet meaningful slices. The numbers running on the screen are blurry, far away and unreadable. But certainty beats upon my temples, being heard a little and disappearing a little. When the aneurysm will explode, something terrible will happen, blood will brazenly wash my brain as if in a storm, pressure my being and threaten my life.

Fine is The Line

Fine is the line
Almost invisible
Like the blink of an eye
Like a single hair
Like the fill of a capillary
Which beats at the rhythm of the heart
And whispers:
I am here,
Here is oxygen,
We can survive
Some more, and more.
Thin is the capillary
Will it withstand the howling of the heart
Absorbing its roar
Embracing the flow
Of the blood
Which brings life
As long as it remains
Within the boundaries of the allowed
Between thin
Transparent walls
Through which death looks
Awaiting to tear them,
To set my blood
Free ...
And send me, to my death.

BALANCES

We have a ceremony every half a year. We get an MRI scan, for a detailed three-dimensional picture of the brain; an MRA, to receive information regarding the blood flow in the brain's arteries; and now an MRV is added, to check the blood flow in the brain's veins. When Prof. Govrin asked to add to the MRV test for the veins, we learned that the tumor, probably a meningioma, has started to put pressure on the main vein which drains blood from the brain. Even on the back side of my head, my brain has to deal with challenges which are not simple.

We have a ceremony every half a year. Without delay we set a meeting with Prof. Govrin, for a private consultation in order to hear from him, concerning all the findings and ramifications from the different imaging readouts. We go up to Jerusalem to meet him and hear from him his analysis of the different images and his conclusions. We arrive on time and wait an hour or two. When we are called in, we find him ready and his two big computer screens filled with one section of the brain or another.

We have a ceremony every half a year. Prof. Govrin shows us that the tumor has grown and explains that the longer we wait to deal with it the less options will be available for treatment. He carefully studies the interaction between the tumor and the wall of the main vein and shows us that the tumor has not yet damaged the blood flow in it. "This is on the one hand good news, and not good news on the other. The good news is that there is good blood flow in the main vein, and no blockage should be expected in the near future." I have already learned not to ask what "the near future" means, because his look will say it all. In the end he will be sorry that his open face communicates with our beseeching eyes. "The bad news is that since the flow is sufficient right now, the body does not build any bypasses and secondary, complementary paths for itself. Therefore, when the blockage will occur – not 'if' but rather 'when' – the brain damage will be terribly large."

We have a ceremony every half a year. We look at the screens and follow his words, his finger, and his face, which tells us much more than he would like them to relay to us. Prof. Govrin recommends doing the surgery "before it will be too late." Immediately afterwards he repeats his statement regarding the unstable situation of the aneurysms and my brain in general. Seeing the aneurysm, which is not fully closed, and blood flowing into it continuously – thank G-d! – he clarifies that one should weigh the surgery damage vis a vis its benefits. He states his opinion: to do the surgery, the sooner the better.

We have a ceremony every half a year. Prof. Govrin looks at me, looks at my eyes which follow his finger, at my face which challenges the dogmas and acceptable truths, the fears and dealing with concerns and deliberations. He smiles a slightly shy, half smile and says, "I know that none of this is new to you. The tumor will continue to grow. At some point you will have no choice but to operate and have it removed. In my opinion the sooner the better. But..." he raises both his eyebrows in wonder and continues with a light laugh on his face, "I know that you are above luck (mazal) and detailed medical risks. I know that you handle your life on a different plane, detached, or maybe only removed and separated from the statistics and risk analysis that we bring to you. All considered, I, as a doctor, can only recommend what to do. The decision is yours, and I assume that this time you will again decide that the operation on the tumor can and should wait."

We have a ceremony every half a year. After the tour of the tumor area in the right, back lobe of the brain, we move to the right frontal lobe. There we meet the aneurysm, which is unwilling to die. The aneurysm is active, and its open neck keeps growing. "I understand that because of this aneurysm the neurosurgeons are not keen to operate on you. But nothing is going to disappear, not the aneurysm and not the tumor. There is nothing which can be done regarding the aneurysm, but the tumor, at least, can be operated on and taken out." I nod my head. Yes, I do understand that they are both an inseparable part of my brain, but no, I do not want anyone to touch my brain, to open my brain, to cut into my skull, at least as long as it is possible to wait.

We have a ceremony every half a year. We finish the meeting with Prof. Govrin and go upstairs to see Prof. Hezkeyah. Prof. Hezkeyah spreads the different imaging pictures in front of us on three screens. He examines the tumor, with no interest, and recommends that we do not deal with it. He checks and re-checks the aneurysm and its open neck full of blood. In his opinion there is nothing to be done at this time, and it is good that it is so. "Your brain has gone though so much trauma in the last few years. I do not know anyone in your situation, simply because people in your situation would have died a long time ago. The traumas in the brain take a long time to heal, as much as such healing might be possible. Give your brain the rest it needs so very much. Brain surgery is traumatic and causes not only functional damages but also changes in personality. There is no rush to operate. On the contrary, it is best to delay the surgery for as long as possible, and in the meanwhile live!!! Do all that you want and love to do. Do not relinquish anything. Enjoy life and do not think about what is happening in your brain. It cannot help, so what is the use of the heartache, the pain in the soul and everyone's fear?" His warm, thinking, deciding, and recommending eyes, which quiet the pressure and fear which caress my eyes every day of my life, moves to Abe's eyes. His eyes stay there for a minute, for the presence, for the connection and joining with Abe's mental state, and his hand rests on Abe's shoulder with love and wonder. It seems to me that in every visit and in every conversation with us he admires, respects and honors Abe more and more. He knows and understands that it is harder to be the one loving the person at risk, than it is being the person at risk himself.

We have a ceremony every half a year. We leave the hospital. Silence and inner contemplation fill the space which wraps around us. We get into the car, buckle up, start the engine, exit through the gates of the hospital grounds and breath deeply. Breath into a heart which has expanded with fear and hope. We exhale into the mutual space and breathe in the "togetherness." We look at each other's eyes and say, "We need to celebrate." Abe steers the car down the roads, finding a place for us to sit and enjoy good, tasty food with no effort on our end. We raise a glass of water, click glass to glass and say the blessing "That has been created with His word" – and that His word was "get out of the hospital." I got out. We got out. We are back to our half a year routine. The routine of life itself in our pleasant and spacious home. To the blessed routine with Abe coming home from work and finding me happy, loving and most of the time functioning, at one level or another.

We have a ceremony every half a year. May it remain like that, an identical ceremony every time. On this matter we both pray for boredom and repetition. We have a ceremony every half a year, and we pray that it will continue so, until a hundred and twenty. We have a ceremony every half a year. A ceremony of forgetting the ceremony that just took place, until the next ceremony (half a year later).

The tumor on the right side of the brain is putting pressure on nearby areas, and this causes my left arm and leg to become weak. The left leg affects only my swimming. I do not swim in a straight line. It is not terrible, because it means that there is a need to focus on staying straight, and walking – swimming – in a straight path is in any case a great and important mitzva. The weakness in my left arm means that I cannot balance a plate, so I must concentrate so that it does not fall from my hand while I put a plate full of food on the table. It means that I cannot serve a plate to the dinner table using my left hand. I serve scolding hot coffee cups one at a time, because to carry a hot cup of coffee in my left hand almost guarantees a burn and a broken cup. For all the impediments from the weak hand I find solutions, and all this does not affect my peace of mind. The situation is harder for Abe. He would have liked for us to remove the tumor and for me to return to perfect, outside functioning. But, in the meanwhile, I stand firm in my position.

Even Abe is affected by what can be seen from the outside, more than from what is happening on the inside. A weak body – it is felt, present, noticed, brings forward the handicap, the limitations, the hardships in movement and in performing in the material world. The brain – slower, focused for only shorter intervals, halting once in a while – such a brain is hidden from the eye. The hardships from my brain are strongly present in my life. In every study, in every writing, in every plan, in every conversation and in every correspondence, and it becomes worse when my brain is tired. And my brain is getting more and more tired. Sometimes it is as if someone unplugged it from electricity, the brain shuts off and the body wants to close its eyes and sleep. Sleep for the brain is much more than rest for the body. I live with this brain all alone, almost hidden from sight.

• • •

Many months of a good and relatively stable routine are cut off during a hasty and reckless examination. Due to the appearance of blood in my stools, our health insurance insisted on a colonoscopy. In conversations with the family doctor, it was clear that in light of my medical situation, the risks in such an examination are several levels higher than the risk that the blood is an indication of anything more than hemorrhoids. At some point, the pressure from the health insurance on our family doctor is so high that he asks me to visit a gastroenterologist, so that he can be the one to decide what to recommend due to my complex situation (including the epilepsy). Our family doctor writes a referral-question-consultation letter to the gastro expert.

The expert doctor has no doubts – the examination has to be done. Due to my medical condition he decides to do it in a hospital and not in a clinic.

My gut feeling is not good, but I do not listen to it. I go into the examination room. The doctor is sitting with his back to me and does not acknowledge my entry. "I am inserting a needle for the infusion," says the man who is standing next to me.

He asks: "Thirty-five?" "Thirty-five" arrives the answer from the doctor who has his back to me. I am sinking, not hearing, and not knowing a thing.

I wake up all sore, pounded. I attribute it to whatever was put into my veins and to the examination itself. My head hurts badly, like after an epileptic attack, but I have no reason to suspect that I actually had a seizure.

The doctor passes by and asks me how am I feeling.

"I am all sore," I reply.

"We had quite a struggle with you during the examination. Next time I will conduct the examination only under total anesthesia."

"What happened?" I ask.

"In the middle of the endoscopic examination your body went crazy and convulsed, and the technician had to use a lot of force to keep your head from moving, so that I could continue the examination. In the end I had to get out quickly and I did not complete it." His words do not travel from my ears to the brain, but rather stay somewhere in the space between them.

I go back home and try to go to sleep. My neck is screaming with pain, and my right arm is not willing to move. Every position is painful and this does not enable rest, let alone sleep. The situation becomes worse during the evening and night, and I cannot move my right arm and my neck at all, in almost any position.

An orthopedic doctor, an X-ray and ultrasound for the shoulder, all cannot find something which can explain the situation.

"I hope it will go away on its own," says the orthopedic doctor and moves onto the next patient. The situation does not get better. An X-ray and ultrasound to the neck, a few days later, show pressure on two vertebrates in the spine. This pressure could explain the pains and heavy limitations on movement. The orthopedic doctor tries to understand what has happened, what could have caused such a major trauma to the neck. We tell him about how the gastroenterologist described the course of the examination.

Shock shows on his face. "During an epileptic attack, it is forbidden to try to stop the convulsions, it can cause major damage to muscles and joints. It is absolutely forbidden. It is the ABC when you learn how to deal with a person during an epileptic attack."

Everyone knows it. We too, obviously. We feel great disappointment due to the fact that the gastroenterologist did not consider my medical situation in a careful and professional way, and recommended the examination in spite of it. Even more so, he did the procedure using light anesthesia, with no presence and monitoring by an anesthesiologist. An anesthesiologist would have most probably demanded to do the examination using full anesthesia. A simple medical inquiry could show that he acted in malpractice, but who has the energy to sue? We need our energies to function and live well.

In the weeks following the seizure, I do all that I can to rehabilitate my arm and neck, under the guidance of an excellent physiotherapist and some other treatments. It is very hard for me to deal with these additional limitations, which have been caused unnecessarily. After two months or so, most of the activity in the arm returns, and the pain in the neck subsides.

Now, when the pains are weaker, the complex picture which was hiding behind the motor injuries becomes clear.

The epileptic attacks are more frequent, longer and harder, and their effects carry on for two or three days afterwards. My slow and partially functioning level becomes even worse. There are more and more days in which I need to invest more and more internal energy in order to stay balanced and functioning, with joy of life and thanksgiving. From where do I draw the strength? I do not know.

Maybe it stems from the fact that I hope to stay "balanced" forever, just like I was before the examination. I was not mentally ready for any further damage or deterioration.

In an unexpected way it ended up that the harm in the right shoulder, arm and hand, and the fact that I could not use them, are great gifts from heaven. I have to do everything with my left hand. Get dressed, brush my teeth, bring food to my mouth, to use the mouse and to write on the computer. My left hand, which has become quite lazy because of its relative weakness due to the brain tumor, has to move, function, do. Slowly, slowly, I bring it back, and communication with it becomes healthier, it does more and it accepts more. How wondrous are the ways of G-d and His gifts, who can count?

The family doctor is worried, because of the deterioration in my level of functioning, and sends me urgently to the neurologist who has been treating me. I try to get an appointment to him, to no avail. Having no choice, we make an appointment with a neurologist we are not familiar with. We walk into her room, and she loads up my file onto the computer. She reads it slowly and I notice that she becomes angry. "I am a neurologist, what can I help with here? It is all neurosurgical and endovascular matters!"

I am silentWhat can I tell her? That she is right but there is nothing that can be done? She moves on to study the situation from the follow-up of the previous neurologist, over the last four years. I am silent. Her nervousness increases and is expressed in her hands, her eyes and in the wrinkles on her forehead, and it is clear to me that she has reached the difficult stage. The stage where all the surgical options for the aneurysm have been exhausted, and the aneurysm is still open and active. A situation where nothing can be done, and yet clearly something has to be done.

"You cannot live like this! With a ticking bomb in your head! One cannot live like this; you have to do something about it! This is not something which you can just leave as is and not treat it." Her voice changes from a tone of fear to a tone of panic. "What can I do here? Increase the levels of medication? OK, I will, but what does it help? Your life is in great danger, don't you understand that?!"

I wish to tell her that one can live "with this" and that I am living with this. That despair will not help. Will not help at all. I wish to tell her, but how can I say it in such a way as not to hurt her? Instead, I say to her quietly, "There is nothing further which can be done with the aneurysm. This is the opinion of Prof.

Hezkeyah, and this is also the opinion of international neurosurgeons whom we have consulted with and are experts in this field."

"You have to keep on looking for a solution. You may not stay in this situation as you are in deadly danger. Do you understand that? You cannot just simply sit and do nothing about it!"

I am not sitting and doing nothing. I am living and loving life. I am studying and writing, photographing and editing. I am visiting the children and grandchildren, and I pray. But I have no strength to tell her all that.

"Did you consult with any other neurosurgeons in Israel?" she asks.

"Yes, both in Hadassah and in City Center"

"In Medical Center?" she asks. I nod my head to say no.

"I am giving you a referral to the endovascular clinic in Medical Center hospital. Ask for an appointment with Dr. Peter. Let us see what he has to offer, because something has to be done."

I mumble something about that fact that it will not help, that experts have already studied this case from all the different options and angles.

"So, you do not want to even try?" I understand that as far as she is concerned, if I do not go for another opinion, I will be seen as insane or with a clear suicidal tendency.

"I will certainly try. I will go to him for a consultation."

With a sigh of relief, the neurologist transfers the matter to the endovascular unit in Medical Center.

"Thank you," I add, as matter of courtesy.

What will Abe say when I will tell him about the conversation with her? He will probably be angry at her for her unprofessional way of handling the mental and emotional aspects of my medical condition. To my surprise, he calmly says to me, "This is truly your situation. There is no reason to be surprised or frustrated by the neurologist. She simply told you the truth. The truth which we try to repress. The truth which makes me fear leaving the house every day, because I do not know in what state I will find you when I return. The truth which you push aside in order to continue to function, to do, to live. Her response to your condition was totally normal. You are the exceptional one, the surprising and wondrous one. You live in a constant miracle which is renewed daily, and I pray to G-d that you will have many more miracle days like these".

I am silent again, this time withdrawing into myself. Asking myself again, what is the most important thing for me to do? What are the things which, if I do not complete them, will be lost in the netherworld? I need to decide what is not so important to complete, and will bother me the least if it does not come to fruition, or will not be shared or passed on by personal example?

What do I really think is the most important thing to do "now," today, tomorrow? When I go up to heaven, on what things will I be asked "Why did you not do them?" When I, and my life, will be judged, who is the "real Sara" inside me? Who was I supposed to realize? What was the real purpose and goals of my life? In my world? In the worlds of others, both near and far? To what level does my life today bring me closer to the essence of my life and mission on this earth? These thoughts do not bring me sorrow. On the contrary, I am happy to wrestle with them. I feel that they help me focus and delve inside myself, to discover a real awareness of the value of life, and of the fact that life is not only a gift, but also contains a responsibility to do with it acts of goodness and loving kindness.

Teach Me My Lord to Pray
Teach me my Lord to pray
Grant me my Lord the ability to appreciate
Let me hope and pray
For all those wonders of G-d.

To hear the song of the morning
Greeting with peace
The hush of the night Which is your glory.

To listen to the singing of the due
When it drips like myrrh
From the petals of the flower,
silent In their joy of being.

To touch the cords of the day
Stretching across the firmament
And echoing from the end of the world
To its end,
Until my last day arrives.

The Essence

There is no time left, but for the essence.
To listen to the heart which is begging to hug
The whole world that is dear to you,
And to touch everyone with the hands, with the eyes.

To caress a cheek, a shoulder, the top of the head,
And to let the space between them fill up with vitality
Which waters and quenches and interfaces with the breaths
Which mix with the vain pleasures of the world
In the rhythm of the inner drum
That is stretched thin and vibrating
Under the fluttering touch of my hand
Between the hidden lines of my life,
Crushing between its fingers the threads of wool.
Some are thick and coarse to touch,
Others are soft and the soul snuggles inside them.
Some are thin and stretched like cords,
And some are hanging loose on the window seals
The eyes that are wide open and see nothing.

There is no time left, but for the essence.
To know to distinguish between the desirable and the necessary,
Between what builds and what destroys,
Between the free choices and duties.
Only duties of the heart are truly important,
Only they will accompany us to the end.

Only they will remain scattered,
Like floating fireflies
Like pulsing stars
In the fields I have walked
Seeing and not seeing,

Giving and never missing,
Connected yet separate.
Because only I know,
With an inner, essential, and demanding knowledge,
There is no time left, but for the essence.

There Is No Poetry Within Me
There is no poetry within me,
Only a prayer which entwines from my life strings,
Threading threads
And trying to get through the needles eye
What is entwined here
Through to the 'There' which has not yet arrived.

There is no poetry within me,
Only hope which gathers the letters of my being
The notes of my life
And tries to build a broad horizon
Which starts "Here"
And sprawls all the way to "There".

There is no poetry within me,
Only heartbeats
Which wash my body with blood
From a yearning heart
Which is trying to nourish my life
From the energies of today
Without pushing me to the world to come.

A COINCIDENTAL MEETING /
A BRIEF ENCOUNTER

What do you do?

I am Alive.

Pleased to meet you, I am Rivka.

My name is Sara, not Alive.

Oh, I thought you said Alive.

Yes, when you asked me what I do, I answered "I am Alive."

A deep swallow of saliva. A breath, and another one. A look of pity for someone who is not completely sane. I smile, relaxed. A look of bewilderment.

I mean what I said. I say it with joy, the joy of life.

Oh... wow. So ... so what do you do while you are Alive?

(silence)

So, you are at home all day?

Most of the days I am at home. There are times when I study in a Midrasha and with Chavrutot.

So how do you pass the time? You must be terribly bored.

I do not "pass" the time. I live it. I barely get done a tenth of what I plan to do in a day.

I do not understand. What have you got to do all day? What are you trying to get done? What do you do with your days?

I study Torah, Talmud, Ethics, Jewish philosophy. I prepare a weekly Shiur on the portion of the week and the preparation takes me long, full days. I am writing a book. I am learning coaching. I write poetry with words and photography. I am a mother. I am a grandmother. I am Abe's wife, with him and beside him, with great love and peace which is wider and deeper than the sea.

Wow. How do you find time for all of this? Where do you find the strength for all this?

From where do I get my strength?
    The question echoes in the spaciousness of my being, thrown from one side to the other, from one space to another space. With every touch or hit, the answer became a present and real face and body.
    The strength to live? The love of life? The closeness to G-d? These are all childhood friends. Thanks to them I am still around. Thanks to them additional lives came to this world. These are childhood friends who have enabled me, throughout my whole

life, to choose and act according to the guidance of my inner voice, even when it did not fit the opinion of "the majority" (or "everyone") or to the opinion of "the experts."

PART TWO

From Where is the Strength?

I am walking on smooth sand. A strip of sand that the water kisses again and again, calling it to glide onto the infinite, and retreating only in order to attack again, tempt again, and kiss again, with passion. One step follows the other. Observing the rising heel leaving a dimple of existence, which evaporates in the next wave, or the one after it. Walking and there are no footprints to mark my path, my choices.

My foot sinks into soft round niches full of sea water, and I know that I have walked this way before once or twice. I might have forgotten, but my body has not. I might have erased it, but my experience did not.

The previous choices in my life have widened the scope of the horizon, have deepened my insights and built them as solid foundations for the choices which came after them. Hard choices. Almost impossible choices. Choices of life, even if not perfect. Choices in which inner quiet is found, in spite of the high, noisy waves around. Choices with which we lived, and we live, feeling the soft, round niches their footprints left in the wet sand of my life.

I let my feet find their way to the road signs of the past, and to the gifts which have awaited me along that road – strengths and insights.

Solid Foundations

I met Abe in Jerusalem, on Mount Zion. I met him at a posh wedding where my best friend, from Belgium, married a young man from Brazil. We were the only two friends of the bride at the wedding, my friend Chen and I. All the other invited guests were family members of the bride and groom, who had arrived to Israel especially for the wedding. The two of us stood and talked. After some time, I went to bring us both a cold drink from the bar. When I got back, I found her talking in English with two young guys, whom I assumed were "from the side of the groom." I stood next to them listening to the conversation. After a short while Abe turned to me, and thus "transferred" his friend Rick to talk with Chen.

For the next three hours we, Abe and I, spoke about many interesting and meaningful topics. We spoke of children's education, on the required content, and more importantly, about the level of freedom we should give them so that they would develop a sense of responsibility on one hand and a constant wish to learn on the other. We spoke about developing their inquisitiveness and imagination while maintaining their natural curiosity as children, and about making space for creativity in every educational framework, first and foremost in the home. We were raised in very different homes, but we were both the first born, and thus we had some similar points of reference.

Abe told me how he and his friend came to be at the wedding. "We are not invited guests. We just heard the music from up the hill and came in. Music next to King David's tomb is a wonderful thing. We have just studied in the *yeshiva* (a place of Torah learning) about King David's harp, which hung above his bed. The wind would play on it in the middle of the night, until King David awoke and played his praises to G-d on it. There is a wedding taking place in the yeshivah tonight, but we do not really know anyone there. So, after the *chuppah* (the four pole canopy under which the wedding ceremony takes place) we went out for a stroll, heard the music and ventured in."

"Which yeshiva, and how did you get there?" I asked.

"Diaspora Yeshiva," Abe answered. "And how did we arrive there? That is already a long story." I asked him to please share it with me.

"The two of us, Rick and I, are from Atlanta, Georgia in the USA. We finished college and planned our summer break trip to Europe before we would begin our graduate studies in the university. At some point my mother asked me if we are planning to visit Israel also, and I said that we were not. Our plan was to buy a Euro rail pass and travel though all of Western Europe.

"'If you will include Israel in your trip, and stay there for at least two to three weeks, I will pay your round trip plane tickets,' my mother said.

"I had no reason to say no. I had no negative feelings towards Israel. I basically had no feeling at all towards Israel. Israel was not in my thoughts in any context whatsoever. I succeeded in convincing Rick to come with me to Israel. We traveled through all of Europe for six weeks, and then we flew to Israel. We were in the north, the Galil, the Golan Heights, and we went down south. We spent a few days on the beach in Nuweiba, and then we took a bus back to Jerusalem.

"We were sweaty, we had not taken a shower for four days

and it was hot, terribly hot. With our heavy backpacks on our backs, we were dying to find a place to shower and sleep in Jerusalem. Every place we found was fully occupied. At some point I had no more strength to continue our search. I decided that this was just the right time to use my credit card and to pay for a place to sleep, even in a hotel.

"Throughout the whole trip had we managed on a few dollars a day, so in my mind I could afford to splurge. We stopped someone on the street and asked about the closest hotel.

"'You are right next to one,' he said, pointing to the King David Hotel.

"We went into the hotel lobby but were quickly escorted out by a gaurd. 'There is no room in this hotel for you people,' he said, and left us tired and disappointed, but not despairing. I went back in and told them that they had no right to discriminate against us. My credit card is as good as anyone who walks in here, and the dollars it represents are the same American dollars. This time, after we insisted, the manager came out to talk to us. I made it clear that I would not agree to any discrimination based on our clothes or backpacks. The manager made it clear that he could not allow us to walk through his elegant hotel in our current state. The solution was simple. He took my credit card and paid for a room for us with it and brought out the keys. He directed us to enter the hotel through the service entrance and from there we went directly to our room."

"The King David Hotel, as you probably know, is an elegant five-star hotel, one of the fanciest in Jerusalem. The room was spacious, and the bathroom was gigantic, even larger than the room. We showered, peeling off layers of sweat and sand and who knows what else, and then we went to sleep.

"Our torn short pants and worn-out shirts made way for another set of pants and shirts, and towards the evening we went for a walk, with the goal of arriving at the Western Wall. Later, around midnight, after absorbing the golden spirituality of the "wall" and its bright, large stones, we began our walk back to the hotel. A pickup truck came from a around a corner and the youths inside threw at us rocks and bottles. We ran away without knowing where to, and at the end of our retreat we found ourselves outside the gates of an ancient structure. We had no idea where we were, and we did not know what direction to continue in order to find our hotel. We looked around for someone to ask. At a distance we saw a man with a beard and a rifle at the entrance to a structure. We walked to him and asked him if he could please give us directions to the King David Hotel.

"'The King David Hotel? What for? Here, right here, is located the holy tomb of King David.' These words were the beginning of a long night. A night full of stories about King David and King Solomon, about prophets and high priests. Mesmerized, we sat and listened to him. Sometime before dawn we turned to say goodbye.

"'Where will you be on Shabbat?' he asked. 'If you want you can come to us, to the Diaspora Yeshiva, for Shabbat. A free bed, meals and a lot of spirit and soul [*Ruach* and *Neshama*],' offered Wolf, from the yeshiva.

"Around sunrise, Rick and I finally returned to our room at the King David Hotel. We sat on our beds and we talked. We were excited, riled up, energized by some unexplained, powerful force. We spoke about Wolf's invitation, the man with the rifle, the beard, the *Tzizit* (four fringed garment) and the *Kippah* (small, symbolic head cover). It was clear to both of us that if we were to accept the invitation and stay in the yeshiva for Shabbat, it would change our lives.

"After much deliberation and soul searching, we decided to accept his invitation and spend Shabbat at the Diaspora Yeshiva. We were warmly received by the young men and teachers.

176

That Shabbat was full of prayer, songs, stories and more songs. On *Motzey Shabbat* (the end of Shabbat, when tree stars can be seen in the sky) there was an *Havdala* ceremony (marking the move from the holy Shabbat to the week days) accompanied by different musical instruments, and later a crowded and joyous *Melava Malka* (a meal accompanying the 'Shabbat queen' out) with singing and dancing.

"We were invited to stay in the Yeshiva for a year and to study Torah. We were both very excited, though we knew deep inside that this decision would change the fabric and essence of our lives. We both wanted to study and learn about our roots, to live in Jerusalem and to get to know it intimately through its stones and paths and through its Biblical stories.

"We have been at the Yeshiva already for several days. We passed the fast day of The 9th of Av, and today the Yeshiva erected a Chuppah for a *Ba'al Teshuva* (a person returning to his Jewish roots) student who is marrying a *Ba'al Teshuva* woman, both from the USA. We are still new and we are learning to get to know the guys, but they have already started to introduce us to the study of *Talmud (discussions of Jewish principals by sagesput into written format almost two thousand years ago)*. In the Yeshiva they learn Talmud all through the day until late at night, with other subjects dispersed in between.

"This is a very meaningful time for both of us. It is not simple. We are learning, in English, a text which has been written two thousand years ago in Hebrew and Aramaic. We do not know Hebrew, except for a few words such as 'Shalom' and '*Toda.*' (thank you) This is an incredibly special experience, and to study the ancient texts inside ancient buildings, some of them are hundreds of years old, is absolutely fantastic."

Abe's eyes were shining. He was enthralled by the miraculous path which he himself had just described. There was a broad and high-level curiosity in his eyes, with a great desire to deepen his hold on what is truly important. He wanted to be a Jew who lives like a Jew, a real Jew.

It was time for me to start my way back to my place. He walked me to the bus stop and waited. We waited a long time. "May I have your phone number?" he asked.

"No, you may not. I do not give the number to people I have just met," I answered in the strict tone of someone who lives in a defined set of rules, and believes that they are the most important sets of rules.

"So how can I reach you? How can I stay in touch?" Shock and fear touched his voice.

"Send me a letter," I answered. The bus could finally be heard around the corner. I gave Abe my dorm address at Bar Ilan University. The bus arrived, the door opened and swallowed me into it, and Abe disappeared behind a stone wall.

I arrived at my room long after midnight, tired but unable to fall asleep. I was too excited. Meeting Abe and the conversation we had had touched the depth of my soul. In the morning I told my roommate that I had met a very interesting and special guy. Later, she would tell me that my whole face shined when I mentioned his name, and she knew already then that he was not "just an interesting guy."

A few days later, a letter arrived from him. I carried on a correspondences with several people. Letters were the form of communication between those who wished to stay in touch. A phone? There was a public phone on the wall at the entrance to the building. Whoever was close to it when it rang would pick up the phone, find out who the call was for, and call her name out loud: "... you have a call." The receiver would remain hanging, swinging until the one, whose call it was, picked it up, or until someone passed next to it and returned it, beeping, to its cradle. Needless to say, the whole conversation would take place at the entrance to the dormitory building, which was busy at all times.

I kept a strict rule and answered my letters in the order they arrived, first one first and last one last. But when Abe's letter arrived I read it right away and immediately wrote him a long and detailed reply to the issues that he had raised. Now it was even clearer to my roommate that this person was a very special guy for me, the most special of them all.

It was summer. The winter semester would start only after the holidays. That summer I worked as a lab technician helping a Ph.D. student in Dr. Brown's lab. I carried out measurements on scientific equipment, which was located on the fourth and last floor, in a room at the end of a corridor.

A day after I had mailed the return letter, in the early afternoon, a guy showed up at the entrance to the scientific equipment room. "Hello, you remember me?" he asked.

"No," I answered tersely. I had no room, time or energy in my life for the guy-girl games hinted at in every corner of the university. He was not the first, and probably not the last, that will try to "hit it off" with me, I said to myself.

"I am the guy who you spoke with at the wedding in Jerusalem, some two weeks ago. I am Abe," A beseeching look in his eyes, as if saying – please recognize me. Remember me. You have to remember me.

"Oh, yes, of course I remember you," I said happily. I remembered everything which was said between us, but I did not remember what he looked like at all. To my shame, I have never remembered how people look, and it will probably stay this way for all my life. "How did you find me?"

He sighed a sigh of relief and explained. "You remember Rick, my friend? We sent, each of us, a telegram to our parents, in which we asked to stay for a year in Israel and study Jewish law, before we return home to study law in university and start working as lawyers. I registered for law in several universities, and I am still waiting for an answer from one of them. Rick received a short tempered and angry response from his parents, saying in essence that he should get on the first plane back home, because if he does not come home quickly, he will 'kill' his father. So today, I escorted him to the airport. Once we were separated, I realized that I am all alone. So, I came to look for you."

He saw the question mark in my eyes and continued: "You told me that you work in the labs. So, I inquired where the biological lab building was, and went to check every room in each corridor one by one. It was just my luck that you would be working on the top floor, in the last room of the corridor," he said with a shy smile on his face. "But at the end, I found you," he stated the obvious.

"I need to work until six o'clock, only afterwards we will be able to talk. In the meanwhile, you can go to the library and read until I finish my work," I concluded the conversation and went back to the test-tubes and samples. I was being paid by the hour, and therefore my time during work was not really mine.

I found Abe in the library, engrossed in reading a thick book: "The Abridged History of the Jewish People from the Days of Conquering the Land During the Time of Joshua Until Our Time." We dined on bread and cheese – both staple foods subsidized by the government, and therefore within my meager means – and we talked. We circled the university grounds many times that night, talking about things that were important to us.

I found Abe an empty bed in the men's dorms, so he had a place to sleep. During the next day I worked, and he sat in the library and read his history book. In the evening we met, dined on bread and cheese and continued the conversation from the night before. That night we also circled the campus many times talking, while being fully attentive and internalizing the things that were said. The connection between us started to pulse like a heartbeat of a being within a being. Without speaking about it, it pulsated in our hearts, and we knew that we would not want to live without the new being, which had formed "us."

Abe had to go back to his room in the Diaspora Yeshiva. The yeshiva was almost empty, but that was his only home, and there were a few other guys with him who had no family in Israel, and no relatives or friends to visit. Before he left, I invited him to my parents' home for Shabbat. Only after the invitation I realized that I could not "just" bring him over for a Shabbat. I had never invited any guy to my parents' home for Shabbat. If he would be the only guest, then it would be a clear statement that "this is serious," and I was not ready to include my parents in this special relationship. In haste I invited three more friends, two girls and a guy. This way I could tell my parents that I had invited "a few friends" for Shabbat. Either way, it left my mother wondering, as I have never, ever had friends, boys or girls, over for a Shabbat meal. More than that, I had never invited anyone to my parents' home for Shabbat.

Abe and one of the invited girls arrived for the Shabbat. It was a somewhat tense Shabbat, but went by mostly in peace. Abe was interrogated about his family, studies, plans for the future and everything else. Lucky for him, my friend also received equal attention, so that there were breaks in his interrogation. The Shabbat meals at my parents' home, which have always been long, where especially longer that time. My sisters, all younger than me, where not happy about it, not at all.

We continued to talk and write to each other. The month of Elul (the last month of the Jewish year, with the high holy-days of the new year, right after it.) arrived and Abe delved into his yeshiva studies, thankful to be able to deal with such an important matter. He slept in an eight-hundred-year-old room. The thick stone walls kept the room cool in the summer, but with the shorter days and cooler nights, the temperature in the rooms dived drastically. Abe came down with a bad cold. With no source of heat, his cold became even worse as the days turned frigid, and he sat and studied in his coat and gloves, wearing a woolen hat and scarf.

I knew that studies in the yeshiva would end right after Yom Kippur and resume on the first day of the month of *Heshvan*. I asked my parents if I could invite Abe for the first day of Sukkot, and maybe a few more days of Chol Hamoed. I explained to my parents, "Because he has no one in Israel and he has no place to be." We sat in the Sukkah from morning until evening and talked. My sisters walked in and out of the Sukkah, and always received a bit of his attention. He learned their names quickly, and made them feel that each and every one of them was special and worthy. This was a new experience in my parents' home – a worthy existence for each one, just because she was herself. The atmosphere around him was pleasant, and the little ones cuddled next to him whenever they could. When I helped in the kitchen, Abe conversed with my father, and the rest of the day we were together.

"They talk incessantly," my mother commented. "How do they have so much to talk about?" she added. Later, she would tell me that she already understood then that we were in love and would eventually want to get married.

Every year during Chol Hamoed we used to go to my grandparents' house in Zefat. My uncle and his wife and six children also lived in their large stone house, built with local Galilean stone. I loved being there. The cousins were always happy, creative, full of life and loved hiking. That year Abe came with us. I only realized what bringing him meant, when we got to Zefat and I introduced him to my uncle's family. Everyone saw him as my future groom, and they liked him. As far as the family in Israel was concerned, I had found my future husband.

Dealing with his family, in the USA, had to be done in a more measured pace. Abe sent his mother letters every week. In every letter the description of our relationship "moved up a notch." At the beginning I was a nice girl. Then a special girl. In the following letter I was already a very special girl. In the next one I was a very, very special girl to whom he was developing real feelings for. In a slow, persistent drip, his mother learned about me and about the mutual commitment that grew between, and within, us.

• • •

Abe asked for my hand in marriage. I told him that he had to ask my father for my hand. He thought I was kidding, but the look in my eyes made it clear that I was dead serious. In our home it was always clear who was the head of the family, the boss, the one who had the final word on all matters including the future of the children. I did not give the matter much thought. I was sure that it would be merely a formality, but Abe came out of the meeting with my father disappointed and distraught.

"Your father said that I cannot decide that you are the woman I wish to marry and build a home with, while I am here in Israel, disconnected from my parents, my natural environment and all the friends which I grew up with," he said. When he saw my teary, shocked eyes he collected himself and added, "Your father said that if I still want to marry you after I return home, then he will agree to the marriage."

We sat, worried, on the stairs in the back yard. Abe only had a return ticket back to Atlanta. All of his savings had been drained during his trip in Europe and his stay at the Diaspora Yeshiva. The situation was quite gloomy. All I could say to Abe was that my father meant every word he said, regarding his obligation to go back to Atlanta, to his parents' home. My father would not go back on his word.

"Do not worry," Abe said in the end. "I will book a seat on the earliest possible flight and go to my parents. I am sure that my parents will be happy with my happiness, and will not oppose our marriage in any way. They also know that it is not dependent on them. It is my choice. They have always respected my choices and my decisions. I will explain the whole situation to them and ask them to let me return to you, and they will purchase a ticket for me to return to Israel and to you. If they will not, then I will go to work at any job I can find, to save the money needed for a ticket back to Israel. I will come back to you and we will get married."

He did his best to sound more certain of his ability to come back than he actually felt. The truth was that we had no choice.

In January, Abe flew to Atlanta, and I remained by myself, waiting to hear from him. The days were long, the nights were even longer. There was no communication between us except for letters, airmail of course (it still took a week or so to arrive). In his first letter, which he wrote the day after he landed in Atlanta, he told me that his parents were very happy to see him, and that he had not yet sat down to speak to them about me and us. He added that he was sure that his mother knew why he came home, because from the many letters that she had received, she understood that he had met a very special lady and that he loved her.

The yearning and longing were mutual. The following letter was longer and very complex. He had already sat down with his parents and spoke to them about everything. They had no objection to him getting married, and of course they wanted him to marry his sweetheart. But, in their opinion it was irresponsible to get married before he completed his studies and received his master's degree in law and had a profession and a steady job. When he tried to argue, they reminded him of the facts of life. As long as he is home, unmarried, they would pay all his tuition fees and his living expenses. As soon as he got married, he would be on his own, and solely responsible for himself and his wife. Therefore, it would be both unwise and financially irresponsible to get married now.

He explained to me in the letter that no argument on his part was of any use. "This is the American mentality. As soon as we get married, we will not see a cent from them. Not even the amount they have saved for my studies. I want you to know this and to tell me what, in your opinion, is the right thing for us to do. As far as they are concerned: wedding – yes, but a wedding now will not be understood at all."

I took a deep breath, but I was still short of air. I never imagined everything becoming so complicated. Lucky for me, the letter did not end with this question. On the other side of the page, he clarified that he did not plan on waiting and was ready to get married right away. Economically, we would manage with whatever job he could find. Regarding the cost of the ticket back to Israel, he still did not know what would be. In light of this, he had no idea when he would be able to fly back to Israel and join me.

When I read about the expected financial hardships, I was relieved. I knew that I would be able to manage through periods of hardship and shortage. As a family, we were on welfare for more than two years. From my study stipend at the university I helped at home as much as I could, but it was, unfortunately, very little. I was able to study at the university only thanks to the academic scholarships which I had received. I was hoping that Abe would be able to adjust to a simple life, poor in money (yet rich in love). I believed that love and a great wish to build a home together would enable us to overcome, when they came up, any trouble or hardship that would arise. This might sound naïve and unfounded, but that was the truth. I felt and believed that our love was stronger than all the hardships which awaited us in the very near future.

In his third letter Abe opened with the words "I cannot believe it! They do not wish to see you!" I read these words over and over again, and still, I did not comprehend them. Abe described his parents as good and reasonable people. He had a very high regard for his mother, and he had great confidence in her help to navigate their approval for marriage.

"I sat with my parents. I told them that we want to get married as soon as possible, and that the wedding will be in Israel, because this is where your family lives, and it is a very large family. My parents made it clear that if we want a wedding in Israel, then the wedding must be postponed to the summer (the letter was written in January), when my father will take his yearly two weeks' vacation. I asked them if they would like to meet you before the wedding. They said they trust me and my choice, and it is enough that they will meet me when they come to Israel for the wedding."

He sounded extremely disappointed, but he moved on to good news. "My parents said that they will pay for my ticket to Israel. They would like some time with me, and G-d willing, I will be able to return to you in a few weeks."

I felt blessed with our good fortune. Abe would be back, G-d willing, in a few weeks. More than that I could not have asked for from G-d. Beyond that reality, nothing was more important for me. I knew with a deep, inner knowledge – which might seem irresponsible or ignoring reality – that we would be able to manage everything. I knew that with G-d's mercy, as long as we would be together, coping as a couple, we would be able to find the good in every challenge and hardship which would come our way.

With all this mental-logical thinking, something sat in the pit of my stomach and weighed on my soul. His parents did not wish to meet me. They saw no need to get to know me before the wedding. They do not wish to meet me?!

The next day, while working in Dr. Brown's lab, the phone rang in her room. She answered and called for me. "The call is for you. I could not understand what else he said, but he asked for you."

I was surprised, Abe called me on the phone! In those years, the cost of long- distance, international calls was so high that the phone was used only for short and absolutely necessary calls. I was relieved that as soon as Dr. Brown realized the call was from Abe, she walked out of the room and closed the door behind her, leaving me alone.

"Come! Come to Atlanta! I do not know how you will come, but please come! My parents want to meet you. Though they said that would not pay for the ticket, but please come." Abe ended the call. The receiver was left in my hand. I put it back in its cradle very slowly, as if to try and have a little time to absorb what Abe said, before I went back my other world.

I was very excited, yet emotionally confused and uncertain. I did not know what to do. In his letter, he explained in detail that he had not succeeded in convincing his parents how important it was to meet me in Atlanta. He knew that I had no money for a ticket, not even for a part of the cost. Maybe I did not understand him? Maybe I did not hear right? I had no way to call him back. An international long- distance call was not accessible for most people, and I could not ask Dr. Brown to call from her office phone. I did not understand what had happened. What was happening? How did he think that I would come? How could I come? The semester wad ending that week, so I would not miss classes, but that was the only clear fact in my mind. The thoughts swirled around themselves, asking for, and not finding, an answer.

I collected my things, apologized, and left the lab. There were two things I had to do. To find the cheapest ticket possible, and to find a way to finance it. I decided first find out how much the cheapest ticket would cost.

A friend, a distant relative, studied that year at Bar Ilan. I told her the story. She got very excited. She was jumping up and down with joy. As far as she was concerned, this was a sweet story of a prince and princess. Her uncle was a travel agent and she spoke to him. Begging, she got for me a really cheap ticket. Yet still, cheap as it was, I needed to find the money to buy it. The only option I had was to ask for an advance on the monthly stipends that I was to receive until the end of the year. The stipend was part of a special academic scholarship which I had received for two years in row. This sum would enable me to buy the ticket.

I went to the office which dealt with students' scholarships and I explained my request. I do not remember what I said to them, except for telling them over and over again that I had to go, because my happiness and my whole life depended on it. They did not like the idea at all, because the scholarship was intended to enable me to study without working for a living. In spite of it, something touched their heart, and they allowed me to withdraw the needed sum. That basically meant that I would not have enough money to live on for the rest of the academic year.

Two days were left before the flight. I sent a telegram to Abe: "Arriving flight 111. Landing 18:00 this Sunday. Sara," and I took the bus home to get organized for the flight and to say goodbye to my parents.

My father said nothing, but my mother was very worried. "You are going for almost three weeks. How do you know that they will accept you in their home? What will you do if you will be miserable with them? And what will you wear there? It has been years since you bought anything new. And what about a coat? Abe did say that the winter there is not harder than the winter in Israel, but you still need a reasonable coat and warm clothes." She talked and she repeatedly asked, but to no avail, as I had no answers to her questions. I could not even relate to a situation where his parents would not want me, or that I would feel terrible in their home. They are good people, they are Abe's parents, they even told him that they will help pay for his ticket back to Israel.

I received a short telegram. "Excited. Waiting at airport. Abe." I was also excited, extremely excited. I packed a small suitcase with the winter cloths that I had. Because my coat was not in a presentable state, and definitely not for overseas, I discarded it and instead wore, on top of my shirt and the sweater, another sweater, thick and warm.

I do not remember a thing from the long flight. My first memory is Abe running towards me excitedly, stopping himself close to me and saying, "I love you so much. I am so happy you could come," His parents greeted me with warmth. I did not expect the meeting to be any different. I made a mental note to write to my mother that all is well, thank G-d, and that they are good and normal people.

Abe's father said that they would wait with me for my suitcases. He had a hard time believing me when I told him that the small suitcase was all I had brought with me, but his mother pulled on his sleeve and walked him towards the car. Behind them the two of us walked, Abe carried the small suitcase and skipped with joy the whole way. I was exhausted. As far as my body was concerned, it was already morning in Israel. I had been traveling for over twenty-four hours.

In their kitchen a fancy meal awaited, with many delicious foods. Some years before my arrival his mother had koshered the kitchen, with the help and advice of a rabbi in Atlanta. I was hungry, but was even more tired. I waited until it was polite to leave the table and go to sleep. I fell into a deep and needed sleep. Eventually I woke up from excitement and jet-lag, in the middle of the night.

When the American morning dawned, Abe told me what led

to that short phone call from him. "Good friends of my parents had come to visit, and heard that I was getting married in the summer.

"'Have you seen the bride? Have you met her?' they asked.

My parents said they hadn't. 'So, when will you meet her?' they continued.

"'When we arrive to Israel for the wedding,' my parents answered.

"'What is the matter with you?! Are you crazy? We cannot believe that this is what you are thinking. How many children do you have? Three. How many times in his life will Abe get married? Once. Abe is going to live all of his life with this girl, and you do not think it is important to get to know her before the wedding?! Why don't you invite her to come visit you? This way she will also get to know you, she will recognize you and know you are the groom's parents when you come to the wedding.'

"My parents' friends were not willing to leave our house until my parents committed to inviting you to visit. They are very good friends, and my father really appreciates them, this is why, in the end, he agreed you should fly over, but at your own expense."

I told Abe how I financed the ticket. We were both silent. I was happy I came, but we had no idea how I would live when we return to Israel.

Things clarified over the next two days.

Abe registered for *aliyah* to Israel (to become a citizen under the Law of Return) and would attend a Hebrew *ulpan* (a special class for teaching Hebrew as second language) in Herzliya. That way he would have a place to live and would learn Hebrew. We fixed the date for our wedding, taking into account Abe's parents, and were going to get married exactly one year from the day we met, the fifteenth of Av.

Unfortunately, he would not be able to complete the whole year-long Ulpan due to our wedding plans. Once a week an

Aliyah *shaliach* (helping Jews plan the move to live in Israel) arrived in Atlanta, and we arranged a time to meet with him. We learned that since Abe would be making aliyah during his studies, the state would pay his tuition for a graduate degree, as long as he would start his studies within a year of his aliyah and continue in the same field in which he studied before his aliyah. This was wonderful news. Abe would be able to complete his studies for a MA degree and would be able to acquire a profession he could use in Israel, as long as he remained in the field of structural engineering.

Abe knew that he had to give up his dream to become a lawyer, as it would be impossible for him to be one in Israel because of his lack of Hebrew. Now it was final – he would be able to get funding for his studies only if he studied structural engineering and worked in the field in which he already had a bachelor's degree from Georgia Tech – a very prestigious engineering institute, similar to the Technion in Israel.

As time went by, his parents learned how I financed my flight, and they decided to cover the cost of the ticket. Now I had a way to live until the end of the academic year. Good friends of his parents invited us to buy clothes in a storage warehouse, where they stored their merchandise until they were ready to sell them in the market. I chose clothes both carefully and frugally. The clothes were cheap, less than a tenth of the cost of simple clothes in Israel. I ended up buying several outfits for a ridiculous price. When I walked up to the counter, they asked me if I was done, as there was so much merchandise in the warehouse, and I should really help myself to more. I said that what I had picked out was enough for me. They did not hide their surprise, and happily gave me everything I chose as a gift.

Friends of his parents wanted to meet me and asked when the engagement party would be. His parents suddenly shifted gears. His mother planned an open house reception on the last Sunday of our stay in Atlanta. They invited all their friends, Abe's friends and Atlanta relatives. The menu was chosen with great care, and his mother's friends volunteered to take part in the preparations. Our excitement rose from one day to the next, until one evening Abe's father asked me, "What will you wear for the party?"

"Marvin", his mother said, "tomorrow we are going to buy dresses for the party. Would you like to join us?" And so, the four of us traveled to a huge shopping center – it was years before the first shopping mall was built in Israel. There was such abundance, the eyes skipping superficially over the huge selection of merchandise, all beautifully and invitingly displayed. His mother walked decisively to the formal evening gowns.

How could I choose a dress here? I stood helpless, baffled and ashamed. Everything looked so fancy and very much not "me." His father settled into an armchair, and his mother started pulling dresses off the hangers.

I went into a fitting room. I put on one magnificent dress and took it off. I put on another and took it off.

"Where are you? We want to see the dresses on you." I wanted to disappear, vanish into thin air. How can I walk out in front of Abe and his father? I tried to choose the simplest, widest, and most modest dress and walked out of the booth.

"Actually, you are not really fat!" his father said. "I thought that you were fat, with all the clothes that you wore when you arrived. I was sure you were fat, and I could not understand how Abe chose you."

I could not stand there with all of these eyes on me, but what choice did I have?

Gradually we reached an understanding of what would be "out of the question." No laces, no shiny stuff, no puffed-up sleeves, no clingy material, no long slit in the skirt. This narrowed the choice to very few dresses, and in the next store we found what we were looking for. A long white dress, with delicate flowers printed on the material. I felt wonderfully spoiled, and I loved this new and unknown feeling.

The big day arrived. The front door of their house was opened, inviting the guests to come through it. The first people to arrive were his mother's excited and warm best friends, who accepted me into their circle with simplicity. Afterwards their other friends arrived, in a quiet flow, throughout the whole magical Sunday afternoon. They walked in, evaluated me from afar, waited for Abe and his mother to introduce us, and said a few polite words and wishes. Some evaluated and judged me, some saw me and accepted me as I was: Abe's choice of a future wife.

Abe was tense. He waited to see his own friends, and to see me through their eyes. They arrived one after the other, awkward, curious and astonished. Abe was the first one to get engaged. His friends had not even started to enter marriage into their life equation. Abe was going to leave his home and them, his friends, and go to a faraway country in order to marry this girl, who was standing here next to him. Who was she? What spell had she cast on him to make him cancel all his plans for university, his profession and a good job? They arrived with their girlfriends or with girls from their age group, all pretty, carefully made up and meticulously dressed. I have never used makeup, and the engagement party was no exception.

Abe's previous, serious girlfriends arrived. It was a strange feeling to know that they knew him much longer that I had known him and that they were close to him in all ways, for long, meaningful periods of his life. But I saw this as an opportunity to hear about Abe, to learn about him from their angle. It was a special experience, and I felt that the party gave me a special gift. It gave me a glimpse into Abe's world of his youth and adulthood, into the world which existed before we had met in Jerusalem five months ago. It gave me a window into his sensitivity to others and into the richness of his long-term relationships with them, even after they stopped going out as a couple. I was so happy with my – our – choice. I had won a goodhearted man, sensitive, loving, grateful and clever, both in the wisdom of the mind and in the wisdom of understanding people.

· · ·

I had met Abe in the summer between the second and third (and last) year of my bachelor's degree. We got married a year later, in the following summer, so that the date would suit his parents' yearly vacation. During this third and last year I had already started my research for a Masters in Biochemistry at Dr. Brown's lab. Therefore, at the beginning of the first year of my masters program I had enough data to put in a request to proceed directly to a PhD. This option, of skipping the need for an MA thesis prior to being accepted to a PhD research program, was new in Israel, and Dr. Brown supported my attempt to get onto this exceptional track. Two of us, a young physics researcher from another university, and myself, were the first in Israel to be approved to move directly to PhD level research. There was no difficulty in widening and deepening the scope of my research so that it would fit the research and thesis requirements of a respectable PhD.

Once we got married, I started working in the lab only five days a week – this was many years before the whole country moved to a five-day work week. We wanted to have some time together on Friday, to prepare Shabbat together and enter it relaxed and happy. It was important for us to have a time set aside for the two of us, together. Half a year after our wedding I got pregnant; we were happy.

When Dr. Brown saw that my belly was growing, she called me to her office and waited for me with a serious face. "I cannot understand how you dare walk around flaunting your belly, letting everyone know that you are pregnant. When I was pregnant, I wore lab coats which were big enough to hide my belly, so that my colleagues and department team members did not know that I was pregnant up until almost the end." I was shocked, I had never thought of pregnancy as something one had to hide.

I gave birth to a healthy boy, and when I came back from maternity leave, I changed my work hours to four days a week until 14:00. This schedule enabled me to keep breastfeeding and to be with our son for most of the day hours during of the week. This was important to me, as this way I felt that I was the one to make the decisions about our son's daily schedule and not the nanny. This change did not hinder my research or slow it down, as in the evening hours I read scientific publications, analyzed data and planned experiments.

I went back to work after the legally obligated maternity leave of twelve weeks. It was hard to leave the baby at home, and also I was not feeling so well, I was suffering from nausea, mainly in the morning. After throwing up for several mornings in a row I understood that I was pregnant again. Abe and I were surprised. I did not know that one could get pregnant while still breastfeeding.

We were still young fresh parents, learning to take care of their one and only boy. The fact that I got pregnant was exciting, yet it was hard for us to fathom that before we got used to one child we would already have, with G-d's help, two.

Basically, I came back from maternity leave – pregnant. This time Dr. Brown was furious when she called me to her office. "You are not some idiot from the market place! Why are you proliferating like rabbits?! Do you not know that there are contraceptives? Do you not know how to use them? You are not dumb! You know that you have a brilliant future in academia, you are on the way to becoming the youngest PhD in history, at least in

Israel. I expect you to do whatever it takes so as not to sabotage your excellent chances for a fast climb on the academic ladder."

Words gathered in my throat, entwined and entangled with one another, creating a feeling of choking, and with that a rising level of fear. I had been raised to obey authority, in all matters, with no questions asked. There was no option of saying "no" to my parents on any issue or topic. They demanded absolute obedience, with no argument or protest. As the eldest daughter I knew what was expected of me, and I feared the anger and fury which would erupt when I did not comply immediately, or in less than a fully satisfactory way. My parents had uprooted the ability to say no from my being. I felt bewildered and helpless. Her words were full of contempt, and her tone of voice left no doubt: if I continued with this pregnancy, she would make my life miserable. I feared that I might even lose my place in her lab.

Surprisingly, I was able to say no. No to authority. No to the head of the lab. No to the person who held my academic life in her hands. No to someone older than me, and with much more experience in the academic world. In disbelief and bewilderment, I told Abe about the conversation. She was a "female boss," who was supposed to understand me better than a "male boss." It was clear to both of us that she would be against me. We did not believe, then, that she would destroy me almost completely.

I was happy with the fetus forming inside me. Thankfulness swelled inside, and slightly blunted the contempt which became my daily bread. As the pregnancy progressed, so did her anger towards me. As the pregnancy progressed, it became harder and harder for me to stand on my feet, even with the help of thick, tight and hot elastic stockings. But despite all the pain and hardship, the awareness of G-d's great blessings, and of the blessed anticipation to the birth of the child growing inside me only became stronger.

My research was successful and yielded scientific articles

which were accepted in leading international scientific journals in the field. I continued to teach students in the learning labs, in order to supplement our income from my research grant.

Abe completed his studies at the Technion in project management, and started working as a novice engineer and as a building supervisor. His salary was minimal, but we knew that this was where one starts, and then one prays to be able to move up and get a higher salary.

We started to build a house in my parents' plot in Zichron Yaakov. A small house, two bedrooms, a kitchen and a bathroom. No living room and no dining room, but with a spacious kitchen and a place for a dining table. The building marked the beginning of a long period, a period of living next to my parents and my sisters, and the beginning of many years of paying back a mortgage.

Winter arrived and with it we had another sweet and perfect little boy. He was quick to arrive and join his brother, who had just turned eleven months old. Our small, rented apartment in Bnei Brak became even more crowded. Abe made an effort to complete the construction of our house as quickly as possible, because paying for both rent and the mortgage at the same time was impossible.

I had more than enough data and publications to warrant a PhD. I asked Dr. Brown to let me write the thesis from Zichron Yaakov. She did not agree. I said that I will come to the lab, based on the needs of the lab and the students there. She did not agree. I said that I was willing to commit to coming to the lab three days a week for the coming year, even after I would submit my PhD thesis to the committee.

She did not agree. I could not help it, and I asked her why.

"You really think that I will let you be a bad Influence on my students?! I expect them to take their work seriously, and put their research at the front of their minds. You are a bad example for them, and I have no wish to see you in my lab. You chose to destroy your academic life, not me." After a short lull in the rain of insults that she hurled my way, she threw in a final sentence: "I will not let someone who is so reckless, someone who puts proliferating like rabbits before academic research, to become a doctor, to get a PhD degree. I am withdrawing my consent for you to do a direct path to a PhD. You can write your thesis and submit it as a Master's thesis only."

I had no breath, and my vocal cords were paralyzed from shock and pain. The shock at her level of hate – or her jealousy? – hit me so hard, I had to collect myself in order to walk out of her room. Before I could close the door behind me, she added poison to the poisonous cup: "And you have no business here anymore. Finish the experiments which you have put up this week, and you can start writing. Your *Master's* thesis of course."

Twelve articles, more than enough data from my original research for a PhD thesis, which could have opened doors for me at leading research labs. But she "allowed" me to submit only one master's thesis. Today, I know that I could have asked the head of the department and the faculty dean to interfere, to ask for justice, but in those days my fear of authority, especially a wicked and threatening one, left me no option of protesting.

NOT MADE OF CARDBOARD

"The brain of the fetus in your womb is not growing. I have been tracing the size of the head for three months already. It is too small, way below the normal range, and it seems that it has not grown at all. Based on the ultrasound, I think that there is no reason to keep this pregnancy. The sooner we do it, the less burden there will be on your body. You are, thank G-d, healthy, and will be able to have more children in the future. But there is no reason to keep this fetus in the womb. A fetus with a small head and a stunted brain will not live outside the womb, and if it does, it will be a distorted life. If you will be lucky, it will be short lived."

We were not able to comprehend his words. How can he simply just decide that there was no value to the life of the fetus inside me, to the life of our next child.

The doctor was a good doctor. He was one of the first to use an ultrasound machine in his clinic. It was thrilling and exciting when he proposed to "see the fetus" on the screen. All we saw were black and gray smears on the screen, in undefined shapes which changed as the sensor moved on my jelly covered belly. I felt frustrated looking at the scrambled screen, but I could not move my eyes from it. All of a sudden, the black lines began to pulsate. Pulsation, at the rate of a fetus heartbeat, was visible on the screen! It was his heart beating. There are no words to describe this amazement at the impossible, to see the tiny fetus's heart beating. To see the fetus, alive. A fetus which had not reached yet the size enabling me to feel its movements in my womb.

It was a wonderful gift. We came back the following month, and again the next one. After the third ultrasound screening, the doctor told us that the fetus's head was not developing.

We faced a new and terrible situation. There was nothing we could do in order to help the fetus develop in a better, more correct, more complete way. We were totally helpless. We wanted to do something to fix it, but we faced an unfathomable situation. We had a gift from G-d, but it seemed to be damaged.

What do you do with a gift that seems, G-d forbid, like a punishment? What do you do when the giver is G-d?

For the first two pregnancies, a follow-up visit to the gynecologist was a technical matter which we did because that was "what one must do." This follow-up visit amounted to listening to the fetus's heartbeat and listening to me say that "I am generally feeling okay, thank G-d, and the only thing that is hard on me are my hurting veins all along both legs." In short, a pregnancy which proceeds as expected, including the expected weight gain, especially in the last months of pregnancy.

This time we had an opportunity to see that which is hidden from the eye. An opportunity which unveiled the pregnancy from its mystery. An opportunity which robbed us, this time, from our simple prayers and blessed expectations and waiting.

The gynecologist decided that because of the fetus's dire situation, and in light of the need to protect me during the upcoming planned abortion, I needed to be hospitalized. I was referred to a hospital close to my home, and I was hospitalized in the women's ward, together with other women with high-risk pregnancies. I was in a weird situation. The women in the room were praying not to lose their fetuses, G-d forbid, and to complete their pregnancies and bring healthy and thriving babies into this world. And I, what should I pray for? The doctors were demanding to uproot my fetus from my womb and throw it into the garbage, in order to save us "unnecessary pain and suffering."

I was restless. At home were two little boys, one and two years old. Who was going to be with them during the hours after the nanny left? Who would take care of the household while I was "laying" in the hospital?

In the morning they collected blood. I asked an intern for which tests they are sending it, but the intern referred me to the doctor in the ward who was in charge of my case. I still had no idea who he was. "At ten there are the doctors' rounds with the head of the department," I was told. After the visit I would ask to see the doctor.

I waited. Time crawled into the unknown. A cardboard file, with punched pages fastened to it, was put on my bed. My name and my ID number where on the front. I picked up the file to open it, but right away the nurse asked me to put it down. "This is a file for the doctors. You are not allowed to read it. It is not for you."

I put it down and waited. The doctors' rounds started on the other side of the ward. I waited. When they got to my bed, one of the doctors picked up the thin file and said, "The patient is destined for an abortion. The fetus is growing but the head is not. The head is probably in a degenerative process. In light of the situation, we should not wait for a natural abortion. I do not see here any blood test results."

"The lab notified us that the blood got lost."

"So why did you not take blood again?" Silence.

"We will wait for the blood tests and then schedule the abortion." The doctors, lead by the head of the department turned away from my bed.

"May I ask something?" I asked. A few heads turned around.

"Why am I hospitalized at all? And what are the blood tests for? What are you hoping to learn from them?" I asked.

"You are here because your doctor asked to hospitalize you. Right now there are no lab results, we will wait for them and see." The words remained like a trail behind their backs, moving away from the room in condescending silence.

I was left to wait. I waited. "The intern who is supposed to take your blood is done with taking blood for today. Tomorrow morning, he will take blood from you again."

I waited. The night was long. At home, the two little ones were with Abe, and he needed to go to work in the morning. It was his first job after completing his studies, and he shouldn't miss days, but now everything was on his shoulders. And I? I was lying down-sitting-reading-going crazy, not knowing what to pray for, what to ask for.

The next day the intern arrived and took blood again. The thin, cardboard paper file was put at the foot of my bed. A small group of doctors came for the doctors' rounds. They open the file.

"The lab results arrived. They look normal. One test is missing. What happened?" the question is heard.

"The test-tube broke in the lab."

"So, did you take blood again?" asked one of the doctors.

"No, I did not, I will take it after the visit."

"OK. We can schedule a time to induce the abortion, in the meanwhile, continued rest." The faces, which have not seen me, not even for a minute, turned their backs to me and started going out of the room.

"Why do I need to rest?" I asked.

The voice came from the last doctor to leave: "Because this is what the senior doctor said."

I could not bear anymore the total and meaningless answer, which was given to me offhandedly as if I was just a nuisance.

My whole fiber protested against being treated as an object, as a womb carrying a damaged fetus with no thought of me as a woman, a mother, a person, a human-being. But the worst of all was that they were making medical decisions without asking me, seeing me, or looking me in the eyes and thus recognizing that I was laying in the bed next to which they were talking.

The cardboard file was still on my bed. I hid it under the blanket. I went to the public phone at the ward entrance and called Abe at work.

"Please come to pick me up, please. I am going home." Something in my tone of voice left no room for doubt or questions. I took off the hospital gown and put on my cloths. I put the cardboard file in my bag and left the ward. One of the nurses saw me next to the exit door. "Where are you going? The doctor has not released you!" she called.

"I am no one's prisoner, definitely not of a doctor who does not even know me, or speaks to me. I am not staying where all that I am is a cardboard file, and that is that." The ward's door closed with one less patient, and no one was going to be amiss of anything because of it.

I waited for Abe outside, on a bench by the bus stop. A bag with my personal items lay at my feet, and in it the thin, cardboard file. I did not open the file until we arrived at home. I was afraid that if I would open it, someone would come to shout at me and tell me it was forbidden. But no one came out to find me, and no one shouted at me, at least until I arrived home.

"What are you doing here? Are you out of your mind?! One should never leave the hospital without a release letter from a doctor. Now they are not responsible for anything that happens to you! This was a totally irresponsible act on your part." My mother wrung her hands over and over again, as if trying to wash away any contact with what was, in her opinion, the hasty move I had made.

"This was the first responsible action I have taken since they diagnosed our fetus as missing a mind, a brain or both," I answered, exhausted, and did not wait to hear her response.

I had no strength to continue the conversation and did not wish to explain. I hugged the children and spent the rest of the day being a mother to two wonderful boys with normal brains and sharp minds. In the evening we searched for a top gynecologist. The recommendation was for Prof. Altman in Haifa. The following evening, we sat in his private office, Abe, myself and the cardboard file. I presented the sequence of events to him, as a gift handed over the cardboard file and we asked for his medical opinion.

Prof. Altman looked at my face, his eyes met mine and he asked: "What do you feel? What do you think is happening inside your womb?"

I was surprised. I remained silent. For the first time, I tried to feel what was happening with me, without relying on external findings and measurable parameters. What had not been said found its way to my tongue, to my palate, to my lips: "I feel good. Pressured only because of what the doctors are telling me. I cannot believe that G-d would give me a present and I will throw it into the garbage. I feel blessed and not cursed. This whole pregnancy is a blessing."

I looked at his face. It remained sealed, but to me it seemed to be warmer, more accepting. I did not know if this was the kind of answer he was expecting. I did not know if my answer was "logical" or "scientific enough" for him. I did not know what his response would be. The essence of belief was shown on Abe's face, and inside me a source of warmth, full of light and love, was lit. I was pregnant, I was excited about the birth of the fetus inside my womb, and I wanted to keep it and guard it to the best of my ability. While taking all the above into account, I still knew that it was forbidden to ignore the medical opinion.

Prof. Altman asked that I be hospitalized in "his" hospital for a short time, to test in an organized manner all the measurable parameters of the pregnancy and the course of fetal development. Blood was taken, a careful and detailed ultrasound was done and with a follow-up of the fetal heartbeat.

On my second day in the hospital, Prof. Altman arrived at my bed, leading the doctors' rounds. He listened to a report by one of the young doctors, and then asked him what his medical recommendation was. "It is clearly an abnormal case, of a head which is not growing. In my opinion there is no reason to continue such a pregnancy, especially not where there is risk for the mother, such as clot formation in the veins in the legs and an embolism in the heart or in the brain."

"How do you feel?" Prof. Altman asked me.

"I feel good and want to go home," I said.

"And what do you think?" he asked the group of doctors, which hung upon his every word. The doctors' responses, both as individuals and as a group, were fascinating. Some of the doctors agreed right away with the doctor who presented my case. Others, the more cautious ones, were afraid of a trap, and thought there must be a reason why Prof. Altman was asking for their opinion before to revealing his own. He did not give in to any of them. At the end, they all recommended to end the poor pregnancy.

Only then did Prof. Altman begin to speak. I learned from him a great lesson in humility on one side, and the importance of experience on the other. "If there was no ultrasound, would you have recommended to stop this pregnancy?"

The doctors looked at him with sheep's eyes, and bafflement ruled their faces. You could see their thoughts running back and forth, back and forth. The professor was recommending to ignore, even if for just a minute, the most advanced and astonishing medical information. How could one do such a thing?

How could it be that a doctor would be allowed to ignore new data which the developing technology was giving him? Could it be that the professor was already old and did not feel comfortable with new technologies, and therefore suggested to ignore them?!

One could touch and feel the silence in the air, rough to the point of being painful. One could taste it on the tongue, its taste was of rust. A bent ear was asking to hear the thoughts, or at least the wheels, of the brain turning, but to no avail.

Eventually, one of them succeeded in getting some syllables out of his mouth: "What does the distinguished professor mean?" as if saying, 'It's not possible that we heard you correctly. It's not possible that you want to ignore the severe findings concerning the state of the fetus's brain.'

Again, silence overcame the whole group, this time heavy, thick and slightly burning.

"Is there one finding, except for the ultrasound, which is abnormal? Which causes us to suspect that there might be a problem with this pregnancy?" the doctor, who had the file in his hands, opened it. All the doctors stretched their necks to see the data. "The truth is that 'no,' there are no other abnormal or worrying findings."

"So, without the ultrasound, is there a reason to have any concern regarding the pregnancy or the fetus?" all the heads nodded, as if saying in screaming silence, "No. We would not have thought to even bring this pregnancy for a discussion. The pregnancy looks perfectly normal, and the mother feels good."

"That means, you think that the pregnancy should be stopped based only on ultrasound pictures. You are suggesting killing a fetus, which according to all the other parameters is doing well, only because of a new imaging system. The fact that it is new does not mean that it is not good, or not important. It means that we do not have a lot of experience with it yet. I suggest releasing this woman to her home and receiving her in the maternity ward in due course, when the birth is ready to happen naturally."

The doctors nodded their heads in agreement in unison, albeit slightly hesitant. The young doctor closed the file in his hands and said to me, "I will prepare the release letter as soon as we complete the doctors' rounds," as he left the room last.

I did not go to any further ultrasound tests, even though the doctors had a great interest in following the fetus's progress. I did not wish for this pregnancy to be different from the other ones. I wished to be wrapped with the cloak of the invisible One who sees, and let the baby be born and seen in its own time, at the time set for it by the creator and king of the universe, who breathes, with each and every breath, life into every human being.

A beautiful and sweet baby girl was born, with a small, but normal, head. She developed nicely, according to all the measurements and graphs in the mother and child center, except for the head's circumference. Today she is a leading gynecologist who is highly regarded by the medical staff in her department and by the women who are treated by her.

• • •

My second PhD, this time in Immunology, I did at the medical faculty at the Technion, Prof. Johnson's lab. His research budgets shrunk with the years, and at one point he was forced to give some of his lab space and research area to a young researcher who had come back from a post-doc overseas. This researcher brought into the lab research involving factors which affect the immune system of mice, and their cages occasionally would arrive to the lab. When he started working in our-his lab, I was already extremely pregnant with our sixth daughter.

When I gave birth, her sister was one year old, and my PhD

thesis was in the middle of the writing stage. Since we had a nanny who was at our house, I could go over to my parents' house and write there quietly. The tiny baby was with me all the time, breast feeding according to her needs and wishes. I wrote while she slept. I wrote while she breastfed. I developed a system to relax and comfort her when she was on my knees. I would rock her gently, holding onto her with my left arm and writing with my right. My maternity leave went by in this manner, and towards its completion my thesis was ready to be submitted.

Following the long and arduous writing process, the feeling of relief was not a true relief. I was tired and weak, and with less and less strength to do household chores, large or small. I was not fit to function as necessary, a mother of six who was supposed to go back to work after her maternity leave. I lost weight and did less and less. It was clear to us that the weakness stemmed from the most recent, and frequent, births and my foolishness as to the way I "rested" during the convalescence period. Therefore, we had expected things would get better soon, and that I would regain my strength and come back to myself. Had I not done so, again and again, in the past?

But things did not get better. I kept on losing weight and I became weaker and weaker. Based on the results of some blood tests, I was referred to the hematology unit at Hadassah Medical Center. The head of the department saw me and looked through all the blood tests. He questioned me thoroughly about the possibility that I had been exposed to a viral infection, because the picture did not fit any of the known infectious diseases which damage the immune system. My answer was adamantly negative. He seemed concerned and worried. I waited quietly for his opinion.

"I am sorry, but I cannot explain your blood results, niether the deterioration in the number of normal cells which are needed for a functioning immune system, nor the increase in the amount of abnormal white cells in the blood. I do not know what name to give it, but that does not change the situation. In the direction and pace that your immune system is going, you do not have many months left to live, and your level of functioning will continue to deteriorate. I am really sorry that I do not have any good news, and that I have no way to help you. I do not know how to slow the deterioration, let alone stop it, and unfortunately I have no idea how to get the system back to its normal state." He got up from his chair, marking the end of the meeting, and said again, "I am so sorry that this is the situation. I am really sorry."

I cannot explain this today, but the whole way home I was thinking about the fact that I was not willing to give up, that I was not willing to stop living and not willing to stop functioning. And since I was not willing to die, then I would not die, because I would live. Instead of fear of death, I decided in my heart not to die. Now it sounds silly, rude or both, but then it seemed to me the most natural thing in the world. The problem was that I had no idea, not even a sliver of an idea, how to do it. The answer arrived from an unexpected place, from my mother-in-law in Atlanta, Georgia, in the USA.

In a telephone conversation that night we told her what the hematologist said, and also that I was not willing to give up, but instead I wanted to get stronger, better and go back to functioning as normal.

"Come to Atlanta," she said. "There are excellent doctors in alternative medicine. I will find out who are the best, and make appointments for you. Maybe they will have an answer, even if conventional medicine has none. Here, you will be able to rest, because I will come over to help you. Let me spoil you and take care of you from close by."

The offer was tempting, but not practical. I, a mother of six little ones, could not get up and go away to Atlanta and leave them here alone, without me. Should we go? How could one even think about it? Abe had his own thriving office in structural engineering and building supervision, right under our house.

But, in spite of all the facts and the technical details, we wanted to try and bring Abe's mother's proposal to fruition. Why? Simply because there was no other offer on the table, and the idea of giving up did not even enter into our thoughts.

With G-d's mighty hand, the opportunity was not late in arriving. Abe heard that one of the large construction companies that he worked with were looking to develop outside of Israel. He suggested that they establish a daughter company in Atlanta, and that he would manage it for them. They traveled together to Atlanta to check the feasibility of the idea. Abe's connections, as someone who was born, raised and educated in Atlanta, were good and promising. Shortly after, a contract was signed with Abe, and he flew to Atlanta to find us a house to live, in walking distance from the "Ohel Avraham" synagogue and community lead by Rabbi Lev. There wasn't an apartment for rent whose owner was willing to rent it to a family with six children. The only option was to buy a house. Abe found a typical house, not too big, fifteen minutes' walk from the synagogue, and signed the contract to buy it. The money from selling our car in Israel was enough for the down payment on the house. He took a mortgage for the rest of the sum. He came back immediately to pack us up, and arrange the transfer of our large and sweet family to the city of his birth.

We knew that whatever we did not bring with us we would need to buy there. We looked for an airline which flew directly to Atlanta, not via New York, and would let us take more luggage on the plane. I did not succeed in convincing El-Al to let us take three suitcases per passenger, and the European airline KLM was the only one who agreed.

We were allowed to take twenty-one suitcases with us. Now,

we had to decide what to take and what to leave behind. I did not have the strength to do the packing. I sat in an armchair and directed my sisters and my mother. My strength was dwindling, and I got tired quickly, but I had a goal to reach, and put all the energy I could muster into preparing for our flight and transfer to the USA. Each child had a little bag with surprises and activities to keep them busy while on the plane during the long flight from Amsterdam to Atlanta.

Each child had "accompanying luggage" which went on the plane with him. In those suitcases were cloths and diapers for the night's lay over in Amsterdam and the long flight over the ocean the following afternoon. In the bags there was food for the day's wait in Amsterdam and for the flight, during which all that would be served to us was kosher food packaged in trays, which had been prepared days or weeks before the flight.

The last Shabbat at home. The last Shabbat in the synagogue in the village. The last Shabbat with the view of the sea, from a beautiful and plentiful garden. The last Shabbat with the extended family. The last Shabbat with one of my sisters living on one side of our house, and another sister on the other side. The last Shabbat for the children with their cousins, playing all together in the large yard which connected the houses. The last Shabbat in Israel.

During that Shabbat, we repeatedly told ourselves, again and again, that we were going for a temporary stay; that we are going for three years and no more; that we bought the house there due to a lack of another option, but not as property in the *Galut* (diaspora). We said it to each other. We said it to the children. We said it to my parents, my sisters, my brothers in law, to the uncles and aunts and to the grandparents from my mother's side. We said it loud and clear, on every day since the decision to travel had been made.

There was another time, in the past, when we had had to

protect ourselves decisively against getting lost in the US diaspora. Then, as a young couple, despite great promises of help from Abe's grandmother, we did not go back to the US after the wedding, even though we led a very simple and poor life in Israel. This time we are going straight into the lion's den of comfort and plenitude. We are going back to Abe's place of birth as a family with six children. Our flight to Amsterdam was leaving on Sunday afternoon.

It was winter. Thankfully, it did not rain on the day of our flight. We arrived at the airport with several cars, some of which had only luggage along with the driver. At the airport, the cars unloaded the luggage, and us, and went on their way.

We were quite a rare sight. One man in charge of twenty-one big suitcases. Two boys, eight and nine years old, carrying on their back their own personal bags, and pushing a cart with eight more bags which were destined to accompany us onto the plane. Two "big girls," five and six years old, with personal bags on their back, were holding onto the two sides of the small stroller, where an almost two-year-old girl was sitting, and their mother was pushing the carriage. Another girl, almost three, with a small bag on her back and without a place to hold onto the stroller, was jumping up and down excitedly. An active and full of life little girl, holding on to a strap which was tied to the stroller... the voyage had started.

The flight left towards the evening. The children were very excited and there was a need to keep them busy with different activities and games. They drew and colored and glued. They read books and listened to stories that we read to them. The four and half hours flight passed with active parents' supervision, and with peace and quiet for those around us. When the passengers got up from their seats, after landing, an elderly couple turned to us and said: "We did not even know that there were children behind us."

It was a complement which we carried with pride, until the next flight. It was clearly an impossible standard to hold onto during the next flight, which would be twice as long, all of it during daylight, but at least we had something to strive for. The luggage stayed at the airport in Amsterdam and would be transferred to the belly of the plane which would take us to Atlanta. Two parents, four "big" children, two little girls, eight carry-on bags (which were on the plane with us) and one stroller – were transferred to a hotel in the city by an airline vehicle. We got to the connected rooms towards eleven o'clock at night. We were all very tired and we all fell into a deep and uneventful sleep.

As healthy children do, they were all up before the sun, regardless of the late hour in which they went to sleep the night before. What does one do in Amsterdam with six children, ages two to nine? It was obvious that we had to do something with the happy and full-of-life children, prior to the long flight, which would be in constant daylight as we flew west. The flight was scheduled to leave at two in the afternoon. The solution: going out to walk around the city. Getting some fresh air, coupled with seeing new and exciting sites – which hopefully would excite them, too – and would served as a way to move the clock's hands faster, so that the waiting would end quickly and well. We put on our coats, a hat for the little one in the stroller, and we went out.

When the outside door of the hotel opened, the cold hit our faces. Within a few minutes the tips of our fingers started hurting from the cold. Another street, another turn, and we were all unhappy. We were cold. Very cold. Mist from our mouths hung between our lips and noses, dense, thick and heavy. We were stomping our feet trying to warm up, to keep the toes from the painful cold. Shoes for an Israeli winter are fit, at the most, for Dutch springtime. Here we needed fur-padded shoes and thick, warm socks, but we had none of those. It was clear that we had to find a heated place where we could walk around. What could be better than to visit a museum? Abe walked back to the hotel to find out where we could find a museum which would be good for little children, and we walked behind him slowly. We were cold, and we were quite miserable. Abe came back from the hotel, and his face held no good news.

"All the museums in the city are closed on Mondays," he said. "The concierge tried to be helpful and said that in the street parallel to this one, there are good restaurants where we could sit and have a good, hot meal. There was no use in trying to explain to him that we cannot eat anything in these restaurants. Sorry that I do not have any better news. What are we going to do?"

We went to the parallel street and started marching. Because of the terrible cold, we tried to not stop, but it was impossible to keep this up for a long time. We had two hours or so before we had to return to the hotel and travel to the airport. On one of the street corners there was a small, uniquely designed coffee house. Two small tables, which could be seen from the street window, had people sitting at them, drinking, eating and talking. It was a unanimous decision, without words and without voting: we were going into this coffee house to drink something hot and warm up.

When we opened the outside door of the coffee house, one woman looked up and raised an eyebrow in wonder. When we also opened the inner, entrance door of the coffee house, everyone turned their head towards us. We came in and stood in a line, one after the other, in a narrow passageway between the tables and the counter. When we were all in, all conversations stopped. Nothing was heard, except for the wonder which was spreading on the faces of those sitting in the restaurant. The waitress wiped her hands on her perfectly white apron and pointed for us to go upstairs to the second floor of the coffee house. The stairs were very steep. The children walked up happily on their short legs. Abe went up first and sat them down at one of the small tables in the upper space, which was just as narrow as the one downstairs. He whispered a strict warning for them to behave themselves and "sit nicely," and went back downstairs to help me climb up as he carried the little one in his arms. To our relief, the waiter allowed us to leave our stroller folded under the stairs on the entrance level.

Needless to mention, those sitting on the second floor also followed every child who came in with a questioning look. I could hear those sitting there thinking to themselves: "Does this line of children end somewhere?" After a few minutes of defrosting, we all took off our coats. Two adjacent small tables were now full with our family. The conversations had not yet resumed at the other tables, when the waitress came to take our order. "Eight large glass cups of hot chocolate please." The sounds of her footsteps signaled to everyone to resume their conversations.

Six children and two adults sitting in a long and narrow space, at two little tables, and on the tables, a small bowl with brown crystals that looked like candies. "Ima, what is this?" they asked.

"Brown sugar crystals."

"Ima, may we take one?" they continued.

"You may."

"Ima, may we take another one?" they continued.

"You may."

"May we take another one?" they added hopefully.

"OK."

At long last, the sweet, steaming hot chocolate drinks arrived. We hugged the cups and sipped slow, small warming sips from the familiar sweet brown drink. Even a hot drink eventually cools off and it can be drunk in full. The cups emptied. The clock showed that we had another hour until it would be worthwhile to return to the hotel and leave for the airport. The bowls with the brown sugar crystals were empty.

Abe looked around. Those sitting at the other tables looked at him and signaled that he could come and take the sweet, golden crystals from their tables. He got up, took the bowls and thanked them.

When the waitress came to see how we were doing, she found eight empty cups, a few empty bowls which once contained crystals of brown sugar, a tired woman barely sitting on the hard wooden chair with no padding, six little children sitting and listening, and one man whispering a story in English. Without removing his eyes from the children, he pointed at the empty sugar bowls. The waitress nodded and collected the cups and the empty bowls. The children kept on listening with their mouth open. The little one settled into a warm, soft place in my arms and fell asleep.

The magic of the story was broken by the waitress, who brought to the table two bowls full of brown sugar crystals. Without asking, they sucked, chewed and sucked, while talking quietly in the silence of the coffee house, which was almost empty now. After another round of hot chocolate, the time had come to walk back to the hotel. Abe went down first, with the little one in his arms. After him a line of sugar-stuffed children came down the stairs, and at the end of the line one mother, tired and weak yet functioning (as there was really no choice). We put on our insufficient coats and marched quickly and decisively to the warmth of the hotel lobby.

It was a long flight, and the children were up most of the time. We made figures from playdough. We made up stories and plays with the playdough figures. We solved riddles, drew pictures, colored, and filled workbooks of all sorts. Finally, we were getting close to Atlanta. The plane made circles in the sky and did not start its decent. The pilot told us, over the intercom, that due to heavy fog above the Atlanta Airport, we would need to land in a nearby airport. Abe and I exchanged glances. It meant landing more than a two-hour drive away from Atlanta. No one would meet us. No one would be able to help us with all the heavy and plentiful luggage. We were already so exhausted from the constant activity with the children, making sure they did not disturb one another or the other passengers, we had no ability to cope with the implications of landing in a strange and unplanned location.

After some time, which seemed like an eternity, the plane started descending. A grayish white, thick and almost palpable fog enveloped the plane. Suddenly, with no prior warning, the wheels banged, touching the ground. The invisible plane had landed in the thickness of the fog.

"Welcome to the United States. We have just landed at the Atlanta Airport..." a sigh of relief rose from every seat on the full plane, and within that crowd the largest sigh of relief came from two parents, who were on the plane with their six children, a ton of carry-on bags and a huge number of suitcases in the belly of the plane.

At the exit, Bubbie and Zadie waited for us (this was how we lovingly called Abe's parents) with some of their friends. Two very large luggage trolleys, heavily loaded with suitcases and large boxes, arrived behind us, pushed by porters. We were extremely tired and very excited. With the help of their friends and their large vehicles, we arrived at Bubbie's and Zadie's house. A homely smell of chicken soup greeted us as we entered Bubbie's kitchen. All we wanted to do was to go to sleep. The children dropped down wherever they found an empty spot and fell asleep right away. It was quiet. A quiet which I knew would be broken sometime during the middle of the night, when their bodies would let them know it is morning, morning in Israel, which was seven hours ahead of us.

Abe went with friends and unloaded our considerable, heavy luggage in our waiting and empty home. The bags we took with us on the plane were set to last us through sleeping at Bubbie's and Zadie's house for a night or two. We could not retire to our bedroom before we shared with everyone the experience of the flight, and we ate some of the rich and hot chicken soup. By the time everyone had gone to sleep, a weak winter sun had already risen in Israel.

The next day we tried to minimally furnish our house, where we would live for the next three years. Abe went to pick up a big table and eight chairs from an elderly couple who did not need them anymore. I called to order eight simple beds, with a metal spring frame and a simple mattress. "We can deliver the beds to you tomorrow. To where should we deliver it?" asked the lady on the other end of the line.

"To Little Court," I answered.

The following day the phone rang. "Ma'am, the truck is on Little Court, but the driver cannot find your institution."

"We are not an institution; it is for a private home. I see the truck; I will go out and wave to it." The silence on the other end of the line filled my ear, and shock could be seen on the face of the speaker, even through the phone receiver.

We moved to our home on the third night after our arrival. Abe went to register the children for the schools and kindergartens associated with the synagogue.

Bubbie was a teacher in that kindergarten, so we were blessed to have her as our younger children's teacher. By Shabbat, we had gotten over the jet lag and on Monday, a week after we landed in Atlanta, the children went to school and to kindergarten. The little one stayed home with me.

At the beginning, Bubbie came to us every day after work in the kindergarten, to help me and lighten the burden. Upon her request, and with her help, we found a woman from the community who was happy to watch over the little one during the morning hours, so that I could rest, sleep and try to gather strength for the busy afternoon and evening hours.

Bubbie took me to the first appointment in a clinic for alternative medicine. The doctor prescribed different herbs and tinctures to strengthen my immune system and myself. The passage of time, the herbs and tinctures, the love and peace and quiet – all allowed me to slowly get out of the deterioration process, and to begin to climb the long path to healing and eventually to good health.

A SCIENTIFIC TIME BOMB

When we got to Atlanta I was exhausted and very weak. In the first months I did little, only tasks of utmost necessity, and these too with Bubbies' help. The treatments to restore my immune system helped, and I slowly got back to myself.

In the summer I started looking for a lab to do my post-doc, and I found Prof. Anderson from Center University, who was looking for post-docs. I went for an interview with him, and on the way to his office I passed through wide and clean corridors, stretching between his labs, which were large and full of light. In front of him were lying my scientific CV and copies of all the papers I published during my PhD work in biochemistry and in immunology.

The conversation was pleasant and relaxed. He told me about the two main research areas his labs were working on. The first was relating to the heart muscle, for which he had had a large and active laboratory for many years. The second was in the field of AIDS-HIV, using monkeys. This laboratory was being built and set-up as we spoke. Prof. Anderson had a budget for a post-doc in both fields, and he invited me to choose.

"What would you recommend for me to choose?" I asked.

"There is almost no AIDS in Israel," he said. "And in the post-doc stage it is worthwhile to build a foundation for new findings in a field in which you could fit into the academic world in Israel.

Therefore, I would recommend for you to choose the heart muscle field. The lab in this subject is already up and running, and it has many researchers who could help you get into your own research, once you have studied the field in depth."

He gave me two thick files, one on each subject, and requested that I read them and decide during the coming week. I was supposed to get up, thank him, and leave the room. But I could not. The question burned on the tip of my tongue, and I was afraid that if I did not ask it I might, G-d forbid, mislead him, and that he would hire me without taking into account all the relevant implications.

"Prof. Anderson, before I leave, I have a question. Why did you not ask me how would I be able to do good, efficient research with six children?" I was concerned that he might have overlooked that fact in my CV.

His whole face smiled, and he said: "If you have accomplished all that have until today, with a large and growing family, then I have nothing to worry about with regards to your abilities and output. It would be great if you will be able to publish as much as you have from my lab also."

Even before I got home, I knew that I wanted the bigger, more challenging, more intriguing, and newer option. A lab at its building stage was, in my eyes, a plus and not a minus. I first read the heart muscle file. It included many publications and a hugely ambitious research proposal submitted to the National Institute of Health (NIH), which gives out only a few research grants every year, after a tedious and detailed scientific evaluation process.

I realized that I would not be happy dealing with this subject. It was too comfortable, to cushioned, and the research has been built on careful, measured steps from one aspect of the research to another, in a predetermined path. I put the file down and moved onto the file on the research proposal for investigating AIDS in monkeys, so as to better understand the course of the disease and to study the different modes of coping with that viral infection. It was fascinating, challenging, novel and in the process of establishing a new way of thinking. In addition, the work was with monkeys – something that was not possible at all in Israel. A post-doc overseas is meant to be an opportunity to get to know systems which do not exist in Israel, so that one can come back and inspire research using new methods and tools.

When I entered Prof. Anderson's room, a week later, and told him what I chose, he smiled a big smile and said, "I knew that you will chose this one, the bigger challenge and less charted territory, which is at its first steps, on a road no one has paved yet. I am happy with your choice. Good luck."

It was the first time in my life that my daring was not met by severe faces and a heavy important question: "Don't you think this is a little bit too big for you? Why take a risk when you can go in a clear and predefined path?" I knew that here, in this lab, I would truly start my scientific life.

We agreed that I would start two days after the opening of the upcoming school year. I asked to be at the university only four days a week, and to finish my day at three in the afternoon, so that I could pick up the children from school and kindergarten and to receive the others as they arrive home. It was a very unusual and unconventional request. Prof. Anderson seemed surprised. For real and serious researchers, the research is the center of their life, it manages them more than they manage it. I explained to him that this way I am with the children for most of their waking hours during the week, and that it was important to me. This way I could talk with them about their day's events soon after they came home, when everything was still fresh and bubbling in their minds.

I saw that he was not comfortable. He wanted me to work with him, but he had no idea how to handle a woman like me.

"I understand, Prof. Anderson, that you are surprised to hear my unusual request. It is important for me to enter the research in a way that will enable me to keep the close connection with my children, without diminishing it. I plan to continue my research at home, after they go to sleep. Reading relevant articles, summarizing and analyzing data from the experiments I run, and planning the next experiments. This way I can arrive at the lab the next day, ready to start running the experiments right away, and the use of my lab time will be maximized. Please let me start, in this setup of formally working only 60% of a position, and also pay me accordingly, only two-thirds of a post-doc salary. Let us see how things develop, and we will see if I can increase my weekly working hours, and when."

Prof. Anderson leaned back in his chair and said with a smile, "Working with you is going to be interesting. I agree to the terms you have set, and I look forward to your joining my lab at the end of the summer. Good luck." He got up and walked me to the door. "This is going to be interesting... really interesting..." he said, smiling, and he wished me good luck again.

The summer evaporated in burning leaves, and autumn gave way to winter. At the beginning we were only two in the lab. Bill was doing an MD-PhD degree. He was a bright, hardworking, pleasant young man, and a fascinating partner for scientific brainstorming. We were both trying to understand why one species of monkeys, when it became infected with HIV, got sick, developed AIDS and all the symptoms, then experienced deterioration leading to eventual death. Another species of monkeys stayed perfectly healthy, in spite of being infected with the very same virus.

Some unexpected results were showing up in our research. The monkeys were being categorized as infected or not infected based on a blood test for viral antibodies. We started our research using the monkey species which did not develop AIDS even when infected with the virus. The monkeys who tested negative in this antibody test served as controls in our experiments.

In one experiment after another those "seronegative" monkeys had a measurable immune response against the virus. This was unexpected, and against the leading paradigm at the time, i.e. that everyone who got infected generated antibodies against the virus. I repeated the experiments over and over again, and the phenomenon repeated itself. Monkeys who had no antibodies against the virus, behaved immunologically as if they were infected with it. I asked to get blood samples from other seronegative monkeys from the same species and colony. The result repeated themselves in the additional monkeys. It was not possible to ignore the results nor their implications.

I did not wish to ignore them, specifically because of what they inferred. "Maybe," they whispered in my ears, "the established, well-founded and accepted scientific dogma, that whoever does not have antibodies is not infected, is not always true?!"

I was facing a gigantic challenge. I wanted to try and formulate my own interpretation of the data. An interpretation which refuted all the immunological dogmas and paradigms of this time, around HIV in particular. I went to Prof. Anderson and explained to him what I thought, based on the repeated, unexpected experimental data.

"I think that these monkeys did get infected with the virus, but they did not make antibodies against it, and that is why they are not considered carriers (of the virus)."

"I am assuming that you know that this is against everything we know about the immune system response in general, and of its response to viruses in particular." It was the opening remark in a conversation, not a closing one.

I went on to put forward a hypothesis, that since all the adult females have antibodies against the virus and the virus was in their blood, their fetuses already had gotten infected in the womb. "Maybe they are tolerant to the virus, and do not fight it because they encounter it in the womb, in an environment which gets to be defined as part of "self" by the immune system."

"But if they are not fighting the virus, then they should be dying from it even faster, sooner than the other monkeys, which are infected with the same virus," Prof. Anderson said, and his fingers started taping the edge of his table as his face closed up, focusing the thoughts inward, and I could see the wheels in his brain turning fast and steady.

"Prof. Anderson, their mothers are also infected with the virus, but do not get sick and do not die of AIDS. Maybe they also got infected in their mothers' womb and therefore they also did not make antibodies in the earlier years of their life? Maybe it is the ability to *not* respond to the virus with antibodies, at least not early on, which offers the best way of coping with it? At least in this species of monkeys?"

The question, the proposal, the thought, the theory and the possible conclusion all hung in the room, absorbing the air into an unattainable space of their own. Prof. Anderson's mouth opened as if it wished to speak, but was actually only asking for air. Familiar air. Air in which the basic assumptions laid by others, greater than us in science, are undisputed. On their shoulders, we stand and build possible models and design experiments to be proven.

What I proposed as a model of thinking and a way to analyze reality was revolutionary and hard to digest. To my surprise, Prof. Anderson did not reject it on the spot. "You could be right," he said. "But you will need to prove your hypothesis unequivocally. You will have to fight with all the researchers in the field of AIDS monkey research, and it is a small group. Without their support, your life will be very complex and hard. They will demand more and more proofs for your claim. They will not give in, not one iota, on the way there." He stopped talking, as if weighing to add another warning. "You also have to be aware of the fact that your claim could be considered a major insult to the head of our primate center. He will not collaborate with you and will not help you."

Over time, it became evident that the head of the primate center not only was not happy with the results of the subsequent experiments, but that he was willing to do anything, really anything, to try to disprove my interpretation of the data, totally ignoring the clear proofs which had been obtained through each set of experiments.

I developed a new system, in which I pushed immune system cells, which recognized the virus but did not generate antibodies in the body, to produce antibodies in a culture. In this way I proved that they did get exposed to the virus, and that the immune system did recognize it, but "chose" not to react against it. It was an earth-shattering finding, and it strengthened my hypothesis that the results pointed to a new and radical dimension in our understanding of the immune system. Every experimental data and answer gave rise to more questions and put in front of me more challenges.

A very important question troubled my mind in those days: are the "negative" monkeys still infected? I presented the question to Dr. Williams, a European virologist who had joined our lab, and asked him to look for the virus in the seronegative monkeys. By patiently and stubbornly experimenting, he did prove that the virus was still in the blood of those monkeys, who were considered negative according to the existing and currently acceptable testing used to identify carriers of the virus.

With great excitement Dr. Williams prepared the amazing results for a conference of all the researchers dealing with the monkey model of HIV and AIDS, some two hundred people. The researchers listened intently, and many hands were raised with questions at the end of the presentation. Most of them tried to question the credibility of the results and the presentation. There was no solid base for any of the criticism, but they still undermined the data in the eyes of the whole scientific crowd there. This left me restless. Not because many tried to reject the results as not logical or as faulty from the start. On the scientific level, the results clearly showed to me that some of the axioms and paradigms which ruled the AIDS field were not true. I was facing a giant challenge – to put together, and prove via experiments, new and different axioms and paradigms. This called for thinking out of the box, deep resolve and mainly, courage. I had no idea how much courage it would demand, and I did not know if what I had was enough.

Prof. Anderson was by my side the entire way. He believed in my groundbreaking research and was not afraid of thinking differently. But the road was full of obstacles. The head of the primate center was furious and felt betrayed, as I had disqualified his clear-cut division in his monkey populations. He made every possible effort to undermine both my results and myself. Prof. Anderson warned me, and re-warned me, that it was not good to have the head of the primate center as my enemy. My wonderful mentor did a lot of work 'behind the scenes' to lower the flames, distancing and protecting me by putting himself as the go-to between us.

A critical and scary question remained: are these monkeys, who test negative with the existing blood tests, but have been shown, with the system I developed, to be infected – are they infectious? Can they infect other monkeys? In order to answer this question, we needed to transfer blood from those monkeys, which the head of the primate center had been claiming are negative and have no virus, to monkeys which had never been previously exposed to the virus, and see if they would get infected. The head of the center was sure that the answer would be negative.

We proposed an experimental set-up to him, which would enable him to refute all our (Dr. Williams and myself) claims and conclusions about the negative monkeys who we claimed were still carriers. He swallowed the hook with the bait. He was willing to set aside, for this experiment, four fresh monkeys who had never encountered the virus before and made it clear that all the work with the monkeys would be done at their center. We would only get blood samples for testing. Prof. Anderson managed the whole process and agreed to all the terms.

In the days and weeks following this transfer of blood from the "negative" monkeys to fresh monkeys, it was hard to think of anything else, let alone focus on other experiments. Every other subject seemed trivial compared with the huge question that we had put forward. Everyone tensely waited to see what the results of the experiment would be. I was sure that the blood from the negative monkeys would infect the fresh monkeys, and that they would become carriers of the virus, but I did not know if they would eventually develop AIDS – a question no one in our lab dared say out loud, yet.

Because I thought that the results would have medical, clinical and diagnostic implications in people infected with HIV, my tension was real, palpable and blinding. I tried to push those thoughts to the back of my head, until after we would get the initial results.

The results arrived, and what I hoped for, happened. What I feared became a reality. Three of the fresh monkeys, who had received blood from negative monkeys, started making antibodies against the virus. Initially these antibodies could be found only using the system I had developed, but after a few weeks they became positive according to regular testing, too. After several months, the fourth monkey was also proven to be infected and a carrier. The experiment results also showed us that the system I had developed enabled detection of the infection in the monkeys, weeks before it was possible to identify this using the regular methods. In other words, the current diagnostic systems did not identify all of the carriers, especially not those recently infected, and those were found to be the most infectious.

I held in my hands a scientific and public helath time bomb. I could not sleep at night. It was clear to me that if there were monkeys who were carriers in spite of testing negative, then there were also people like that. This meant that there were people who were infected with the dangerous HIV virus, but this was not detected by the current methods. This had diagnostic and medical implications, also for the safety of blood units. According to my findings, it was dangerous to rely only on the current testing, because it missed carriers. In the current situation based on the current testing, hidden carriers of HIV were allowed to donate blood.

One day I gathered up my courage and went to Prof. Anderson's room and sat down heavily across from him. I did not know what his response would be to what I was about to ask from him, but I knew one thing for sure: everything which he would say would be said with complete honesty and respect. I told him that I have a request which was far from being simple. He sat up in his chair and said he was listening.

"If there are monkeys like that, negative yet dangerous carriers, then there are also people like that!" To my surprise he nodded his head and said that he agreed with me.

"But," he added, "there is nothing we, as scientists, can do about it."

"I want to check blood samples from people at high risk for HIV infection and see if there are hidden carriers among them. Maybe the system I invented can be used to identify them, make a correct diagnosis and provide appropriate treatment."

Prof. Anderson remained silent for a few, long minutes before he said to me, in an understanding but determined voice: "Look,

Sara, HIV in monkeys is an experimental model. You have, and will have, those among the researchers who will oppose you, but all the arguments and discussions will be scientific. You are a good scientist, and you will have no problem dealing with researchers in the field of the monkey model of AIDS. The scientific world is your world."

He took a deep breath and continued: "HIV is a whole different story. In AIDS and HIV there is more politics than science. Do not go there. Do not leave the pure, basic, science. The politics of AIDS is not pure and not clean. It is dirty, and it is only becoming worse and more terrible. Already today one man is willing to destroy another if he is touching the model which he has determined to prove as correct."

I understood every word he said, and I agreed with his assessment of the hardship and risk, but I could not give up. Not yet. "But there are people like that, they are a risk, from infections through blood units in the blood banks, to the population's safety. If there are people like that, they are being told that they are negative (and thus not carriers), and they go back home and see no reason not to be careful or warn others, so that they will not infect those around them, especially those they love the most."

"And if you find such people, what will you do with the results?" he wondered.

"First of all, I will publish, so that it will be known that there is such a phenomenon. Also, I will be able to point out, in the article, the fact that there is an answer to the problem which I am reporting, which is changing the way we test for HIV antibodies, therefore enabling early detection of hidden carriers."

"This will not be simple," he was clear and determined, but his eyes did not leave mine, and my frustration was all there to be felt and seen. "Sara, listen to me. You know that I have great respect for you, and a high appreciation of you as both a scientist and as a person. I am telling you, going into the field of HIV in humans is like walking into a wasps' nest with no escape exit. I do suggest that you stay in the purely scientific area of the monkey model. There I can help you safeguard yourself, and find ways to overcome the obstacles which scientists will surely put in front of you, as they are conservatives by nature."

"But Prof. Anderson, if I do nothing with these findings, then I leave the human population exposed to infections from HIV carriers who have not been detected by the current tests. Prof. Anderson, to remain silent and avert my eyes to my own scientific comfort zone, seem to me like a betrayal. A betrayal of humanity, and especially of the weaker populations, where the epidemic is spreading super-fast, and terribly. To remain silent means to risk people's lives. Please, help me to not to remain silent."

Prof. Anderson was quiet. I thought I had crossed the line. To imply, even in the slightest hint, that he might betray the well-being of people was a grave insult, and he did not deserve it. He was an MD and a researcher whose goal was to help save lives and increase the chances of healing and recuperation from a cardiac stroke.

"Again, your uninhibited Israeli straight forwardness. When will you learn? When will you become more moderate?" I scolded myself during the long silence in the room.

Prof. Anderson broke the silence. "Do you have a proposal for an experiment which could provide initial data about people and HIV?" without waiting for my answer he cleared his desktop. I spread in front of him the experimental set up which I had planned as a feasibility study for my theory and method which I had developed. He commented and improved upon it, we changed and added until both of us were happy with the result. Now the true obstacle remained – where were we going to get blood samples from people categorized as high risk? At that point Prof. Anderson got to work calling in favors from some doctors who were friends. I left him in his room calling people, and I went back to the lab.

After a few days Prof. Anderson called me to his room. "After quite a few calls, there is a possibility of getting some two hundred blood samples from the hospital in downtown Atlanta," he said.

"Just as in all big cities, the populations at high risk for HIV/AIDS are the weaker populations, who come to the public hospital. The samples which we will get will be left over from samples taken for a blood count, so that there will be no need to draw blood especially for the experiment – as that would require the approval of the Helsinki committee. It was agreed that all identifiers will be removed from the test tubes, and the experiment will be anonymous. The samples will be transferred to our lab, and there we will keep the plasma for regular tests, and transfer the cells to the culture system you developed. The two samples, the original one and the one treated in culture, will be sent to the hospital lab, where they will run antibody testing in the routine assay, and the results will be sent to us. I agreed that if there will be scientific publication of the results, the head research doctor at the hospital will be the lead author, despite the fact that she was not the initiator nor the conductor of the experiment."

I did not know how to thank him. He had gone out of his way to help me go into research in a field in which he clearly did not wish to get into, and where he was afraid that I would be crushed by the political wheels in the field of AIDS. He did it out of respect for me as an independent researcher, but also because he was an especially honest, true medical doctor and researcher with integrity to the core.

I could have directed the groundbreaking research in the interesting and revolutionary findings in the area of the monkeys' immune system, who were and remained seronegative and healthy carriers. I could have stayed in the theoretical area of novel immunological models. I could have sat quietly, basking in the respect bestowed upon an inventor who thought out of the box, and decided to remain silent. But is was not really or truly possible. Can a person behave like Cain, and not hear the blood of my brother screaming form the earth, and still remain human? What could actually happen to me? What could be a good reason to bury my head in the sand and ignore the spreading epidemic? Was I actually allowed to focus only on my personal peace, as if saying "May there just be peace for me and my research?"

I sought humility which would keep me away from the edge of the cliff, but it was not there to be found. I was so sure that I could save lives, so I saw no option of folding up, giving up and remaining in the confines of the "pure research" lab. After the soul had risen to the heights of science, to the place where science and life meet and give life – or take it away – I could not be confined to the golden cage of research using only animal models for AIDS.

I thanked Prof. Anderson, and we moved on to finalize the technical details of the blood samples and testing. I respected him more and more, because in spite of the fact that he thought it was not a good idea for me to get into the wasps' nest of AIDS medical politics, he respected my decision and request, and did everything he could, and more, in order to enable me to run the study I requested.

I was fortunate to have a great man as an advisor, towering over many, as a researcher and as a medical doctor, as an employer and as a scientific mentor. He made room for me and for my request, even though we looked at the world from very different angles, and my priorities were also very different than his. He respected me as a researcher, and he speared no effort in order to enable me to ask the scientific questions which I sought to ask, seek and answer. Later, I learned that as a young researcher who was relatively new to the university, he also took upon himself great risks. At that point in time, he had no supporters for doing any research on people with HIV. Everyone thought he should stay on the safe, stable and high ground on which his research had stood until that time.

After two weeks, the leftover blood from blood samples started to arrive in our lab, and the first study to identify hidden (silent) carriers of HIV in people commenced. These were the last weeks of my seventh pregnancy. I finished compiling and analyzing the data on my estimated due date. At Prof. Anderson's request, I presented the results to the faculty heads on a Friday afternoon, when I already had contractions. There was a lot wondering and surprise in the room, and many questions were asked. But the results were very clear and significant: among the people who were infected with HIV, there were people who tested negative with the current assays, and we could identify them using the new and innovative system which we had developed. Everyone stood and clapped their hands. I left, with no delays, to finish the preparations for Shabbat and for the birth. I gave birth the following Wednesday.

When I came back to the lab, after a vacation for recuperation, I was told that Prof. Anderson had asked his lab manager, a very sharp and smart woman, to try to repeat the results I found, using a different high-risk population of drug users. Prof. Anderson understood how important it was to confirm the results with the help of more hands, more samples and another population. He understood the pressures which we would face and acted to protect us by fortifying us in advance. Her results were identical to the ones we found in the first study I conducted. Everyone in the faculty was greatly excited.

The faculty dean called me in for a meeting. It was a rare situation to receive his attention as a post-doc in general, and for sure one who was only in her second year of research.

"I am going to a big international conference on HIV, which is going to take place in Los Angeles, and I will present the results there of the silent carriers of HIV research. Clearly it is inappropriate that such important results would be presented by a beginning researcher. Please prepare a presentation for me with the results."

I prepared the presentation, and I went through it with him. It was clear to me that he would be able to present the presentation well, but there was no chance that he could answer the technical and scientific questions which would come up after the lecture. He did get a time to present the data in the slot preserved for

"groundbreaking news," but he was not familiar with the small/large details.

I shared none of this with anyone. With Prof. Anderson there was no need for words. I knew that he tried to convince the faculty dean to send me to the conference but failed. It made him a little angry. He thought it was right, respectable, and fair that I would present the groundbreaking research and that I would get recognition and appreciation for my work. But I was still excited for the recognition and attention I received from the dean for a discovery which he thought so much of that he wanted to present it himself.

I knew that the results could mean saving many lives. I knew that beyond the scientific discovery, all the rest is in other people's hands. I was just a young researcher doing her post-doc, in a prestigious university in the big United States. I was not deserving of all the truth and good that G-d had bestowed upon me in His mercy. All I could do was thank G-d for enabling me to come to this amazing discovery and pray that He would enable this discovery to spread its wings beyond the limits of the lab and the university and to save lives, as many lives as possible.

Prof. Anderson's lab was not set up or ready to start research with HIV, and therefore I could not continue to work on the early detection of HIV in humans.

I went back to the monkeys' immune system, and my head was full of intriguing research questions which had arisen from the surprising results we achieved about the different ways the different monkey species handle the infection of HIV.

• • •

It was time for me to write a big grant proposal to the NIH, with Prof. Anderson's help and encouragement, and to ask for funding for my research for the next few years.

Only a person who has prepared a grant proposal for NIH funding knows the huge scope, and the tens and hundreds of hours required for the scientific writing. While writing, ideas are clarified and sharpened for the writing scientist too, and the proposed research plan becomes refined and more developed with time and endless drafts. However, the end arrives a day before the final submission date. One stays up most of the night, and the next morning some copies leave to the NIH via special courier, who has to hand them over on the very same day and get a confirmation of submission.

After the loud sounds of preparation, the thin sound of silence, of waiting, began. A time for introspection and prayer, together with continued blessings and various doings. The experiments yielded more and more important results, fascinating results, results which would put together a more complete picture of the way the body and its immune system copes with the invasion by the virus. Results which could support in the future a continuation of the grant funding we requested, and maybe even enlarge it.

The answer was received after many months. As the date approached, tension and expectations were felt in the air. All the leading researchers in the department and in the faculty relied on research budgets from different sources, of which the leading one was the NIH. Only a small percentage of the proposals gets funded by the NIH. After a stringent and detailed review of the proposal by several scientific advisors, there was a meeting to discuss it in a larger forum of reviewers. The final accumulated score would determine if the proposed research would receive the requested funding.

An envelope was laid on my desk. I did not need to read the name of the sender in order to know that this was the answer from the NIH. I was very excited, but I knew that the competition was tough and that all the scientists which submit are excellent. My chance to get such large funding on my first proposal, without a positive history with this huge funding institution, was minute. I have never run away from hard challenges, but I was never good at handling disappointments.

I opened the envelope, opened the folded piece of paper and read it. "We are happy to inform you that your research proposal has scored a very good score, and funding for this groundbreaking research has been granted according to the following sections."

The proposal has been granted! I had millions of dollars, over several years, available to me. The proposal was written from Prof. Anderson's lab, and without his close help and his rewriting of meaningful sections of the scientific discussion, I would not have been granted this funding, but he insisted that my name would be the first one on the proposal, so that I would be the senior researcher in the proposed research plan.

"It is based on your experiments, and it is a proposal about what you propose and want to do with the findings in your hands, in order to move this field forward. Therefore, it is your proposal. I am only an enabler, and not the researcher." He said this and was not willing to change his mind even on the last day before submission. Not even after a sleepless night and adding many changes and corrections which were small but important, until the last minute and almost beyond it.

I rose to go to Prof. Anderson's office to share the good news with him and thank him, but he was already on the way to my desk. "Mazel Tov, Mazel Tov," he said in Hebrew with a heavy American accent. "I am so proud of you!"

I was speechless – a pretty rare situation in my case. I tried to say thank you, but the words were not heard outside the space in my head which was full, stormy, confused, happy and not believing, yet fully believing. "You already know? How? From where?"

"My friends from the NIH were so excited that such a young researcher of mine got such a large grant, so they had to share it with me on the day of notice. Their call just beat the envelope in your hands by a few minutes."

There are moments that you know you will never come back to, but that you will never forget. There are moments that you know are an axis, on which the coming years of your life could be moved and changed, even 180 degrees. There are moments where you actually float above them, and when you try to hold onto their memory, it is hovering above you, touching but not touching, even today. The moment of receiving the letter approving the huge grant for my research was such a moment.

It was a once in a lifetime chance. A chance to take off in the academic world as high as I could ever wish. I had never even dared to dream of getting such an opportunity. I was overwhelmed and dizzy from happiness and excitement, from the wide and wondrous horizon which opened in front of me. However, I could not know where all this would truly take me. The letter which rolled onto my doorstep created the need to choose a life of faith in our destiny as Jews, or, G-d forbid, loose the right Jewish way for me, for us.

238

My findings made waves in the entire Center University Faculty of Medicine. When the funding was granted, I was the talk of the day, of the week and of the month in the faculty, in the community and in the wider family in Israel. Sometime after receiving the notice from the NIH, Prof. Anderson called me to his office. He was very excited. "Your work, your extraordinary findings, their meaning as far as the spread of AIDS in the population, their ramifications regarding the safety of blood banks and on CDC monitoring – are enormous. The fact that the NIH saw in your proposal an important horizon of new understandings regarding the immune system and how it works, and approved the full funding you asked for, add to your prestige. Well done!"

Prof. Anderson had never expressed emotions in front of me. He had always been attentive and easygoing, and I could not understand why he would call me in order to tell me what we both already knew. "They called me from the university management, to ask my opinion about appointing you to the position of senior researcher, with professorship and a lab of your own."

"Obviously, I gave a warm recommendation. You will be the first case where a researcher is offered a chair at such an early stage of his scientific life. I am very excited; this is a once in a lifetime opportunity. The committee which deals with your case has asked for you to come to them tomorrow. Good luck. You really deserve this."

I went home, trying to let the words seep into my soul, into my inner being. That evening Abe and I celebrated over a glass of wine. We both knew that I would continue devoting time to the lab with the format we had chosen, four days until three pm, so that I could receive the children when they came back from school and from kindergarten. We already knew what I could accomplish within this framework. In the lab, at the moment, I conducted the experiments. At home, after putting the children to sleep, I continued reading scientific literature and planned the experiments for the following day. In such a set-up the university's proposal was exciting and promising, and it was clear to both of us that I would accept the proposal when I appeared in front of the committee the next day.

The morning hours crawled by slowly, I was excited and could not focus on anything. Many faces waited for me in a room covered with mahogany wood, with dark wood furniture and a deep carpet. Faces I was not familiar with. The committee members wished to get to know me a little. They wanted to hear about Israel – "It is dangerous to live there, right? All your family is in Israel?!" – about me being an Orthodox Jew – "This does not bother you to do research, especially of a disease such as AIDS?" – about seven children – "How do you manage at all? Who helps you at home? Unbelievable!" – about my research – "Amazing! Groundbreaking! You have courage, you dared and succeeded, admirable" – about the plans to continue in the new field I had created and develop the new research tools I invented.

The head of the committee addressed me and said: "I am happy to inform you that the committee met last week, and it was decided to invite you to be part of our academic staff. The university will create a special chair within the School of Medicine for you. We will build and equip a lab based on your needs, so that you can proceed with the groundbreaking research which you have started."

All the faces were staring at me, and they were all nodding in agreement while he spoke. When he was done, they all clapped their hands.

"Thank you. This is a great honor, too great an honor. Truthfully, I have no words to express my feelings and my excitement."

"Then, we will transfer our decision to the rector so that he will officially accept the appointment and will allocate the space, time and budget in order to get your lab ready as soon as possible. I know that you came to us as a post-doc, and thus for a limited time. Now you will not be limited, on the contrary, the condition for accepting the chair is that you will stay at the university for at least five years."

I was young. I was quick to respond. I was dogmatic and set on the time frame Abe and I had decided – three years in Atlanta and then returning immediately. How could I stay any longer than what we had agreed on ahead of our trip?!

I was mother to a boy who was going to have a Bar Mitzva in another year and half, becoming a responsible person for his actions in the eyes of G-d. I was a mother to all our children and wanted to raise them according to the laws of the Torah while preparing them in the proper ways of the world. There was no good way of doing this in Atlanta, at least not with the older children. I was the wife of a man who grew up in Atlanta, fully American, and who knew "everyone" in the Jewish community in this big city. His temptation to stay in Atlanta would be very strong and could drag us into a life in exile for an unlimited time.

I was the eldest, with many younger sisters who looked up to me to learn and to do. I was a daughter of the people of Israel, living in the Land of Israel, in the state of Israel. I knew that the most important thing which I needed to do, in order to keep my family and myself Zionists, was to make sure that we would all get on a plane after three years with no delay. The chair, the new lab, the honor and the wonderful scientific challenges, they all meant a commitment for five years, which will bring the total years in exile, out of our homeland, to seven.

I thought, decided, and spoke without pausing to absorb the new situation. "We came to Atlanta for three years. Almost two years have passed, and this means that we will go back to Israel, G-d willing, after another year and half, as planned."

The silence in the room was screeching, loud and hard. I have never been sensitive to nuances in people's speech. I have never learned to handle myself around people. I never learned to read the body language or facial expressions of the people in front of me. I was ignorant of how to deal with people, especially in politics of any sort. Despite all this, the surprise, shock and the total disbelief that I actually rejected their offer – even I could feel it.

But I did not see any other way. I told them my truth, and they could not understand how a person could be "stuck" with his truth to this degree. Who could even imagine rejecting such a fantastic offer, which has had no equal in the whole history of this old and respected university?

It never occurred to me to say to the committee "yes," and not really mean to keep the promise they required. I did not think about the possibility of dividing my time between Israel and the U.S. I was a mother and wife, and these are roles one cannot play from afar, inconsistently. The big mission of my life was for Abe to be stronger in Torah, in keeping the commandments and for the children to grow up in Israel with a life based on both Torah and work, Torah and a proper way of living in this word, as proud Israelis in the State of Israel. I wanted them all to be Zionists, and that Zionism would be an important and necessary part of their lives, as children, as adolescents and as adults. I knew that all these goals would fall to the wayside if I would say "yes." I could not lie to my soul. I could not lie to the many and different circles around me. I could not betray the Zionism, which burned inside me and never died, not even for a minute.

After my negative answer, the committee did not delay, and it ended the meeting without any further response.

The news got to Prof. Anderson before I returned to the lab and to his office. Even today I have no words to describe all that has passed through his face – the shock, doubt, sorrow, frustration, disbelief, and disappointment in me. The greatest of all these was his inability to understand, or at least accept, that there were other things which were more important to me than my scientific and academic advancement. Science was his entire life and the essence of his being.

How could it be that it was not to be so with me, too? I was so smart and successful. One should not put this to waste, not for anything else in the world.

In spite of all his words, and in spite of the pain and sorrow which I caused him, I had no doubt that my ideals as a Jew, as a citizen of the State of Israel, as a mother to six children born within seven and a half years – overpowered everything, including an important and illustrious academic career in science. In addition, Abe was a ba'al teshuva, choosing to lead a religiousway of life only as an adult. Without another source of support and light to show the way, I was obligated for his Torah life and to walk with him the whole way. It was not clear to me at all how can one be a wholesome Jew in the diaspora when you have a place in the Land of Israel. Abe also knew this and understood my decision.

Today, I am not certain that he realized, then, the magnitude of the opportunity which came my way, how rare and out of the ordinary it was.

This decision has since shaped my entire life. My last day at Prof. Anderson's lab was my last day in groundbreaking research which redefined boundaries and was thoroughly exciting. From the science point of view, going back to Israel meant a death sentence for my career as an academic research scientist.

Over the years, I have been asked many times about this detrimental – and stupid in the eyes of many good and dear people – decision. When I came back to Israel, my professional-scientific life was hard, disappointing, nearly one of despair. Despite it all, it was clear to me, throughout the complex and perplexing road, that it was the right decision. As a matter of fact, it was the only free choice I could make, and remain true and honest to the things I believed in most. It was the only way to stay true to my soul, to who I was, to who I chose to be, with a deep faith in the Land and State of Israel and the Torah as the only right base for building a family in the Israeli-Jewish nation.

I thought that this would be the hardest choice I would ever have to make, but G-d thought differently, and in a major way.

A DOUBLE AND TRIPLE MIRACLE

I had arrived in Atlanta with clear doctor's instructions not to get pregnant. My poor immune system, which a pregnancy could depress even more, G-d forbid, was in terrible state. Even after I regained my strength, my immune system remained depressed, and I continued to take contraceptives, as we both believed that we were better off saying thank you for the six treasures which we already had, and not to risk my health or, G-d forbid, my life.

My amazing results with the monkeys were accompanied by feelings of weakness, tiredness and a general state of "not feeling so good." After a few weeks, when I started throwing up every morning, I understood that I got pregnant in spite of the contraceptive pills which I was taking. I worried. We were worried. We knew that the doctors saw a pregnancy as a life-threatening situation in my case. A visit to an obstetrician confirmed that I was pregnant. In light of the poor state of my immune system, he recommended to abort the pregnancy.

We went to ask Rabbi Friedman, the Rabbi of the Orthodox community that we belonged to. He listened attentively, asked many questions, and said that it seems that I could abort, based on the law against *Rodef* (as the fetus was risking my life), but since this was a matter of life or death, he would send the question to the head Rabbinical court in Jerusalem.

In the meanwhile, the obstetrician sent us to a specialist in fetal ultrasound, in order to do a thorough screening of the fetal organs and systems. He was concerned that the virus, which had shattered my health, might cause defects in the fetus, especially in the heart valves. My body was scared and my mind in revolt.

In the clinic, the expert obstetrician saw us. He did the obstetric ultrasonography, paying detailed attention to the tiny heart of the fetus. "Everything looks fine in the heart. Now I will examine the rest of the organs and I will send you home."

More jell on my belly, more moving back and forth on the skin which was already slightly stretched. Again and again the examination went back to the head. I did not know how to read a sonogram, but I knew that something was not right. After long and heavy moments of silence, the doctor raised his head from the screen and said: "The examination shows that there is no damage to the organs which we were afraid would be harmed by the virus. This is good news, but we have to remember that there are many defects which we cannot see, not even with the latest instruments."

Abe and I sighed with relief, and our souls were happy with a simple happiness. The doctor took a deep breath and said: "I did not expect to see such a thing, but it seems that there might be an area in the brain which is darker than it should be. I do not know what it means, and it could be nothing. Please tidy yourself up and both of you come to my office."

The doctor was sitting at his desk and writing an answer for my obstetrician. He raised his head and signaled for us to sit down. "I will be done shortly," he said, and his eyes returned to the pen and paper. When the letter was in an envelope, he gave it to us and clarified: "I mentioned in the letter the unclear finding in the head of the fetus. I recommend that you come for another ultrasound next month."

Rabbi Friedman notified us that the Rabbinical Court in

Jerusalem returned a verdict that I may abort the fetus, as it endangered my life. I told Abe, "I am allowed to abort, but I am not obligated to do so. Are we really going to stop a G-d given gift of a wondrous fetus developing inside me?" Abe trusted me and our joint belief that all of G-ds actions are for the better.

A month later I went to the ultrasound by myself. Abe was extremely busy at work, and I already knew the way to the clinic. This time a technician did the ultrasound and went through the whole fetal body. I thought that there was again something dark in the fetus's head, but I was not sure.

The technician left and I waited long minutes until her return. She came back a little confused and said that this was a new piece of equipment and that she was less familiar with it. She requested, if I would please agree, to move to the other room, where the old and familiar unit was located, the one she was thoroughly familiar with.

I did not understand, but I knew in my heart that something was not right in the fetus's head. I went to the other room. My body laid on the bed and my soul sought a place from which to observe and try to understand. Again some jell, and again some gray stains moving on the screen. The technician left and the doctor came in. He also moved the apparatus over the tiny head again and again. The minutes were long and heavy, clinging to the existence of my body laying, as if bound on an altar. With the slow and experienced movements of his trained hand, even I could see that in the head there was an area which was black, instead of gray. Upon making eye contact with me he asked that I tidy myself up and come to his office. How can one "tidy oneself up" when everything inside me was full of turmoil and bewilderment?

His mouth sounded the words, but on their way to me, they sank into the swamp of fear and reached my ears dirty and damaged. I heard every syllable, every word, every sentence, but

I could not contain them, and they remained hanging between heaven and earth, between the vibrating sound and the eardrum. Unwilling to enter, and the body unwilling to let them in.

"The examination today shows, beyond any doubt, that part of the brain is full of liquid instead of brain tissue. According to the location of the black area, it is probably the rare phenomenon which is called Dandy-Walker Syndrome. It seems that the cerebellum, the area which controls breathing, is damaged. This means that the baby might die soon after it will be born, because it will not be able to breathe on his own. If it will live, it will be a short and miserable life, both for him and for you."

He waited for me to say something, but I had no words. "You have to hurry up. According to the length of the pregnancy, you have only two more days in which to legally abort in the State of Georgia. Afterwards you will have to cross the border to Carolina, where they allow a legal abortion for another week. I am sorry to have to tell you all this, but at least this way you will be spared unnecessary suffering and risk for you, your family, and especially for the fetus, which, if born and if it can breathe on its own, will have to live with difficult and miserable defects."

Silence. His words tried to fit inside me within a sane medical frame. He asked me to wait until he wrote a letter stating the urgent need for an abortion, so that I would be able to stop the pregnancy right away, tomorrow morning at the latest.

I have no idea where my spirit stored the words. Where it put the medical meanings. The soul curled into itself, hugging the light growing inside me and comforting it.

I just know that I had arrived safely home. The children walked in one after the other, pouring out friends' cars who were the carpool drivers for that day. They needed a hug, a listening ear, water to drink, water on their face, water to wash their hands. They needed a piece of fruit and something light to eat so they could survive until dinner time.

Evening came. Serving food for everyone. Feeding the little ones. Showers for everyone. Pajamas. A story for the little ones. To turn off the light. A conversation with the older ones, lights off there, too.

I needed to prepare myself for Abe's return home. How does one get ready for such a meeting? With such a cruel reality?!

Abe came home tired and hungry. I sat with him while he ate, drank some water, and relaxed from the pressures of the long day. When he asked about my day and about the visit to the doctor I did not answer. I had to wait until his mind relaxed before I gave it such a terrible shake.

The time had come when I could not justify the waiting and silence anymore. A spirit in turmoil and a soul curled up, unwilling to look me in the face, or his face. "There is a black area in the brain. An area where there is no brain tissue, probably because of an accumulation of liquids. This area grew in the past month. It is the doctor's opinion that there is no other option but to abort the fetus. According to the laws of Georgia, we have only two more days to abort, legally, here in Atlanta. He recommended to do it, with no delay."

Abe was in shock. I returned to the shock which had stopped at the doorpost of my being as a functioning mother, the shock which waited until I would let it inside me, and now the door had opened. The door to our private hell and to our hell as a couple. The door to oblivion and to the space which could never be filled.

We sat one next to the other on the sofa and remained silent. There was no room for words. We needed to look inside ourselves and search for communication with our inner selves, to seek words of the soul, to pray and hope for a miracle. For the strength to do whatever needed to be done.

I did not know what to ask from G-d. To ask the fetus to die in the womb soon, without our interference? To ask that he die upon birth? To ask that he breathe on its own and live and grow up with terrible defects? That he will live months? Years? That the baby would be granted many years of life and that we would be able to bring it happiness, in spite of all the handicaps and hardships? To ask for the strength to lose the baby? To ask for the strength to raise it? To ask for strength to hold strong the whole family around it? To ask for strength to love him with no limits and to nourish whatever there would be, without dwelling on whatever would be missing?

The questions emerged into my consciousness like big drops of burning salt water on a wound. Every question a drop. Every question a burn and a pain. Every question swinging me between deep terrible abysses full of sharp rocks. Every question drowning me in a black hole which sucked my whole being into it. Miraculously, in spite of all the attempts by this rocking experience, I did not sink into despair, but rather stayed in a state of prayer. I continued to ceaselessly invite G-d to sit next to me and tell me what was His will, what was our duty.

The night squeezed its way in between the window and the curtain, trying to cover up the questions in sweet, tempting webs of sleep. Abe sat next to me, thinking, praying and silent, inside and out.

Suddenly, within the darkness of the unknown, a light flickered. The light of G-d. The fetus kicked inside me, then kicked again. Actually, he did not kick, but rather fluttered on the wall of the womb like a butterfly which had left the cocoon and was trying its wings for the first time. I felt him move, even though he was still tiny. I knew he was alive and that I could not abort him, I could not truncate his fetal life. I could not even think of the option of throwing a gift from G-d away to the garbage. I knew that by deciding to keep the pregnancy and protect the fetus I was choosing life. I chose to believe that everything has a reason and a cause, and that there was a G-d who sees the whole picture. I prayed for the strength to continue and to always believe that there was only good in G-d's plan, and that we needed to search for it and be open to creating it.

I turned my face to Abe, and he turned his face to me. Our tearing eyes met, spoke their secret language and agreed with each other. Gifts from G-d above we should collect unto our bosom and hug tightly. We needed to make room inside ourselves, and to internalize our responsibility for them. We cried and smiled and decided and hugged and cried again. The morning rose on parents who did not despair, and who prayed for the strength which would be needed in order to nurture G-d's gift to the utmost that they could.

The fetus continued growing inside me.

In the morning we went to Rabbi Friedman and shared the decision to keep the baby with him, in spite of the verdict from the *Bet Din* which allowed me to abort within Jewish law/*Halacha*, and the recommendations and warnings of the doctors.

He listened attentively. He listened to the inner voices which peeked between the spoken words. Within his office, a presence of belief and support, of appreciation and understanding, was woven. He understood our choice in accepting and keeping the new life that was growing inside me. He understood our insistence in believing in the good in G-d's world and His creations, even when they were not whole in our eyes and in the eyes of all those around us. He was understanding of our choice, of accepting the gift that G-d had forced upon us like a mountain. We had collected this gift from the bowl and loved it even before it was really a being, before it lived. I did not really know what his opinion was, but I felt clearly his respect for us and for the decision we took.

Over the next month, the black area in the brain grew, and it continued to grow in the subsequent month. The cerebellum area, which is in charge of breathing, was part of the black area. Liquids continued to accumulate in the brain. The natural drainage from the brain to the lymph sinus outside of it did not exist. There was nothing that could be done during the pregnancy. Only after the pregnancy would it be possible to insert an external drainage tube and drain the liquids which were pressing on the brain tissue. It was not possible to know which parts of the brain and which functions would be possible to rehabilitated and which ones would not.

I saw no reason to continue going to the ultrasound and see the black spreading and the frustration of the doctor, maybe even his anger, concerning our irresponsible decision. The only follow up I continued were the routine tests during the last trimester of the pregnancy.

I received desperate calls from the family. "Why are you not looking the truth in the eye? Why do you wish to make everyone miserable, including the baby that will be born – if he will live at all?" everyone wondered.

My sister sent me an angry letter. She saw a terrible irresponsibility in carrying on this pregnancy. "You have a beautiful family, six wonderful and healthy children, thank G-d. Why are you determined to destroy it? Is this pregnancy worth the risk of your children becoming orphans? Is it worthwhile for you to make the whole family miserable and bring it into a lasting nightmare, for this defective fetus? How can you behave in such an irresponsible manner? How can you do this to all of us? You know that the pregnancy carries a great risk for your life. It might have perhaps made some sense if you took the risk in order to give birth to a healthy child, but for a distorted child that might not live at all? Is it worth it? What is wrong with you? Get a hold of yourself! Be a responsible adult! You have all the required approvals, both religious and medical, to abort, so what are you waiting for?" Two pages full of pain and frustration, great fear, and an inability to see my side of things, not even a bit.

We were alone in a bubble of difficult predictions and a whirl-wind of great faith. Abe, Rabbi Friedman and I, we were the only ones who knew that there was a need for prayer, for a lot of prayer. But what should one pray for? I did not know what Rabbi Fried-man prayed for. Abe and I did everything in our power to contain this difficult story within our "togetherness" and not let it burst out. Abe prayed that all would be well. And I, I did not know what to ask for. I collected all the faith and desperation which threat-ened to sneak in. I wove together all the hopes and wishes, all the words and syllables – and threw them to the heaven.

"G-d, you do the asking for me, because I am too little to know what to ask for." Only one prayer accompanied me all those months, weeks, days and hours until the birth: "G-d, please give me strength to bear and handle whatever you intend to bring upon me. Give me the strength to do all that will be needed. Give me the strength to see the good in every situation that will come, and the ability to show this good to all those around me, both in the family and in the community."

I received strength. Strength to carry the pregnancy, while doing my work and advancing the research. Strength to carve a new road in my scientific field. Strength to point out a built-in fault in the system for identifying and monitoring HIV carriers and the transfer of the infection to others. Strength to form an idea and to develop it into to a possible solution to the problem I had uncovered. Strength to carry a hard, complex, dangerous and wondrous pregnancy. A wonder too sublime for our under-standing. A wonder of a gift from G-d above. A wonder of form-ing a life and its development in the depth of our being and our awareness on the personal, couple, family, medical and rabbin-ical levels.

We started preparations for the birth. Since I would need to be with the newborn baby in the hospital for long periods of time, we needed to find someone who could be at home with the other children and lend a hand with the household chores, when I would not be there to do so. We needed to bring an *au pair* (live in help) into our home. Someone who would live with us and help with the children, someone who would be an additional address for a hug and a kiss when someone fell or got hurt. We learned about this option from friends, and the details of the terms of employment for such a young woman, who usually came from overseas.

It was clear that we needed someone Jewish. It was important for us that she would speak Hebrew, in order to keep the holy language as their mother tongue. It was also clear that she needed to be observant and keep a completely religious life. I sent my parents a letter, requesting that they ask my youngest sister, who was finishing her twelfth year in the *ulpana* (a high school for religious girls), if there might be someone in her class who would be interested in an au pair position with us, for a year.

The answer was quick to arrive. My sister wanted the position. She would come as soon as possible after completing her matriculation exams, so she could become familiar with our house and the children's routines before the imminent birth. We were very happy. We hoped that it will be good for her and thought of how to make things pleasant for her, in spite of the hardships and challenges approaching our doorstep. We expected the birth in the month of Av (August), in the middle of summer vacation in the US. Until schools and kindergartens would start my sister would have a full-time job.

The time had come to bring into the story an obstetrician who would, G-d willing, deliver the baby.

We chose an observant, G-d fearing Jew from our community, and we shared the mysteries of the pregnancy with him, with all its black and problematic parts. The mutual decision was that in order to give the fetus the best chances of living after the birth, he would conduct the delivery in a large hospital with a level C neonatal unit, the highest support level for newborns, which included breathing machines. In the hospital he chose for us, there were neonatal neurosurgeons and a complete support team for newborns needing surgery, including brain surgery.

Once this decision was taken, I felt that I had done all I could do at that point in time. There was nothing else for me to do, . Now there were four of us in the inner knowing and acting circle.

My sister arrived, excited and anticipating "overseas" experiences, to a different family atmosphere than the one she knew at my parents' home.

The ninth month arrived. On Friday, at the beginning of the month of Av, I went to the doctor's house for a routine urine test. The result was good. We could continue to wait patiently for a natural birth. I was happy. I smiled at him and was going to leave his home office, but he stopped me and said, "I just want you to know that I will do the delivery in the nearby hospital, and not in the big, central one."

"What are you doing?! In the nearby hospital there is no neonatal life support level C! What, do you want my baby to die?! I thought that you would take care of him, protect him from the general hospital system. How can you decide not to give him a chance to live?" all the tears that had waited, that hid, that were pushed to a corner, gushed and ran down my nose and my cheeks onto the big dress, which covered the fetus and myself comfortably, like a tent. He handed me tissues and waited for me to calm down a little.

"I spoke with Rabbi Friedman about it. The situation is complex, and after examining the options –this is his *halachic* recommendation."

"But what will happen if the baby will not be able to breathe on his own? Then the Rabbi is willing to let him die? I thought that you supported me. That you cared about me and that you would respect our decision, Abe and myself. I thought that you would do everything in your power in order that our baby would live. What happened to change your mind?"

Patiently and quietly, he tried to explain to me that it was because there was a chance that the baby would not be able to breathe on his own, that it is important not to give birth in a hospital which had level C incubators. There, they would connect him to a breathing machine and that would be it. There would be no more choice. He told me that he promised Rabbi Friedman and he promises me, too, that if needed he would ventilate the baby with the manual ventilator for as long as it would be necessary.

"Please understand, as long as the baby is ventilated manually and not by a machine, there is the possibility to weigh the options and chose the one we want. Manual ventilation requires changing the person ventilating once in a while. This change involves moments in which there is no ventilation, and therefore the connection to the next person to ventilate does not have to happen if the situation is such that there could not be life without ventilation. Ventilating this way provides the ability to choose, to decide when more becomes known, instead of putting the newborn into a situation from which there would be no return, no room for choice."

I understood nothing, yet I understood everything. Those around me were sure that the baby would be born extremely damaged, and they would like to keep for us the option to stop fighting for a life which could not really be a real life. I could not connect to their point of view. As far as I was concerned, when G-d gives a gift then together with it, He gives the way to receive it and keep it. I believed that things would be okay. Not because I did not understand the facts, but because it was clear to me that there was an existence beyond the seen and measured existence. I believed that whatever would happen in the delivery room and afterwards, strength would be found to turn it into good, to light, to miracles of faith. Until this moment, I never believed in miracles. This time, I believed that miracles were a sure thing.

Somewhere, in the place that the soul interfaces with "being," I knew that all would be well. A knowing, which relied on nothing from this world, but stood firm and clear in the world of the soul, on one of the rungs of the ladder which stands on the earth and its head reaches the heaven. This inner conversation with G-d was beyond words, beyond consciousness, in a place where complete acceptance merges with "being" and completes it. I only asked G-d to "grant peace."

"Grant peace, goodness and blessings, grace, benevolence and mercy inside me, inside us, among us. Lay your hand on your tiny creation and give him peace, too."

I went into Shabbat terribly conflicted, but still organized, in extreme turmoil, but calm, totally cracked, but whole. I went into a Shabbat where there was room for both a queen and a king at the same table, where there was room for all of us, father and mother, all the children and my youngest sister. Like a small piece of the world to come. The Neshama Yeterah embraced my soul, and added to it more light, more prayer, more faith, more acceptance, more dwelling in a world which could not be measured, because it was so big, and at the same time so small.

On Sunday morning I woke up, before dawn, with strong contractions. I knew that I had many hours like this before I would reach the actual birth. At the time I thought that my doctor had already risen, I called him.

"Can it wait until after my study time this morning?" he asked.

I answered that, yes, it would take more time. We arranged to meet at the hospital at eleven that morning.

• • •

What do you do with contractions, and six active children on a Sunday morning? We went to the nearby park with six children, one baby stroller, five pairs of bicycles, a father, a mother, and a younger sister, who had already grown up.

We went in two cars so that there would be room for all the bicycles. We parked at the entrance to President Park, where the president of the university lived. Even though there was a paved road going up to his house, the entry of cars was not permitted, excepting for the president and his guests. The park itself was open to the public. The four older children started riding their bikes, even before we were done putting the youngest one into the stroller and helping her sister get on her tricycle. The road into the park started with a long downhill, and only then it became level, winding between grassy fields and circling a picturesque lake.

They were ahead, behind a curve in the road. Abe held on to the tricycle. My sister held on to the stroller, where the youngest one sat. I held my inflated and hard belly and stopped to breathe through each and every contraction. The contractions became more frequent and longer. I was on my way to give birth. Like every woman giving birth, I withdrew into myself, fully enlisted in the mission of bringing a child into this world.

Our daughter came running down the road, calling for us to come quickly, because her sister had fallen from her bicycle. For a minute we continued walking. A fall from a bicycle was always followed by screams and cries from the one who fell, and in the case of this one she would be screaming even at the slightest hurt. When we realized that we did not hear her screaming, we started running.

Bruryiah lay on the path, moaning soundlessly. The older ones had not seen her fall, they only heard her. There was no way to know how she fell. We decided that I would take her home and call a pediatrician to see her. There was no reason to start packing all the other children. I sat next to her and asked her what hurts. She pointed to her belly. Abe brought his car, the smaller of the two, inside the park and she moved into it slowly, moaning the whole time but barely able to be heard. She did not look good and she did not sound good. On the way out of the park, I had to take a right turn to go home, but I decided to take her to the emergency room at the Children's Hospital by the University, which was right around the corner on the left. I turned left.

On a regular weekday there was almost no way one could make a left turn on the wide, eight lane road, which wound through the city with the university buildings on both sides. But on this early Sunday morning it was empty. A left turn and immediately another left, and we were at the entrance to the emergency room. During those two minutes I spoke to Bruryiah, who was lying on the back seat, but she did not answer me. I stopped the car, turned to her and saw that she was gray and unresponsive.

I got out of the car screaming "Emergency! Emergency!" Before I even made it to the door of the emergency room there were already more than ten people from the medical staff running out. They brought a rolling bed and oxygen gear with them.

"She fell from the bicycle," I said. To another question I answered, "No, no one saw how she fell. But she has a mark on her upper stomach."

The team spent time examining her neck, afraid that her neck vertebrate might have been damaged. They transferred her to a hard board, strapped her up and lifted her to the bed, where she remained strapped to the board. She moaned in pain.

"This is not good for her. She is suffering. It hurts her to lay like this. She got hit in her stomach. It hurts her this way." No one paid me any attention, the doors were pushed open and I went running after the bed.

"Please stay here ma'am, we will stabilize her and then update you."

"I am not leaving my daughter," I said, but no one responded.

"I am a doctor," I said – as "doctor" means both a physician and someone with a PhD. Without waiting for a permission, I pushed into the emergency room and stood directly by her head. She was in terrible pain.

"Please give her something for the pain. Can't you see that she is suffering?" I asked.

"We must first make sure that there is no head injury, only then we will be able to treat her pain."

She lost consciousness, and I thanked G-d for his mercies. The pains were beyond what a human being could bear. They rolled her to the MRI room. They stopped me at the door. No entry to pregnant women. In my case, there was no need to ask. My belly stuck out as if protesting to make sure that it could not be forgotten. From the moment I jumped out of the car calling for help, the contractions disappeared as if they had never been.

The corridor outside the MRI room was white, without any picture to break the emptiness of the space. The space started filling with a silent prayer. I asked G-d to save her. I asked G-d to heal her. I prayed that she would not suffer, that it would not hurt her, that the healing would be fast and complete. Her condition was so dire. Even with the oxygen she remained gray, cold to the touch and unconscious. I prayed and begged for a miracle. "I am asking for a miracle. A huge miracle. Please make my child better now, fast, right away and completely, with no scars remaining."

I did not promise anything. I did not vow anything. I did not enter negotiations with G-d. It was clear to me that I had nothing to offer. No previous rights or credits, no promises for the future. It was clear to me that if anyone could enter into a discussion with Him, into any negotiations, it was only Abraham our forefather, he has done it before. But, how would Abraham our forefather know me? Me out of all people?

In my mind, all our forefathers seemed distant, uninvolved and non-intervening. There was only One who was there and was attentive, present and understanding to me, only G-d. Only me, and Him, and the white walls.

Back and forth in the cold white corridor. Hugging myself from fear, cold, helplessness and loneliness. Breathing in a deep breath and filling up with hope. Only G-d could save her. I knew that He was somewhere in this nameless and shapeless being of mine. I ask Him not to move, not even a millimeter, not even for a split second, there was so much at stake at these moments. A figure appeared from around the corner, Abe.

"I saw that you turned left instead of right and understood that you decided to go to the hospital. I just wanted to know what the situation is. I thought maybe you were being delayed with the paperwork, and maybe you would like my help. The children are all in the car with your sister. Would you rather I take them back home and then return here?" –my pale face stopped his words in their tracks.

"Bruryiah is in there for an MRI. They did not let me in with her. She is unconscious, and they do not yet know where she is wounded and what is the extent of the damages." I had no energy to cry. I had no opportunity to cry. I needed to be completely focused on her needs, and not mine. Abe was in shock. He said that he would take the children and my sister home and come back immediately.

One of the doctors came out of the MRI room. "It seems that there is no damage to the vertebrate and no pressure or damages to the brain. She has major internal bleeding, and we called in the senior surgeon from his home. He will speak with you in more detail."

I requested that they give her something for the pain. They

made it clear to me that she was unconscious, but that they would deal with the pain as soon as things would become clearer regarding surgery.

Abe arrived. Together we waited for the senior doctor who was called in. The light traffic of a Sunday morning enabled the doctor to quickly arrive at the hospital. He went into the MRI room to look at the situation and try to understand the whole picture. When he walked out and approached us, he made sure that we were the parents and explained what were the options for treatment.

"Her spleen was torn, probably from the bicycle handle. She lost, and continues to lose, a lot of blood, which is flowing to the abdominal cavity. The surgery is very complicated because one cannot stitch a spleen. I can only bring the torn pieces close together, with sponges, in order to give the spleen a chance to heal. The other option is to wait on the surgery and start giving her blood. In the surgery we will also need to give her blood, at least eight units. We could give them to her and see, perhaps the bleeding will stop on its own and we can avoid surgery".

Looking into our eyes, he continued: "Surgery in the abdominal cavity is always complicated. She is a healthy child, and her young body has good healing powers of its own. I recommend that you consider treating her without surgical intervention for now. It will always be possible to take her into the surgery room and try to put the spleen together with internal supports. The decision is yours, and I will respect whatever you will decide. They called not only me, but also the whole team necessary to prepare the operation room and carry out the surgery. Should the need arise, we will be available to operate even in the middle of night."

Abe's eyes asked me what I was thinking. His mouth asked me to decide. It was clear to me that if we could leave it in the hands of G-d, without the need for a messenger to operate on her, that this is what should be done. We gave the doctor our decision.

He was happy with the decision, and again made it clear that he was staying close by for as long as necessary.

We pushed the bed to the intensive care unit. We decided that Abe would be with the children until the evening, and after everyone goes sleep, he will come to relieve me so that I could sleep a little, as I needed strength for the birth. Only then did I share with Abe that I had no contractions at all. It was unbelievable. A birth does not stop "in the middle," but in those hours I had no contractions.

In a private intensive care room, adjacent to the trauma room, they connected Bruryiah to different monitors and instruments and she had IV units in both hands. To one of them they connected a bag of blood, and dark red liquid started its way into her vein. The bag emptied and another one was hung on the pole and emptied in a steady pace into her body. Repeated tests at short intervals showed that the level of red blood cells, the hematocrit, kept falling, despite the many blood units. When Abe came in the evening to switch with me, the sixth blood unit was flowing into Bruryiah, and the hematocrit kept on falling.

Abe almost fainted at the sight of the blood and could not stay in the room. I could not leave. I sent Abe home to sleep and gain strength. We were only at the beginning of the road, a long and hard road. I told Abe that I would call when the hematocrit would stabilize and stop going down. And if it would not stabilize, then while the eighth unit would be flowing into her, the doctor must decide whether to take her to the surgery room.

The monotonous throb of the instruments and the variety of quiet beeps, all these summed up the survival ability of a body fighting for oxygen to its tissues and organs. The hematocrit kept on declining. The seventh unit was finished, and it was still going down. Bruryiah was unconscious, so she was not aware that she was approaching the edge of the precipice. A precipice which in a good scenario will mean surgery in the abdominal cavity under the cloud of severe blood loss, and in the other case – death.

The nurse connected the eighth unit. "I am calling the senior surgeon now. He asked to let him know when we get to the eighth unit, so he will have enough time to arrive and prepare the team needed for the surgery."

"I understand," I answered and withdrew into my private inner space, where I conversed with G-d. I asked that He show us His strong hand without a need for the surgeons, the interference of human hands in the wondrous systems that He created. I believed that Bruryiah's body could stop the bleeding, just as the senior surgeon hoped. More than anything, I believed in G-d's benevolence and mercy, and I do not know how to explain the fact that I felt His presence in the cold, sterile and foreign room. I prayed that G-d would have mercy on our little and pure girl, both in her own right and due to her being a daughter of the Jewish people (*Am Yisrael*). I asked for a miracle that even if Gentiles will not notice it, at least some of Jews would see it. I promised Him that I will never forget His mercies, that I will forever sing his praise.

"You will never believe this, but just now the hematocrit stopped falling, during the eighth unit. The internal bleeding has stopped. There will probably be no need for surgery. We are waiting for the senior doctor, he will be here any minute, and we will see what his orders will be."

I did not need to pick up my head in order to see the huge smile on the nurse who spoke to me. When I raised my head, my eyes met four pairs of smiling, hoping eyes. I was happy but not surprised. I believed. The bleeding stopped without surgical intervention. The bleeding stopped with G-d acting directly, without any messengers and go-betweens. This was what I asked for: please show me your strong hand, and He granted us, for a blink of an eye, unfathomable proximity.

We both went to sleep. Me on an armchair next to our anesthetized and ventilated daughter and Abe at home, with six children who would wake up early in the morning, regardless of their father's missing hours of sleep that night. My heart pulsed with a prayer of intertwined thanksgiving and beseeching. In the evening Abe arrived and in the morning he left. In the morning I came and in the evening I left. This was how Monday and Tuesday went by, and during all this time I had no contractions at all.

On Wednesday morning, after the doctors' visit, the head of the intensive care unit came to me and happily told me that they were transferring Beruryah to the ward. "Because of her condition, she will be in the room right across from the nurses' desk, with careful and diligent supervision, but her condition is, in our opinion, stable enough to release her from the intensive care unit."

I was excited, happy and I called Abe to let him know. I walked next to Bruryiah, while holding onto the bed frame by her feet. We walked into the ward full of instruments and beeps and many different tubes, and Bruryiah was awake, relaxed, and heavily drugged. After they set her on the new bed, I felt a kick, and then another one. Within minutes, the contractions came back and within the first half hour their intensity greatly increased.

I felt that I could not wait any longer. I had to get to the delivery room. In the Children's Hospital there was no maternity ward. My doctor asked me to come, as quickly as possible, to the hospital which we had agreed upon. "This is the seventh birth, and there is no way for us to know how quickly it will develop," he said.

• • •

Bubbie, Abe's mother, wanted to be at the birth. I consented, in spite of the fragile state of that pregnancy and of the baby about to be born, or maybe because of it. The solution was to ask Abe's father to come to the children's hospital right away and be with Bruryiah. This was an absolute condition for transferring her to the ward. Someone had to be with her at all times.

The contractions became closer and closer and I could not wait for my father-in-law. There was another bed in the room, with a little girl whose father was busy trying to find a program for her to watch on the TV above her bed. I explained the situation and asked him if he could move the TV so that Bruryiah could also see the screen. "Her grandfather will be here soon, and he will rent for her the TV above her bed and stay with her for the rest of the day. I have to go now. I have to go to give birth."

Abe picked me up and we drove to the hospital. From the car to the ward, I had to stop walking with every contraction, and they were frequent. Abe was afraid that we would never get to the maternity room on time, but there was no way to speed up my pace. The team was surprised to hear that I had walked the whole way from the car to the maternity room, stopping for every contraction.

"Why did you not ask for a wheelchair? This is what everyone does on the way to give birth."

"I am not crippled," I answered. "I am also not sick, thank G-d. I am healthy and I can walk. And I can, with G-d's help, give birth without too much intervention by the staff." I did not add that I had never seen a woman with contractions wheeled in a wheelchair. Walking during contractions is one of the ways which helps move the birth forward.

My doctor arrived. Abe and Bubbie were already in my room. The contractions were hard and continuous. As if the neck of the womb was protesting the fact that it had already made the effort to open up once and was pushed back to the starting line. When

I was getting closer to the birth, several more people came into the room. They introduced themselves but I did not really hear. One was a children's neurosurgeon; another was a neonatal expert. At some point a children's neurologist arrived, too.

Push, contractions, and more push, contractions. The head crowns. Another push and another one, and the head is out. On the next push the whole body slides out. Seconds later I hear a cry. Our son has a voice. That means that he is breathing! Breathing on his own! I started crying from joy. I started crying because of the unbelievable happening.

With the doctors' approval they put him on my belly, "But only for a short minute. We have to take him to do MRI imaging." I looked at his perfect face. I counted the fingers in each hand, the toes on each foot. all were there, perfect and whole, whole and perfect. A miracle! A huge miracle! Our son cried all by his very own! Our son can breathe on his own!

What a great miracle that was!

Tears. Tears of joy, of thanksgiving, of wordless prayer. How can one give thanks for the unbelievable? How can one pray for something beyond one's grasp? How does one give thanks for a miracle? Even our doctors turned away from me wiping a tear from each cheek.

Bubbie cried out load, "I cannot believe it, I cannot believe. He is alive, he is breathing. I cannot believe it." In our hearts we all thanked her for her ability to put into words the thoughts which tumbled in the room, above us all.

The nurse asked me to give her our little son. I did not want to, I was scared. I was scared that they might decide that he "was not good enough to live," and would shorten his life, G-d forbid, or "would not help him live." But there was no choice, we had to know the scope of the damage, and what was more important – what part of the damage could be minimized by immediate surgery.

I asked Abe to go with them, and not take his eyes off him, not even for a second, including in the MRI room itself. Abe promised; it would not have occurred to him otherwise.

"The exposure to radiation is not important, it is important to keep the baby safe!"

The large medical team left right away down the hospital corridors, with a newborn who cried on his own, with a father who was making sure no one would give up on the baby, who cried by himself but has liquid instead of parts of the brain, and with a request from G-d to grant me the strength needed to wait for the newborn to be returned to me, alive.

Left in the room with me were Bubbie, the doctor and one nurse. The nurse cleaned me up and left the room, saying, "I will be back soon."

The doctor asked Bubbie to leave the room for a few minutes.

"I already spoke to Rabbi Friedman before the birth, but there was no reason to mention it to you until after the birth. Pregnancy is life threatening for you. A great miracle happened that you survived it, and it will take time until you will be able get back on track and rehabilitate your immune system. You are forbidden from willingly putting yourself into such a life-threatening situation. Seeing that you got pregnant while on the pill, it is not possible to count on that. The recommendation is to get the tubes tied. This is also Rabbi Freidman's opinion. The easiest way is to do it now, under local anesthesia. I am asking your permission to do that. It is possible to postpone it to a later time, as a separate procedure, but I do not recommend this."

His words brought me back into the reality of my life. A reality which was all here, in the simple world, with no visible miracles. I was still in a process of rehabilitating my immune system, a process which had not yet reached its end, and it was unknown how long the system would remain weak and vulnerable.

We had a daughter who had just come out of intensive care.

Her rehabilitation will be long and complex; we had a one-hour old son who can cry on his own; we had five more children, cute, full of energy and joy of life who were under my sister's supervision at home. Even though I did not wish to acknowledge it, we would never have twelve children. Thank G-d for the wonderful seven.

A wholesomeness within nature. It was hubris to think that we could go beyond nature. We were granted seven children; how fortunate we were and how good is our portion in this world. Abe and I, we both knew that when we decided not to give up on G-d's gift from above, that we would not ask for more children, and would not take unjustified risks to me, to my life.

I gave my consent to the doctor to tie my tubes right then. The nurse came back in with a cart which had all that was needed for the procedure. Within a very short time the irreversible procedure was done, but Abe and the tiny baby had not come back yet.

My conversation with G-d narrowed down to one request. "Please keep him alive and give me the strength to be the best possible mother to him. Keep him alive, and I will gather all my strength to raise him to be the best possible man. Keep him from above, and let me live so that I could keep him here, below." I knew that G-d knew that our partnership in bringing this tiny son to this world was not over yet. I knew that His role had just begun, and that we still had a long road to travel together. I knew that G-d was with me and that I would not be alone with this miracle.

Bubbie came back to the room and held my hand. How special is the comfort, which resides between the hands of two women. How important is this touch, which expresses more than words could ever say. How important is this communication, during a time when the husband is not *halachically* permitted to touch. It was the first time in my life that I experienced this feeling. It was the first time in which I needed it so terribly. But where was Abe?

Abe walked into the room laughing-crying, and after him the whole medical team, smiling with disbelief. Our son was perfect. The liquid which had accumulated in the brain was not trapped there anymore, it was draining. So, there was no need, at this time, to put an external draining tube. The area of the cerebellum in the brain was probably rehabilitating, and this was why the baby could cry and he could breathe on his own. One could not see that large scale areas in the brain were damaged, and thus there was no need to do surgery right now. It was not possible to see the small accumulation of liquids inside the brain in this test, and thus there was no way to know the extent of the current damage to the brain, nor the scope of damage which could develop or be exposed to later.

There would be a need for close follow up by a neonatal and then a children's neurologist. The neurologist gave Abe a business card and left the room. The neurosurgeon and the neonatal expert also bid their goodbyes, and each went his way, with wonderment still on their faces. Our doctor said that he would come the next morning for a checkup, and to approve, G-d willing, my release from the ward, with our tiny son. With our special gift, the miracle.

The three of us looked at the tiny, giant miracle and there were no limits to our thanksgiving and joy. Bubbie decided to leave and said that she was going to spoil her older grandchildren. Abe walked her to her car. Our son, our miracle, was ready to suck, like a real expert from time immemorial. He sucked and sucked and sucked the colostrum and the thankfulness, the prayer and G-d's presence, the acknowledgment of the miracle and the acceptance of the obligation which came from it. He was alive, breathing and sucking, and after some time also sleeping.

Abe came back to the room and said that they would release me sometime tomorrow. The stay was very expensive, and everything had to be paid from our own pocket, as we had not purchased health insurance coverage for pregnancy and birth. Bubbie invited me to come to her house to recuperate for a few days. Abe asked that I go to her, at least until the *brit* (the ceremonial circumcision), which would be, G-d willing, on time, on the eight day.

"And who will be with Bruryiah in the hospital?" I asked.

"We will be with her as needed and Bubbie will also help."

"OK, but what is going on with her? How is she feeling?" I asked.

"Zadie rented the TV above her bed and she watches it a little when she is awake. But she is extremely weak, and therefore she sleeps most of the time." This did not surprise me, after all, she had lost blood at a volume greater than all the blood she had in her body in a normal state.

Exhaustion slowly took over, I needed to let go and let my body fold into itself. In less than two hours the fast of the Ninth of Av would begin, but this year I would not fast. It was a strange feeling, but it did not stop me from falling asleep.

The next day, at noon, Abe came to pick us up from the hospital. When we got to Bubbie's and Zadie's house, Bubbie was waiting for us, all excited. She prepared everything for me as if I was a queen.

"You are a queen," she said when I protested at all the trouble she went to, "You are the mother of a prince." With this, she ended the discussion.

Only after I settled into bed, Abe told me that Bruryiah had a very high fever. The doctors claimed that it was due to the huge amount of blood that drained into the abdominal cavity, which her body now needed to absorb. This process produces toxins, of such a large scope it was a very heavy load on the system. She was weak and needed oxygen to compensate for the lack of blood, and she also suffered pain and high fever.

I so much wanted to be with her, to sit next to her, to hold her hand, but at this time, this present belonged to the newborn and to his just-given birth mother. This, no one could do instead of me. To be with Bruryiah, to spoil her, to make her happy and encourage her – others, important and loving, could do. And they did. Speaking, for her, was hard as it demanded a lot of strength, therefore we did not speak on the phone, even though we rented a phone which was placed by her bed.

After Abe broke the fast and put the children to bed, he came to talk with Bubbie and I about the situation. Many things had happened since Sunday. We spoke about the schedule for the next few days. Abe and Bubbie were not willing to hear even one word about me coming home before the Brit. We decided to have the Brit at our house, as we have done for all the family simchas, including the Brit of our older sons. A Brit at the house, after the morning prayers in our synagogue. Bubbie planed the mitzva meal that would follow and light refreshments for those who would not stay for the meal. Wednesday, after all, is a regular workday for everyone.

I really wanted Bruryiah not to miss the Brit, the joyful occasion, and the meal. I knew that this would be a loss which she would never be able to make up. Bruryiah was still suffering from very high fever and was quite miserable. It was impossible to imagine her coming home in that situation. In spite of it all I was not willing to give up, and Abe started negotiating with the doctors about a "vacation" of a few hours. It was agreed that if the fever went down, and if Bruryiah would be able to sit up, Abe could bring her home in a wheelchair for two to three hours. We added another prayer to our numerous prayers, and we asked that Bruryiah would be able to come for the Brit in a wheelchair.

After Shabbat, Abe came to us and told us an amazing and exciting story. In the last few weeks there had been among the community members three tragic deaths, all at a young age. One man died climbing a mountain, a young woman died of cancer and another young man got killed in a car accident. A week ago, after the third death, , Rabbi Freidman had announced on Shabbat that Sunday, a week later, there would be a community fast in order to pray and beg G-d to lift the bad decrees from the community, and to do repentance on issues of relationships between a man his fellow man. Bruryiah's accident, which happened on the Sunday following that declaration, seemed like another tragedy, which strengthened the need for the community fast and the ensuing repentance.

And this Shabbat, Abe told us, the Rabbi announced that the fast was canceled as two miracles happened in the community. The miracle of our son's birth – alive, breathing and crying, Thank G-d, and the miracle that Bruryiah remained alive after the terrible accident she had, and G-d willing, with many prayers, she would come out of it, become stronger and heal.

When people say that a miracle happened to us, it sounds different than our personal recognition of the miracle. When people tell us that we had two huge miracles, this is hard for us to grasp. The miracles which were "ours" in a small family circle were in our heart and recognized in our souls. But when these miracles became miracles for the whole community, they became huge and incomprehensible. How high can one carry a miracle? How far can a miracle held up high be seen and have influence? We could not grasp it.

The next morning Bubbie woke up with the understanding that there was a practical meaning to the fact that the miracle had become the property of the public: it was likely that the whole community would come for the Brit. There was a need to prepare much more food for the mitzvah meal, and much more food and drink to be served for those that would not stay for the meal.

The amounts from the original plan were doubled. Bubbie's friends volunteered to prepare cakes and Bubbie ordered salads and dips, instead of making them herself. Abe, with the help of friends, brought folding tables and chairs from the synagogue for some of the guests that would come. The parking area next to the house was converted to a function hall. In all those preparations I was a party only through the stories they told me.

In the hospital Bruryiah started to recover. The massive, toxic absorption of the blood in the abdominal cavity was coming to an end. Her fever went down, and she started sitting up in bed a little. Her fast recovery astonished the medical staff. The senior doctor, who suggested that we wait, not go into surgery right away and let the body have a chance to try and stop the bleeding by itself, came every day to see her and kept on praising the natural healing powers that are in our body from creation. He repeatedly complemented us for our brave decision, as he termed it, and explained to the whole staff that the whole recuperation process, without the effects from general anesthesia and complex surgery, would be shorter and better. And we added after every sentence of his, "G-d willing."

On Tuesday I was already restless to get back home, but Bubbie insisted. "It is enough that you are not coming back here after the Brit, I will not allow you to arrive until the hour of the Brit itself. All the preparations are none of your business, and you will arrive as a guest of honor with the baby." When Bubbie insists, there is not a power in the world that can move her, except for a cute smile and eyes begging in thunderous silence. This time even this did not move her from her decision.

Instead of this, Abe and I conducted the negotiations with Bruryiah's medical team. Her recovery rate amazed the doctors, and the nurses did not stop praising her strong will to heal. On Tuesday morning she sat in an armchair for more than an hour, and then again in the afternoon. On Wednesday morning they released her from the hospital in a wheelchair, with clear and detailed instructions regarding all the situations in which we would have to bring her back with no delay. G-d had granted us another miracle: Bruryiah came home a long time before the doctors thought it would be possible.

I was already home when Abe arrived with her from the hospital. I helped her move to the sofa and put on her a pretty Shabbat dress – without raising her arms and without moving her body to help me get to the zipper in the back. The whole area of the sofa and the area close to it was declared a closed survival zone, where no children's activity was allowed. They were all warned, again and again, not to touch her, not to cause her to make a sudden movement, not to get close to the sofa and certainly not to sit on it. The adult family and guests were not allowed to be close to her, too. Bruryiah was kept in a "non-movement" zone. It was important to protect her healing spleen from any movement. We did not want that which had started mending to tear up, G-d forbid, and we surely did not want to have to take her back to the hospital.

The community would never forget this Brit. A Brit which had in it so many miracles. G-d's statement "I have forgiven" echoed between the walls of the house and in the parking lot, which was teeming with men and women who came to witness the miracle, finding two miracles in one house.

The representative of my family was my little sister, who was exhausted from the preparations and from the constant watching over and caring for five children, the oldest being ten and half and the youngest, three and a half. On top of everything, this was towards the end of the very long summer break – almost three months. We got some excited and happy calls from Israel, and many sighs of relief from all those who were worried about us, for the mother, the daughter and the newly born son.

During the pregnancy, after we decided that we would keep G-d's gift and hug it with all our strength and not, G-d forbid, throw it to the ground, we began to think of names. For the previous pregnancies we did not think of names until after the birth. This was not only because we did not know if it was a boy or a girl, but mainly because we felt that we could give a name only after we saw and held the newborn, got to know the newborn, and feel the soul held within the tiny, full of life, body. This time we felt sure that the name needed to relay the fact that he was a gift from G-d. A gift in the sense of being given outside the regular order of the world. A gift which had been planted in my womb in spite of all that we did to prevent it from happening. Matanyah, Netanel, Elchanan and Matanel – these were options that we put on the table. We had decided that the final choice, from among these names, we would postpone until after the birth.

When we held our son, just born, and when we gazed at him, beyond all the questions and wonder about his future and his ability, it was only clear to us then that his name could not explain what was. We understood that his name needed to hold a promise and a commitment to the future. He was born close to the beginning of the fast of the Ninth of Av, a son to a father who was a Kohen and a mother who was a descendant from the house of King David. He was born "almost a Messiah.' He was born in the diaspora, in the comfortable diaspora of the USA, but still a diaspora.

We chose the name Nehemyah. Nehemyah, who was born in the diaspora and rose high in the Persian King's court. In spite of his influential and comfortable position in the diaspora, he made aliyah to the Land of Israel. There he found Jews who did not know about Shabbat and who took foreign wives. When he checked the state of the walls of Jerusalem, he found them breached and crumbling in many places, and some of the built areas were close to falling. Nehemyah recruited all the people in the area to unite in rebuilding the walls of Jerusalem. When there were threats from foreign neighbors, who moved into the

Land of Israel during the first exile, he did not stop the construction, but rather he intensified the effort and told the people that they needed not only to build, but also to defend both what was built and what was still under construction.

Following that directive, the people started working with one hand laying the stones on the walls and the other hand holding a sword. When Nehemyah saw the active commerce on Shabbat, he forbade the entry of merchants into the city on Shabbat and forbade any selling and buying on Shabbat. When Nehemyah was made aware of the sorrow and pain of the poor, and their subjugation to their debts, he demanded that the rich forgo the debts of the poor and the weak, so they could buy seeds for their fields, could rehabilitate themselves and stand on their own two feet. From the scattered, divided people who came to the desolate land from their exile and found the land to be mostly empty – Nehemyah built a new national Jewish entity.

This was our hope from our tiny son, our giant miracle. His name would be Nehemyah Ya'akov. Nehemyah, so that he would be like the Nehemyah of the Jewish return to the Land after the Babylonian exile. Ya'akov, after my grandfather, who most of his life was dedicated, as an architect, to the study of the exact location and structure of the Temple and the Tabernacle, so that the people of Israel would be ready to start building it as soon as the Messiah's shofar is heard – or even beforehand. This little one would become great. This little one will grow and raise the People of Israel in the Land of Israel up high, in the State of Israel, a land in which, G-d willing, will be established and built on the foundation of the Torah of Israel.

From the day that the holy covenant was signed onto his flesh, from the day that Nehemyah Ya'akov got his name, we only looked ahead. Ahead to Bruryiah's complete healing, which would take many more weeks at home, and more months at school with special protections and protective behaviors around her. Ahead to Nehemyah's healthy and normal development.

We came, as required, for a monthly checkup with the neurologist. I could tell the neurologist, even before he checked Nehemyah, that all was well, thank G-d. But we were careful not to discount the doctors' warnings, even though we did not believe their doomsday prophecies. Thus, we performed our part of the deal. An appointment, a checkup, a look of wonder on the face of the neurologist, goodbye, payment and back home, until next month.

Nehemyah grew up, to our joy and to the joy of the whole family. When he was a year old, we moved to a checkup once every three months, when he was three the neurologist and I made an agreement that I would come to him with Nehemyah only if something would seem to me suspicious or abnormal. In his childhood and in his youth, there were complex periods of coping, and he cooperated and took upon himself responsibility at every junction, in which I gave him the choice to take it or not.

All those who know him, know his greatness, even if they are not aware of how fantastic it is, in light of the challenges he had to cope with in the past, and in light of some of them which he carries with him until today, most of them hidden.

At the end of the three years in Atlanta, we sold the house and were ready to go back to Israel. My mother-in-law begged that we do not go "straight into the war." Those were the days of the first Gulf War, and in Israel people sat in sealed rooms with gas masks. We stayed at her home for over a week, but the war was not over.

"Bubbie, if we wait here until there is peace and quiet in Israel, then we would need to wait many more years. It is time for us to go back to Israel. We will cope with the war and missiles just like everyone else. I will order tickets for two weeks from now, and G-d willing all will work out for the best," I said, trying to calm her.

My sister let the Home Front Command know that a family with seven children was arriving on Friday, and they would all need to pick up masks and survival kits at the airport. She would not hear of any other option, and she insisted that everything would be waiting for us, ready, at the airport.

On Friday, our large family landed in Israel, in the middle of a war with missiles landing on its citizens. At Ben Gurion airport a team from Home Front Command waited for us with masks and survival/safety kits for everyone. We were the only family at the arrival hall, and many curious onlookers circled us and our many carts of language.

"Who is this crazy family? So irresponsible to bring children here at a time of war?! So many children. How will they manage when the sirens go off?" That night the sirens went off and woke us all up. We gathered in the sealed room, everyone put on their gas masks, and we joined the people of Israel, in the Land of Israel. We had arrived home.

THE END OF THINGS,

AND THEIR BEGINNING

The tumor in my head started going wild. We had to take it out.

"Exposing the brain to the air changes the personality," that is what he told me.

I prayed that I would wake up "me." But no one prepared me for what really happened.

I woke up with my whole left side paralyzed. I was handicapped and dependent on others for everything. The surgery had caused major cognitive damages to my memory, to my abstract thinking, vocabulary and the ability to concentrate.

I was not "me," and I cried. But I was still "Sara," and "Sara" does not give up.

From the neurosurgical ward I was transferred in an ambulance to a rehabilitation facility for head injuries. There I met the wheelchair and the rehab staff. Beyond the treatments themselves, I worked hard and practiced for many hours. The strong will to be independent in my daily functions, and the need to go back to studying and teaching, to writing prose and poetry, fueled my engine, even after the daily "fuel dose" was finished.

After a few months, in spite of all the hard work and effort, we were told that I would remain in the wheelchair for the rest of my life, and would not be able to learn new things, but I would still be able to play with our grandchildren, with the little ones at least.

The day this was said to us was the day that Abe finally lost it and broke down. It was the day I "knew" that I would walk and teach again.

In the ward I met people who believed that their lot had been cast to be handicapped, or that they "deserved" to be handicapped. Some saw the damage from a stroke or accident as the end of a life worth fighting for. I found hopeful caregivers who accompanied the patients, and also the desperate ones, who were "run down" under the yoke of damages, and the pain of those dear to their heart. I saw patients who wanted to get better but thought that it was up to the professional staff. I was exposed to the pain of families who did not know if their loved one wanted to live at all, and who definitely did not believe that there was a way out of their condition.

"Where do you get the strength to smile, in spite of your condition?" I was asked several times. "How come you do not give up, no matter what they tell you?"

"I believe in the strength within us, in the importance of pushing forward, which willpower can initiate and maintain."

"Yes, but look at you, half a person, how far can you possibly get? How do you fight the despair, the helplessness?"

"Maybe because this is who I am, stubborn and diligent. Maybe because it is not the first time in which I am in an impossible situation, and I do "the impossible." It is not the first time in which I am being told that I have no chance. I prayed to live at all costs, and now I have to create the best and most meaningful life possible in the current situation."

"So, you are something special, but not everyone can be like you."

Questions turned into conversations, and conversations enabled life-changing powers to break through the restraints of being handicapped. I shared with patients the stories of my previous challenges. Together we built small steps on the road to great improvements. I shared with those who accompanied the patients, the pain and hardship that arose every single day anew in the ward. Together, we recognized the fact that not only patients go through it all, but also, and maybe especially, the caregivers and companions. We spoke about the great power which resides in a clear and precise definition of a goal, and in focusing energies and strengths on the way to it. Mutual encouragements, smiles and competitions of "who works the hardest" were added to our life in the ward. We became better people.

We marked a goal together – to stretch out to the furthest possible goal and to make the most of the place that we reach. We all surprised ourselves.

After several more months I walked with support. After a little more than a year I hiked in the Alps. Another half a year passed, and I started giving simple lectures (Shiurim). After a year and half, I gave full-length lectures.

"Who would have believed?" people asked.

"I did."

"But how?"

"I believed that it was possible, and I convinced everyone around me to believe in it, too."

"Why don't you write all this down? Your story gave us all so much strength, others should hear it too."

"Your stories changed our life. Write a book, it could change the life of others, many others."

So, I wrote...

• • •

Thanks

First and foremost a great thank you to Shlomo, my partner for life on all its levels, the head of our wonderful and growing family, who understood that miracles are also a responsibility, and that writing is a mission.

Thank you to all those who told me it was important to publish the book, and those who encouraged me to invest, from my measured/limited time, in completing it.

Thank you...

Made in the USA
Columbia, SC
02 February 2025

53150054R00169